PRAISE FOR

A Deadly Grind

"Has all the right ingredients: small-town setting, kitchen antiques, vintage cookery, and a bowlful of mystery. A perfect recipe for a cozy."

—Susan Wittig Albert, national bestselling author of *Widow's Tears*

"Victoria Hamilton's charming new series is a delightful find." —Sheila Connolly, national bestselling author

"Hamilton's Jaymie Leighton completely captivated me . . . I'll be awaiting [her] return . . . in the next Vintage Kitchen Mystery." —*Lesa's Book Critiques*

"A great new series for cozy fans." —*Debbie's Book Bag*

"Smartly written and successfully plotted, the debut of this new cozy series . . . exudes authenticity." —*Library Journal*

"Fans of vintage kitchenware and those who fondly remember grandma or mother's Pyrex dishes will find a lot to enjoy in this mystery . . . There are several good suspects for the murderer, cleverly hinted at early on, and searching for the identity of the murder victim adds to the well-plotted investigation." —*The Mystery Reader*

BOWLED OVER

VICTORIA HAMILTON

BERKLEY PRIME CRIME, NEW YORK

THE BERKLEY PUBLISHING GROUP
Published by the Penguin Group
Penguin Group (USA) Inc.
375 Hudson Street, New York, New York 10014, USA

USA / Canada / UK / Ireland / Australia / New Zealand / India / South Africa / China

Penguin Books Ltd., Registered Offices: 80 Strand, London WC2R 0RL, England
For more information about the Penguin Group, visit penguin.com.

BOWLED OVER

A Berkley Prime Crime Book / published by arrangement with the author

Berkley Prime Crime Books are published by The Berkley Publishing Group.
BERKLEY® PRIME CRIME and the PRIME CRIME
logo are trademarks of Penguin Group (USA) Inc.

For information, address: The Berkley Publishing Group,
a division of Penguin Group (USA) Inc.,
375 Hudson Street, New York, New York 10014.

ISBN: 978-0-425-25192-8

PUBLISHING HISTORY
Berkley Prime Crime mass-market edition / March 2013

PRINTED IN THE UNITED STATES OF AMERICA

10 9 8 7 6 5 4 3 2 1

Cover illustration by Robert Crawford.
Cover design by Lesley Worrell.
Interior text design by Tiffany Estreicher.

ALWAYS LEARNING   **PEARSON**

Sorrow intrudes on every life, but grief shared transforms into a melancholy bond that needs no words to express. 2012 had its share of sorrow, as well as joy. The release of A Deadly Grind, *Book 1 of the Vintage Kitchen Mysteries, on May 1st was wonderful, but tinged with sadness that one woman who would have loved seeing it so much, Agnes Margaret Simpson, had been lost to our family on January 26th.*

Through the grief I clung to my sister, Mickey Simpson (Mick, to me), and I don't think I'll ever be able to explain how that helped and still does. I can say, at any time of day, "I miss her so much," and Mick will say, "I do, too."

But beyond that, Mick is also the reason I am a writer today; she believed in me when I didn't believe in myself, encouraged me along the path, and gave me the daring to achieve my lifelong goal. She is a wonderfully imaginative and professional writer; I hope I can do for her what she did for me.

ACKNOWLEDGMENTS

There are so many people to thank when any work of fiction comes to fruition. Writing a book is a whirlwind, for the author, and then comes a long, quiet period of fear: that you didn't fulfill your original vision, that the editor will hate it, that when it finally comes out—sometimes a year or more after you turn in your final copy—readers will be disappointed. If you care, you worry.

But no writer works alone, and that is the blessing of being published by an extraordinary company like The Berkley Publishing Group. There are a host of consummate professionals between the author and the reader, and they never let me down.

I have to start with the wonderful Michelle Vega, who gave me a chance and encouragement, and keeps me consistent and from repeating myself. I also want to thank copyeditor Andy Ball, who makes me laugh with clever comments in the margin, and helps me look smarter than I am with much-needed infusions of grammar improvement! There are others too whose names I don't know, but who work hard on the book, making it look and read as near to perfect as I'll ever get.

And at the heart of it is my agent, the one, the only Jessica Faust, my literary soul mate, my sounding board and constant cheering section, as well as the smartest and most professional agent in the business.

Thank you all, from the bottom of my heart.

❧ One ❧

RENT ME, THE sign, written in funky, colored text, read.
Jaymie Leighton propped it up on the glass countertop
and wedged it against the basket with a red plaid Thermos
bottle. She fussed with the picnic display some more, then
stepped back and eyed her arrangement: vintage melamine
dishes in a red gingham pattern stacked in an antique wicker
picnic basket, a stars-and-stripes flag draped over it all and
gorgeous cherry-print linens piled to one side. It made an
attractive display.

Jaymie glanced over at her fellow Queensville townie,
Mrs. Trelawney Bellwood, and watched her examining the
stacks of melamine dishes on the nearby shelf. The woman
would no doubt have some comment; just give her a few
minutes.

A collector of vintage kitchenware—Pyrex bowls, old
utensils, vintage kitchen linens, melamine from the fifties
and sixties—Jaymie had found a way to use some of her

collection in partnership with the Queensville Emporium, a 120-year-old variety/grocery store at the heart of the Michigan town. Tourists could now rent a vintage picnic basket, complete with everything they would need for a day on the river or day-tripping along it: the basket contained melamine dishes, utensils, and a vintage tablecloth for their al fresco picnic. A cooler of delicious locally made food accompanied it.

She hadn't anticipated just how popular the idea would become, especially as the Canadian July First holiday, just the day before, and the Glorious Fourth drew tourists aplenty to the picturesque town of Queensville, with its park overlooking the St. Clair River and Heartbreak Island. There was no prettier sight in Jaymie's mind than a sailboat gliding down the river on a sunny summer day, and visitors to Queensville seemed to agree that a picnic lunch topped it all off just right.

"I know you like the old items, Jaymie," Mrs. Trelawney Bellwood finally said, the wood floor creaking under her chunky orthotic shoes, "but I think that the new dishes are so much prettier. Fresher and brighter."

Jaymie compared the old melamine to the modern stuff that was stacked behind the counter for use in putting together picnic baskets. She had had to rush out and buy up quite a lot of dollar-store dishes when orders had swiftly outstripped her supply of vintage melamine. She was gradually buying up enough of the old stuff to use, and then she could discard the new junk, which she hated. After all, the point was to "picnic like it's 1959," as one of her ads said. "Do you think so?" she murmured, in response to the senior's comment about the new melamine.

"I do!" Mrs. Bellwood said, emphasizing her statement with a rap of her cane.

Shaking her head at Mrs. Bellwood's comment, Jaymie picked up one of the modern melamine dishes in one hand and one of the old ones in the other. "I just can't agree. The vintage melamine, especially the Royalon, Boonton and Russel Wright brands, has real color saturation. The modern stuff is just white with plastic transfer patterns. After a few uses, that pattern will be all scratched off, stained, and look awful. It's cost-effective in this case, but I still don't like it."

"I suppose you have a point," the elderly woman reluctantly agreed. She sighed. "I remember when we used to buy melamine sets for the children to use. Now it's collectible! But I still think the new items are prettier."

Valetta Nibley, pharmacist and catalog-order clerk, had locked her pharmacy at the back and joined them near the front of the store, eyeing the display. "You're never going to get this girl to admit anything new is worth a fig," she said about Jaymie, winking at Mrs. Bellwood. "If it was made after she was born, she's not interested."

"Becca says I was born a generation too late," Jaymie admitted, referring to her older sister, Rebecca Leighton Burke, fifteen years her senior. "But I don't think anybody truly appreciates the stuff that they have and use every day. That's up to future generations. Like now." She got out the order book and scanned the orders, figuring out what all would be needed for the July Fourth rentals in a couple of days. She hoped she had enough supplies! It all depended on that day's rental baskets coming back on time.

Planning the baskets was a lot more fun than she had thought it would be. At first she had just intended to include a cooler with hot dogs and commercial potato salad, but her imagination had taken flight, of course, because she loved food almost as much as she loved vintage kitchenware. She wasn't ready to include "vintage" food with the baskets.

Instead, she had brought in a partner, the chef at the Queensville Inn, to offer the Lover's Lane basket with wine, cheese and croissants; the Family Fun basket with chicken, two salads and cupcakes for dessert; and the Family Reunion basket, a much larger affair that included the food from the Family Fun basket increased to whatever number was necessary.

The business was getting great buzz, with the *Wolverhampton Howler*, a local newspaper, calling it a "grand little tourism boost." The owner of a local winery had called her just that morning, wanting to get in on the idea. He would offer, he said, his grounds for the Lover's Lane renters, and they would get a tour and wine tasting along with their luncheon. She was going to try it out in her next advertisement.

That had gotten Jaymie thinking, and now her mind was teeming with new ideas. Maybe she could include tickets to local events! That would promote Queensville, too. She'd make up a Music Lovers snack basket, with brie, a jar of locally made red-pepper jelly, a baguette, wine and tickets to the Classics in the Park night. And a Day on the River basket would include, along with a lunch, tickets for a ferry ride over to Heartbreak Island and a cruise up the river on a sailboat! The ideas were coming thick and fast; some she could try this summer, but some would have to wait.

The cowbell over the front door clanged, and Valetta looked up to see who was entering. She rushed forward and held the door open as Ella Douglas maneuvered her motorized wheelchair into the store. "We're going to have to get an automatic door opener installed," she said, both to Ella and the store owner, elderly Mr. Klausner.

Mr. Klausner glanced up from the newspaper he was reading with a magnifying glass and nodded. He'd heard it before: modernize or die. At ninety-three, he wasn't in any hurry for either painful procedure.

"How are you today, Ella?" Valetta asked, bending down to the woman.

Ella Douglas, frail and bespectacled, shook her head. "Not too good. If you have a minute, I want to ask you something."

Valetta nodded and the two moved back toward the pharmacy counter, the discussion clearly necessitating Valetta's specialized knowledge as a registered pharmacist. Mrs. Bellwood said her farewells, shouted good-bye to Mr. Klausner—whose bad hearing was selective, some said—and tottered out of the store just as another customer entered.

Jaymie stiffened and riveted her gaze on her basket reservation book. Kathy Cooper—once Kathy Hofstadter, Jaymie's only enemy—had just entered the store. The bad blood between them—mysterious to Jaymie, because she had never found out what had caused it—was so deeply ingrained that Jaymie normally slunk out of the store when Kathy came in. She was a coward—she admitted it freely—but Kathy could be extremely unpleasant when she wanted to be, and it had caused rifts over the years, forcing mutual friends to choose sides in the mysterious conflict.

This time Jaymie straightened her back and took a deep breath. Turning, as Kathy made her way down the aisle, she spotted the little tow-headed boy hand-in-hand with her. This must be Connor, Kathy's nephew. Jaymie had heard about the little boy, though she'd never seen him. It was a tragic story. Kathy's much younger sister, Kylie, had been engaged to a guy in the armed forces. She became pregnant, but the fellow was shipped to Afghanistan before they had time to marry. Kylie bought a wedding dress, planning the wedding while she waited for her soldier to return.

But Drew Walker was killed by an IED on an Afghan road, and his body was shipped home in a flag-draped coffin two days before the baby was born. That was almost three years ago, but Kylie still had not completely recovered from the terrible tragedy. Valetta had told Jaymie that caring for Connor had been left to Kathy and Mrs. Hofstadter, the sisters' mom, especially at first. Kathy had to have some redeeming characteristics if she was so good to her nephew, and Jaymie was determined to mend their broken friendship from school days.

She moved into the aisle in front of her once-upon-a-time friend and said, a forced smile on her lips, "Hi, Kathy. This must be your nephew, Connor."

Kathy turned away, as if she had not heard Jaymie, and said, "Mr. Klausner, did you ever get that Dinkle's Herbal Products catalog I ordered?"

Mr. Klausner looked up, his rheumy eye made huge by the magnifying glass, and held up a magazine. Kathy, her little nephew trotting behind her, advanced to the cashier's desk and took it, then walked toward the back of the store.

It was as if Jaymie weren't there. Anger flared in her, but she calmed herself with a few deep breaths. She would not be defeated. She followed. "Kathy," she said, gentling her voice so as not to frighten the little guy, who watched her with cautious attentiveness. "Kathy, I just wanted to say, I really hope someday we can be friends again. I don't know what I ever did to make you mad, but it was so long ago, can't you forgive and forget?" She'd said it all before, but some day the magic words might work.

Kathy turned slowly from looking at a display of herbal remedies along the pharmacy wall and fixed her brown-eyed gaze on Jaymie. Ella Douglas and Valetta were still talking, their voices low, their attention taken by whatever it was they were saying. "The fact that you can stand there and claim not to know what you did just astounds me."

"But I don't know, Kathy. I've *never* known."

Kathy turned away from her and moved on, apparently intent on the herbal remedies before her. Ella and Valetta were still talking, but Valetta was eyeing Jaymie, eyebrows raised. Jaymie shrugged. She had tried, yet again.

"I just don't know why I'm so dry. I'm thirsty all the time and sometimes my breathing just isn't right," Ella said.

"Have you told your doctor about this?" Valetta said.

Jaymie turned away, pretending to look at the hair-care products while she debated with herself what to do about Kathy.

"I don't have a family doctor yet," Ella replied, her voice thin, with a whiny tone to it. "Bob is picky; he says I deserve the best. He's even looking in Port Huron, now, trying to find a really good doctor who can help me."

"You're lucky to have a husband who cares so much!" Valetta said.

"I know," Ella said. "He's been so good to me. A lot of men would have cut and run when they found out they were saddled with an invalid for a wife, but not Bob. He's a gem."

"But that doesn't solve your problem about a family doctor."

"No, but until I find one, I'm still in touch with Doctor Rajeev in Columbus." She handed Valetta a slip of paper. "I need this prescription filled, if you could, Valetta."

"I'll have it ready in a few minutes. You should tell Dr. Rajeev about your latest symptoms, though." Valetta moved back into her pharmacy office, locking the door after her and opening the sliding pharmacy window.

"I will." Ella used the joystick on her wheelchair to turn, and she examined the line of herbal remedies near Kathy, who had her cell phone out.

"Crap!" Kathy said. "What the hell is this?" She tapped

away at the tiny keyboard while Connor pivoted idly on his heel.

Jaymie considered trying to approach Kathy again but decided against it. Her onetime friend was staring at her cell phone with an angry frown while her nephew tugged at the hem of her T-shirt.

"Connor, let go!" Kathy said, swatting at his hand. "Can't you see I'm busy right now?" The boy began running his hands along the vitamin bottles on the closest shelf, humming tunelessly as he did.

Jaymie covertly examined Kathy's face. It looked like she'd had a shock: she was drained of color, and was still staring at the tiny screen of the cell phone. It was useless to try to sort things out with her former friend while Kathy was so distracted. Jaymie turned away and was about to call out to Valetta that she'd see her later when the little boy screeched and wailed. Ella Douglas cried out and moved her wheelchair rapidly, and the little boy hopped up and down, his face becoming red as tears trickled down his cheeks.

"Connor, Connor!" Kathy cried, whirling around. She knelt at his side, as he moaned and muttered. "What did you do to him?" Kathy said, looking up instantly at Jaymie, then at Ella.

"M-my footie!" the boy wailed, pointing to Ella's wheelchair. "She wan o-o-over me!" he howled, his voice catching between sobs.

"Oh no! I must not have seen him," Ella cried, a look of distress on her wan face, sickly in the fluorescent lighting of the Emporium that glared off her glasses. "Is he okay?"

Valetta came tearing out from the pharmacy just as old Mr. Klausner tapped down the wooden aisle with his cane, his gait a *thump-thump-tap* counterpoint to Connor's crying,

Kathy's shouted accusations, Ella's thin, reedy denials and Valetta's demands to know what happened.

"She ran over Connor!" Kathy yelled, jabbing a finger in Ella's direction.

"Not on purpose," Jaymie said.

"So you know what she's thinking?" Kathy said, straightening.

"Want Grampa! Want Grampa!" Connor shrilled.

"Connor, *no*!" Kathy said. "Your grandpa doesn't want you!"

"How could you say that to him?" Jaymie cried, appalled.

"What do you know about anything?" Kathy said, thrusting her face in Jaymie's.

"Ladies, cut it out!" Valetta said.

"I didn't mean it, I didn't—honest!" Ella shrilled, a sob in her voice. She covered her face with her pale, thin hands.

Connor was silent now, his tears drying as his gaze slewed between the adults, watching the brewing storm with interest on his thin, intelligent face.

"Ella wouldn't have run over Connor's toes on purpose!" Jaymie said, glancing at the wheelchair-bound woman, who was sobbing into her hands. Valetta knelt by her side and tried to calm her.

"Are you calling my nephew a liar?"

"When did I call *him* a liar?" Jaymie asked.

"I didn't see him, really!" Ella cried, her voice thick with tears. She put out her hands in an imploring gesture. "Please, is he all right?" She reached out to Connor, trying to grab his shoulder. "Are you all right, little boy?"

Kathy pulled him away, and he clutched hold of his aunt's leg. "Professional victim, aren't you, *Eleanor*? Why'd you change your name? Hoping people wouldn't remember what a nasty piece of work you were?" She grabbed Connor's hand and tugged him down the aisle. Connor didn't appear to be limping as he trotted after his aunt.

After Kathy was gone, Valetta and Jaymie looked at each other over Ella's head. "What was that all about?" Valetta asked, as Ella sniffled and blew her nose.

"I have no idea."

JAYMIE STOOD AT the deep porcelain Belfast sink in her kitchen; with an old toothbrush and some mild dish detergent, she scrubbed the deep grooves of the Depression glass bowl she had discovered at a thrift store in Canada on her trip to see her grandmother a week before. Maybe she was a little vehement in her scrubbing, because when Becca came in through the back door from the sun porch and set her bags down on the trestle table, she raised her brows.

"You okay, little sister?"

"I'm all right," Jaymie growled, as Hoppy, her little three-legged Yorkie-Poo, who had come inside with Becca, danced around her feet.

She examined the chunky square base of the glass bowl as she turned it over and stuck it under the tap to rinse it off. Why on earth had it been made with a square base like that? One would almost think the thick glass square base was meant to fit into something, but she had already done a little research, and that proved not to be the case at all. In fact, the Depression glass bowls with square bottoms came in nested sets, like her Pyrex Primary Colors, and could be found in other, rarer colors: amber, pink, green, even amethyst. She held hers up: bland, clear glass. Too bad it wasn't one of the pretty ones. Now she was going to have to scour the vintage shops on both sides of the border, because she wanted one in each color. She could imagine them lined up along the shelves in the east-facing window to catch the morning sun.

People were confused by what was meant by *Depression glass*; did it mean created during the Depression, or did it refer to the ridges and patterns most Depression glass had? As far as Jaymie could tell, the name did refer to glass made during the Great Depression, but it spanned a longer time frame, and referred commonly to vintage glass of a lower quality, meant for middle-class consumption.

She didn't care what it meant; she liked it.

"So . . . what's wrong?" Becca finally asked, plopping down the last of her bags.

Jaymie turned to face Becca with a smile, calmer from contemplating her collection and future collecting. Her cluttered kitchen, filled with vintage tins along the top of the cupboards, old bowls on every surface and pitchers, cups and kitchen utensils, calmed her like nothing else. Just when she thought she could not fit another item in her already-crowded kitchen, she found a few precious inches of space to cram in something else. She was able to tell her sister what happened at the Emporium without overdramatizing it.

"Poor Kathy," Becca said, unexpectedly.

"Poor *Kathy*?" Jaymie said. "You should have heard her! You would have thought we were ganging up on the kid."

"Dee told me that Connor is more than a nephew to Kathy; he's like the child she never had," Becca said, referring to her best friend in Queensville, DeeDee Stubbs. Everyone in Queensville liked to gossip, so Dee's knowledge and relentless sharing of information was not surprising. "Kathy would have loved to have had a kid herself, and she did get pregnant once, but lost the baby."

"I remember hearing about it when I was at university,

and you were already married and living in Canada. Kathy was in nursing school, but when she got pregnant, she and Craig got married and she quit school. She seemed really protective of Connor," Jaymie mused.

"Word on the Queensville pipeline is, she's trying to adopt him."

"Really? It was kind of weird; she was all over Ella when the kid cried about being hurt, but before that she was impatient with him and . . . I just don't know. Then she told him his grandpa didn't want him. How mean is that?"

"She must have been talking about Andy Walker, Drew Walker's dad," Becca said.

"I guess," Jaymie said. "I know Kathy and Kylie's dad died years ago."

There was silence for a moment. "I don't know what I ever did to Kathy Cooper," Jaymie mused. "We used to be friends. I just don't know what happened."

Becca raised her brows; it was a very "big sister" kind of look. Jaymie set the dried bowl on the porcelain worktop of her antique Hoosier cabinet, and said, "What, was I some kind of super-brat, like Kathy says, and just don't remember?"

"You were never a super-brat, sis, but you did want to fit in."

There were fifteen years between Jaymie and Becca's ages; sometimes Jaymie felt every minute of those years, and sometimes it seemed like they were just months apart. Right now, there seemed to be decades between them, and not in a good way. "And what does that mean?"

"You were no sterling-silver sweetie pie," Becca said, handing cheese and pork chops from the farmer's market in Wolverhampton to Jaymie, who put them in the fridge.

"Was anyone?" Jaymie asked.

"I know. Forget it," Becca said. She went on to ask about some repairs that Jaymie was having done to the front of their house, a hundred-and-fifty-year-old yellow brick. Jaymie and Becca had co-owned their family's Queensville home ever since their parents had moved to Boca Raton, but Becca also owned her own house in London, Ontario. She was in town for a holiday that would span the Fourth of July sailboat race and picnic in Boardwalk Park, the Queensville park that hugged the St. Clair River. She didn't come back every year for July Fourth, and Jaymie suspected that she mostly wanted her current boyfriend to meet her younger sister.

As they unloaded the rest of Becca's shopping bags, Jaymie detailed the trim work that she had commissioned from the local handyman, but then, returning to their earlier conversation, said, "Becca, what did I ever do to anyone? Was I really so bad in high school?" She plunked down on a chair by the trestle table. The kitchen was furnished in the style of the 1920s, with Jaymie's newly purchased Hoosier cabinet on one wall, displaying some of her vast collection of vintage kitchenware, the rest of which crowded along the tops of the upper cabinets.

"You're a legend at Wolverhampton High, Jaymie; you were the one who came up with Craig Cooper's nickname! I didn't even live here, and I heard about it through the Queensville gossip grapevine!"

Jaymie flushed and bit her lip. Not her finest hour, but it had seemed funny at the time. How was she to know at fourteen that "Pooper Cooper" would stick? The poor guy was called that until high school ended. "Do you think Kathy's grudge against me is from that?" Considering Craig was her husband, it was a remote possibility.

"She didn't start dating Craig until after high school,

right?" Becca said, handing Jaymie the last item from her shopping, a bag of mixed salad greens.

"I don't think she even knew Craig when she started hating on me," Jaymie agreed, jumping up to put the greens in the crisper section of the fridge.

"So, you weren't maybe as nice as you remember," Becca pointed out. "Was there anything else aimed specifically at her?"

"Some insult or injury that's lasted sixteen, seventeen years? I'd remember something that bad."

The phone rang, and Becca picked it up. She talked for a while, as Jaymie rearranged the fridge and looked over her sister's other purchases, then held the phone to her chest. "It's Valetta, Jaymie. She wants to talk to you." She held out the receiver.

"Hey, what's up?" Jaymie asked, taking the cordless phone and sitting down at the table again.

"Just thought you'd be interested," Valetta said. "After you left, Ella's motorized wheelchair was acting up, so I called her husband. Bob came right away and fixed her chair while she poured her heart out about Kathy. He seemed really angry that Kathy upset her so much."

"Yeah?"

"But that's not what I wanted to tell you. I have to say, I was completely taken aback: Did you know that Ella Douglas is Eleanor Grimshaw? Remember the Grimshaws?"

It took a second, but the memory snapped into place. "I do," Jaymie said. "Wow! I remember her, but she sure has changed." Eleanor Grimshaw's family bought a farm near Kathy's parents when they were both about fifteen. Eleanor had been a big girl: tall, strong, hearty, a fresh-faced farm girl in homemade clothes. To see her now—shrunken, frail, shoulders rounded, skin gray and papery—was a shock. It didn't seem possible that it was the same woman.

Valetta said, "Strange how two different people moved back to Queensville just in the last couple of months. Johnny Stanko has moved back here, too."

"Johnny Stanko? Why would he move back here? He *hated* Queensville. I remember when his folks died. Before he left town he made that big speech at the Autumn Fest barbecue, called everyone in town snobs and said he'd *never* be back."

"Well, *never* just arrived," Valetta said, then cackled. "And if I recall, the word he called everyone in town was not *snob*."

"I was trying to be polite."

She snickered. "Gotta go. After that brouhaha, I told Ella I'd call her when her prescription was ready, and Bob could come pick it up."

"What's wrong with her, Valetta? Why is she in a wheelchair?"

"You know I can't talk about that, Jaymie," she said. She might be a gossip, but when it came to professional ethics, Valetta was stern.

"I know, I know."

"You should drop in on her sometime. You were in her class back in the day, weren't you? She seems so lonely since she moved back here."

Jaymie thought about it for a long minute. Something was tugging on her memory, but it was gone before she could grab hold of it. "I might do that. Talk to you later, Valetta."

❊ Two ❊

THE NEXT MORNING, Jaymie woke up ready for her usual tasks. For the last month or so she had been helping Anna Jones, who ran the Shady Rest Bed-and-Breakfast next door. Jaymie's task was the *breakfast* part of bed-and-breakfast. Anna was a couple of months pregnant and sensitive to smells. Eggs turned her stomach, and since it was generally advisable that a bed-and-breakfast hostess not throw up in front of her guests, Jaymie had volunteered to help. Anna's husband pitched in on weekends, but he was in Toronto, where he worked, all week.

Jaymie would have done it for free just to help out her friend, but Anna insisted on paying her, so it had turned into another part-time job. With her duties looking after the family property out on Heartbreak Island, filling in for Queensville shop owners who needed time off, and now with the picnic basket rental business to take care of, she was in danger of having too many jobs.

Since Anna had only two couples as guests, Jaymie was done in an hour, and returned to discover that Becca had gone to Ohio for the day with their friend, DeeDee Stubbs. Dee, who bought sixties and seventies kitsch to sell online, had dragged Becca along to an estate sale in Toledo that was supposed to be fertile ground for her selling empire.

It was good that she'd been left behind, Jaymie thought, looking around her kitchen, since she was getting close to the bursting point on kitchenware. She *should* go upstairs and work for an hour or two on her second cookbook, *More Recipes from the Vintage Kitchen*. Not that she had sold the first one yet. A New York publisher was still looking at it, and after some research Jaymie had figured out it could take months before she heard anything. However, it was best to be ready with a second book, publishing industry wisdom went, because no publisher liked a one-shot deal.

But who wanted to work inside on such a gorgeous day? She sat on the back step of the summer porch and looked out over the carpet of green grass and at the roses bursting into bloom, while Hoppy nosed down the length of the line of holly bushes she had planted that spring. June, July and August were months to soak in the good weather in Michigan. Spring and autumn offered unpredictability, going from blazing hot to frigid within days, sometimes, and winter could be off-the-charts abysmal. It was best to enjoy summer while it lasted.

She just couldn't seem to settle into thoughts of her work in progress, though. The conversation the day before with Becca had left her uneasy. Had she really been such a little witch in high school? She didn't think so, and she couldn't remember any incident that would have turned Kathy against her. They were friends one day, and the next Kathy wasn't talking to her.

Jaymie had tried to figure it out at the time and had pleaded for reconciliation, but then had backed off. She had left things alone too long, she supposed, thinking time would sort it all out, taking her mom's advice to let Kathy cool off over whatever was bothering her. The cooling-off period had stretched to sixteen or seventeen years, with no end in sight. It was certainly too late to rekindle a friendship now, but she could try to at least get to the bottom of the animosity.

If Kathy wouldn't talk to her, maybe the people *around* Kathy would. She'd have to talk to Craig "Pooper" Cooper. Her cheeks burned. How could she have forgotten making up that dreadful, childish nickname? She must have put it out of her mind because she was so ashamed of herself. She hoped her memory was right and it had been an out of character slip-up.

She jumped up, determined suddenly to do something about a dark spot that had bothered her for too long. "Hoppy, wanna go for a walk?" Her little dog did a clumsy spin on the grass and trotted into the house past her with the loping gait that had earned him his name, Hopalong, while Denver, her moody tabby, watched from the safe shelter of the space under the Hoosier cabinet. Jaymie snapped on Hoppy's leash and set out into the beautiful early July morning. The Glorious Fourth was tomorrow. She had to figure out what her contribution was going to be to the picnic dinner that she, Becca, Daniel and Becca's new mystery beau, Kevin, were to share. When she got home she would flip through her old cookbooks in search of a vintage Fourth of July recipe.

She headed to the Queensville Emporium and put Hoppy in the puppy pen to the side of the store, where he could usually meet and greet some of his Queensville buddies and rivals. It was empty this morning, but there were toys and pee-mail, lots to keep him busy. Jaymie entered from the creaky wood porch and waved at Mrs. Klausner, Mr. Klausner's elderly wife. She looked up from her knitting and nodded, her mouth turned down in her habitually sour expression.

Valetta was sorting catalog packages but looked up as the wood floor creaked. "Jaymie! What can I do for you?" she asked, coming to the catalog window.

"I'm on my way to Laskan Cooper."

"Oh. Accounting problems?"

"No, I want to sort out, once and for all, what is wrong between me and Kathy. I know Kathy works for her husband, but she's not actually in the office, is she?"

"She does data entry, but works from home, so she only drops in to pick things up or drop them off. Why? Do you want to see her, or no?"

"I want to see Craig first, so I want to be sure she won't be in the office."

Valetta made a quick call and established that Kathy was out. She leaned back out the order desk window, and said, squinting behind her thick glasses, "That all you need to know? Do you want to know what I think of your plan to befriend Kathy?"

"Not really," Jaymie said. It was her own battle, and she had been stung by her sister's memory of her as a mean girl. She didn't think she had been that bad, but still, she was an adult now, and would do better. Would *be* better.

Valetta shrugged. "Just thought I could help."

"Who is Kathy friends with these days?"

"Dani Brougham," Valetta answered swiftly. "Dani owns a horse farm not too far from here, and she comes into Queensville to the feed-and-tack shop. Today will be her day to pick up her feed, as a matter of fact. She'll be there the moment they open."

"Guess I'd better go see Craig, then hopefully Dani." Jaymie was nervous suddenly and wished she hadn't sloughed off Valetta's offer of advice so nonchalantly.

"Be yourself," Valetta said with a smile twisting her thin lips. "Be sincere. Be honest."

"Should I apologize for coining Craig's nickname in high school?"

Valetta laughed, a horsey *haw-haw* that made Mrs. Klausner frown over her knitting. "I don't think telling him you were the one who thought up 'Pooper Cooper' is going to win you any points."

"You remember that stupid name, too?"

"How could I forget?"

Jaymie left the store and retrieved her dog. With Hoppy by her side, she set out to the street along the river where the office of Laskan Cooper took up the five rooms of a modified cottage. Taking a deep breath, she entered, a buzzer announcing her arrival. Craig Cooper came out to the reception room from a back office and looked around. When he saw Jaymie and Hoppy, he frowned and adjusted his glasses on his nose. "Jaymie Leighton," he said. "Surprised to see *you* here."

"Can I come back and talk, Craig?"

Brows raised, he nodded, and said, "Sure."

She followed him back and took a seat across from him as he settled behind his desk in a room that once would have been a bedroom. It now had no identity but grayness: dove gray walls, steel gray furnishings, charcoal gray blinds. Even Craig was dressed in gray.

"What can I do you for?" he said in a brisk, jaunty tone that no doubt made clients produce folders of tax forms or receipts. He grabbed a sheaf of papers and tapped them into alignment.

She examined his pale, serious face, glasses set high on a beaky nose over thin lips, then took another deep breath, and said, "Craig, I don't know if Kathy said anything, but I had a bit of a run-in with her yesterday at the Emporium."

He nodded. "Heard about it."

She reached down to pet Hoppy and untangle his leash from the leg of the chair. He settled underneath her and curled up on the nubby, mottled gray carpet. "I didn't want that to happen, especially in front of Connor. But it involved Ella Douglas—she was Eleanor Grimshaw back in the old days; do you remember her from school?—and she's in a wheelchair." Craig was about to start talking, and Jaymie put up one hand. "I'm not here to argue over who was right or wrong. It doesn't matter. At least . . . it doesn't matter now. It's over."

She paused, trying to find the right words. "I just want to . . . I really want to put this all . . . the old mess . . . behind us, Kathy and me. Do you think . . ." She sighed and shook her head, then continued: "Do you know how I can make amends to Kathy? Has she ever told you why she hates me so much?" It was awkward, and Jaymie struggled, but she was determined to move ahead.

He tapped a pencil and glanced at his computer monitor, which held an image of a spreadsheet of some sort. When he saw her glancing at it, he turned the monitor away. "I don't know. You were kind of a snob, back in high school. I figured it was something to do with that. Kathy really has never talked about it, at least to me. If I were you, I would just leave it all alone."

That was not unexpected, but she was not going to be so easily deflected. That was what had caused her to let the grievance stew for sixteen years. "Let it alone; she'll forget about whatever it is," well-meaning friends and even her mother had told Jaymie. But Kathy hadn't forgotten about it. Most people would have, but she was cut from different cloth. So Jaymie poured out her reasons for making amends after such a long time, reminding Craig what he should already know, that being "enemies" in a small town made folks uneasy. Mutual friends felt that they needed to take sides. No one invited Kathy and Jaymie to the same events or parties. It was silly. She stopped and watched Craig's gray eyes behind the glinting glass of horn-rimmed spectacles.

He sighed and shook his head. The front door chime sounded just then, and Matt Laskan poked his head into Craig's office a moment later. "Just me," he said. He glanced at Jaymie and smiled, then said to Craig, "I just got done at the insurance agent's office. That little break-in we had last week is not going to be worth claiming, despite the scrambled hard drive and the broken window. We'll have to just pay the costs and swallow it. But we'll have to be more vigilant, my friend, about keeping the alarm on."

"Thanks for taking care of it, Matt."

The fellow glanced at Jaymie, then said, "I ran into Kathy. She seems to think that the move idea is still on. Haven't you had the talk with her yet?"

"Can we get into this later, Matt?" Craig asked, glancing swiftly at Jaymie and then back to his partner with a significant look.

"Okay, all righty. Just sayin'. You gotta keep the old lady in line." He disappeared, whistling, presumably to his own office.

Hoppy, alerted by the whistle, whined a little and stood up, wobbling toward the door to the end of his leash. Jaymie tugged him back, and asked, "What did Matt mean about a move idea?"

"Nothing!" Craig said. "Jaymie, just leave Kathy alone. She's got enough on her mind without *you* screwing things up more." His tone was irritable, where it *had* been calm and equable.

What had happened? She stood up. She was not going to leave it alone, but she didn't have to tell him that she was going to go talk to Kathy's best girlfriend now. Maybe Kathy told her girlfriend things she didn't tell her husband. "I'll let you get back to work, Craig. Sorry to bother you."

He nodded.

But Jaymie just had to ask again, as her brain processed the remark Craig's partner had made. "So . . . are you moving? You guys leaving town?"

"No, of course not. It's nothing important." He didn't meet her eyes and was already tapping away on the number pad of his keyboard, clearly signaling he was too busy to talk.

She glanced at her watch as she left the accounting office. Time for a brisk walk through Boardwalk Park, then to the feed-and-tack store down by the dock.

Queensville, situated as it was on the St. Clair River across from Johnsonville, Ontario, overlooked Heartbreak Island, shared by both Ontarians and Michiganders. The Leighton family owned Rose Tree Cottage on the island, and Jaymie oversaw its cleaning and rental through the spring, summer and autumn months, a task that most cottage owners assigned to a property management company. She stood on the walkway and leaned on the railing, watching a Norwegian tanker navigate the shipping channel, the narrow waterway in the middle of the river that was deep enough to accommodate such vessels. The tanker moved north majestically past Heartbreak Island, and back into the deeper blue of the safer passage in the middle of the St. Clair. The day was warming up. Canada was clear right now, the tiny town of Johnsonville just a green blob on the far shore, but on some mornings in summer there would be a haze near the river, a profound fog so white and dense nothing could be seen. A foghorn would sound to remind ships to navigate carefully.

As she strolled with Hoppy down the walkway, Jaymie's mind drifted to the problem of Daniel Collins. Until recently she hadn't thought much about Daniel, who ran a computer software applications company out of Phoenix, Arizona. Three years before, while driving through Queensville, he'd bought historic Stowe House on a whim; the Queen Anne–style gem of a house was where the Tea with the Queen event was held each May. How rich did you have to be to be able to buy a house like that on a whim? Fortunately for the village, he had become a good and careful conservator of a piece of local history.

Recently they had gotten much closer, and she liked Daniel a lot. He was the kind of man you could depend on, a good friend to have in a crisis. She supposed that what they were doing could be called dating, but she hated to pin a label on what was really just a friendship at this point, at least in her mind.

Daniel had dropped a medium-sized bomb on her a few days before. His parents, who lived near Phoenix, were coming up to see Stowe House. They were anxious to meet her, Daniel had told her. That meant he had been talking to them about her.

Also, he wanted to go with her the next time she went over to Canada to meet her Grandma Leighton, the family matriarch. That, along with his consulting her about changes to Stowe House, had her wondering if he was becoming a little too attached much too quickly. She was just seven months out of a serious relationship and wasn't ready for anything more than casual dating. Joel Anderson had broken her heart into a million tiny pieces in December of the previous year, walking out on their serious relationship a couple of weeks before Christmas. She was just beginning to glue those shards back into something that resembled her heart.

Shaking herself out of her gloom, she walked on, keeping pace with the tanker ship as it majestically slipped upriver toward an oil refinery on the Canadian side. One thing at a time, and no point in worrying about things that might or might not happen between her and Daniel. His parents probably just wanted to see his lovely historic house.

At the end of the park, the walkway descended to the municipal docks and from there to an area of small, old shops, leaning against each other for support like rest home residents. Among them was a bait-and-tackle shop for the fishers who trolled the waters of the St. Clair, and beside it was the Queensville Feed and Tack. She checked her watch. The feed-and-tack shop opened at eleven, and Dani Brougham reportedly was regular as clockwork, their first customer of the day.

As Jaymie strolled toward the feed shop, an old green GMC pickup skidded into the parking lot, throwing up a spray of gravel, and a woman in jeans leaped out and headed toward the door. Jaymie followed, curious to see if this was her quarry.

Her guess was confirmed as she followed the woman in, and a guy in overalls looked up, and said, "Hey, Dani, what's shakin'?" then glanced at Jaymie with curiosity. Jaymie smiled, but kept right on, following Dani Brougham to the back of the shop, where stacks of paper sacks were piled on skids in neat rows. She hadn't thought of an approach, and everything she considered sounded weird and faintly menacing. *So, you're Kathy Cooper's only friend, right?* Or, *Say, Dani, can we talk for a minute about why Kathy Cooper hates me so much?* As it turned out, Hoppy provided the icebreaker by launching himself at Dani Brougham and dancing excitedly round the woman.

"Hey, little guy! Aren't you a cutie-patootie?" Dani Brougham had a pleasantly gruff voice, and she continued to talk as she hunched down to scruff Hoppy's neck until the little dog was wriggling with ecstatic joy. She finally looked up, and said, "He's a cute li'l tripod, isn't he? What kind of dog is he? How'd he lose his leg?"

"He's a Yorkie-Poo, a rescue dog," Jaymie said, smiling down at them. "He was found at a puppy mill, just eight weeks old, his leg caught in the chicken-wire cage. It was so badly infected, they had to amputate. I was just supposed to foster him past the surgery and recovery, but . . ." She shrugged. "That was three years ago."

Dani laughed as she stood. "Who could resist, right? I normally like bigger dogs, but this little guy has loads of personality."

She had never thought she would find herself liking Kathy's best friend so much from the very first moment of meeting her. Every circuitous approach seemed dishonest and sneaky. "You're Dani Brougham, right?" she blurted out.

The woman's smile died. "Yeah, that's me."

"You're a friend of Kathy Cooper's."

Her smile was reborn and lit up her blue eyes. She swiped sandy bangs out of her eyes and said, "Yeah, sure. You a friend of Kathy's?"

"I was, once upon a time. Something happened, though, and there was some kind of misunderstanding, and she . . . we don't speak now. Maybe she's said something about it to you. I'm Jaymie Leighton."

The woman's expression was blank. "Nope, sorry. She's never mentioned your name."

"Not once?"

"Not once." The woman paused for a moment and looked into the middle distance, her eyes unfocused. Then she looked back into Jaymie's eyes. "Hey, did you and she have some kind of run-in yesterday?"

"Um, yes. Yes we did."

Dani sighed and shook her head, then bent down and hefted a heavy bag of feed onto her shoulder, standing with the assurance of a weightlifter. "Look, I'd just let Kathy cool down. You must have really ticked her off," she said, her head tilted sideways to accommodate the heavy bag of feed on her shoulder. "She came out yesterday to the farm, going on and on about how she was going to get back at all her 'enemies.' I told her to cool her jets, but she just said I didn't understand, that some things were unforgivable, and that she'd make sure somebody suffered."

"Who?" Jaymie asked, following as Dani headed to the front of the store. "Make sure *who* suffered?"

Dani passed the clerk, told him what she was taking and said she'd settle up next week, then sailed out the door with Jaymie and Hoppy trotting after her. She tossed the feed into the back of the pickup, then jumped into the cab of the truck and revved the motor, backing out of the parking lot while she said, out the open window, "I don't know who. Her *enemies*, plural, she said, whoever they are. Let it blow over. I'm sure it will be fine. Kathy's really a good egg. Gotta go; I'm on a tight schedule today. Bye!" She tore out of the parking lot in another hail of gravel and tooted her horn, before blasting off toward the highway out of town.

COMFORT FOR JAYMIE'S perturbed spirits was as close as her stack of vintage cookbooks, her fenced backyard and a cup of tea. It was after lunch. She had already taken care of the next day's rental baskets and organized the food pickup for them, so now she had some free time for herself. Denver lay in the shade provided by her Adirondack chair, while Hoppy sniffed the fence line. Her next-door neighbors, Mimi and Grant Watson, were back in town, and their purebred toy poodle, Dipsy, was the bane of Hoppy's existence, but he just couldn't leave her alone. She snapped at him, growled, barked through the fence, and then ignored him when they were in company together. Hoppy was neutered, but Jaymie wondered if his obsession was a kind of hopeless crush on Dipsy.

The Watsons lived in their Queensville home in summer but wintered in Boca Raton, near Alan and Joy, Jaymie and Becca's parents, so they had brought with them a few things for Jaymie and Becca, including a vintage book on Floridian cookery that had a recipe for Key lime pie she just had to try. Her mom *had* been listening to her during their phone calls this past winter after all, Jaymie realized.

Becca and her best friend, Dee, pulled in beside Jaymie's ancient van in the lane behind the house. The Leighton home was one of the old ones in the center of the village, with no laneway in front but a carriage lane and stable behind. The stable was now a garage, of course, weighed down with trumpet vines, orange flowers draped elegantly, disguising the elderly structure. When Becca was staying, she used it for her much nicer and newer car, while Jaymie's rust bucket van baked or shivered in the elements.

"Hey, you two," Jaymie called out, smiling as she noticed how Dee had quite a few boxes of junk to transfer to her car, which sat in the guest parking in the lane. "Did you leave anything untouched?"

"No, so you can come help me carry boxes," Becca said,

unlatching the gate and opening it. "I found a few things you'll like, too."

Oh no, Jaymie thought, getting up and strolling down the stone walkway that bisected the backyard. While she loved shopping for vintage kitchenware, she hated others doing it for her. She knew what she wanted, but others tended to think that anything old and kitcheny was right up her alley. Valetta was particularly bad at this; she enjoyed thrift-store shopping almost as much as Jaymie, but bought more for her friends and relatives than she did for herself. Jaymie had finally had to say that while she appreciated the thought, an avocado green plastic ice bucket from the seventies was not going to find a home in her kitchen.

But she obediently helped her sister unload and carry stuff up to the house. Three boxes contained serving pieces for Becca's thriving business. Rebecca's RLB China Matching could help anyone—for a price—find a replacement for their grandmother's broken Spode platter, or a tea set to go with their Minton dinner service.

Becca's miracle find for Jaymie was a big box of vintage cookbooks, and just a quick look through, as she set it on the trestle table, convinced Jaymie that Becca too had finally figured her out. Some of the titles were kitschy: *The Book of Can Cookery, The Photo Method for Bread Baking* and *Anty Drudge's Cook Book*. She couldn't wait to dig in!

Of course Becca had to spoil her anticipation. "But you had better really go through and get rid of some. I couldn't just take a few because the whole box was up for bids, but we just don't have room for it all."

Jaymie stuck her tongue out at her sister behind Becca's back, and Dee, as she stood watching in the door of the summer porch, smothered a laugh.

"I saw that," Becca said, then chuckled.

It was a girls' evening. Valetta came over after work, and Dee had stayed. They were hanging out with Jaymie and Becca to make the food for the next day's picnic. The plan was to make enough for all their families, so the kitchen, by the time the sun started down, was unbearably warm, and the four women sat out in the backyard with glasses of lemonade, fanning themselves against the heat wave that had just begun to make itself felt across the Great Lakes Basin.

In the kitchen, boiled potatoes and bowls of pasta were cooling to be made into salads. Jaymie had intended to try a recipe from one of the vintage cookbooks from the box Becca had brought home, *The Lilly Wallace New American Cook Book*, from 1943. But looking at it again, it appeared too complicated; she'd have to make not just one but two dressings, homemade French and homemade mayonnaise. Instead, she riffled through her grandmother's well-worn handwritten recipe book and found Grandma Leighton's classic potato salad. Much better!

She also couldn't resist making something quite different, a weird-looking lime jelly mold was chilling in the fridge. Jaymie was fascinated by the recipe's description of it as "elegant enough for guests, nutritious enough for the children, and sure to be the belle of your buffet ball!" There were always lots of exclamation points after such dubious claims. Shredded cabbage and carrot, along with frozen peas, peered mysteriously through the brilliant green miasma of lime gelatin. If she put wobbly eyes on it, it could pass for an alien life form. Like fruitcake, it was doomed to be an inedible conversation piece, but if it got a few laughs, it would serve its purpose.

The topic of conversation turned to Becca's new gentleman friend.

"So, Becca, tell us about Kevin," Valetta said, leaning

forward to pet Denver. The cat slunk away into the slanting shadows beneath the holly bushes.

"Not much to tell. I met him at a show." She was talking about an antiques show, one of the many at which she rented space during the year, to show her wares and cultivate customers. "He's into vintage electronics. He's got the most amazing collection of Bakelite radios and old cameras."

Dee and Valetta exchanged glances. "So, is this husband number three?" Dee said.

Becca threw a handful of grass at her friend while the others chuckled. After husband number two, a charming but feckless "entrepreneur," ruined her credit and left her almost penniless, then fled back to England, Becca had sworn she would never marry again. That oath was two broken engagements ago.

The conversation turned to Jaymie's dilemma with Kathy Cooper. Of the women, Valetta knew her best.

"Craig's partner, Matt Laskan, came into the office while we were talking and said to Craig that he'd seen Kathy, and that she was still talking about the move," Jaymie said. "He asked Craig if he had told her yet that the move was a no-go, but Craig shushed him. What did that mean? Do you know, Valetta?"

Valetta shook her head. Dee shrugged.

"I do know that after Kathy and Kylie's dad died, Kathy tried to get her mom to sell the farm and move into town," Valetta said. "She had a realtor come out and appraise the property, and she even scheduled a guy to come and get rid of the junk. But Mrs. Hofstadter got out her twenty-two and told the appraiser and the junk guy to get off her land."

"Really?" Jaymie said. "Sounds like Kathy comes by her ornery nature honestly. I don't know Mrs. Hofstadter well. When we were kids, Kathy always came to our place."

"Mrs. H. isn't ornery, she just doesn't want to move," Valetta said. "You can't make someone do that."

"I remember how Kathy seemed to me when she came over, when you guys were kids," Becca said. "I felt sorry for her. She always looked like she was afraid to say anything. What made you two friends?" she asked Jaymie.

Jaymie thought about it. "Propinquity?"

Her eyes wide, Dee said, "Wha . . . ? You use the weirdest words sometimes."

"I read," Jaymie said with a faked snooty sniff, and the others laughed. "I mean that Kathy was just always there. I don't even remember *how* we became friends. But she kind of hung on."

"Mom always made sure she had second helpings of cake, and I saw her one day squirrel some away in her pocket. I don't know if it was for later, or what," Becca said.

"She took stuff home for Kylie, I think," Jaymie mused. "They were as close as two sisters could be, even though they were so far apart in age."

"Poor Kylie. I really feel sorry for the little guy, Connor, though," Valetta said. "He is such a sweetie, but his mom is a mess."

"I heard about Kylie's boyfriend dying in Afghanistan," Jaymie said. "How terrible for her!"

"It was two or three years ago, though," Dee said. "She should have snapped out of it by now. She has a child to look after." As a mother herself, the only one of the four women with children, she was inclined to be more judgmental of poor parenting.

"That's why Kathy is so attached to her nephew, I guess," Valetta said. "She had to step in when Kylie was taken down by depression. Kylie is getting better now—she's *really* trying—but as far as Kathy's concerned it's too little too late."

"I'm beginning to feel bad that I haven't tried harder to end this stupid 'feud,' or whatever it is, between Kathy and I. She sounds like a basically decent human being. In some ways." Jaymie shook her head, remembering what Dani had said about her anger at her "enemies." "But she sure can hold on to a grudge." She collected all of their lemonade glasses. "Well, ladies, if we are going to finish the salads and get some sleep before the big day, we had better get moving."

"Agreed," Dee said. "I have to make fried chicken first thing in the morning—in this heat wave! Ugh!"

Many hands make light work, as Grandma Leighton always said. They were done by ten, and the other two women left. Daniel phoned, and Jaymie talked to him for five minutes, then went to bed with a romance novel she was dying to read. She was asleep in five minutes.

❧ Three ❧

WHAT WOULD THE weather be like for the Fourth of July? That had been the hot topic debated in every coffee shop and restaurant in and around Queensville for most of the week leading up to it, despite there being only one way to know for sure. That was to open one's door on July Fourth and look out.

In Queensville, if it was rainy there would be no picnic in Boardwalk Park, no race with colorful sailboats gliding across the water and worst of all, no fireworks. That would be a dreadful downer; no red, blue, gold and green showers reflected in the silken water of the St. Clair River, enjoyed by watchers in Queensville, on Heartbreak Island and even by Canadians, who would gather along the water's edge in Friendly Neighbour Park in Johnsonville, Ontario.

But the Glorious Fourth defied gloomy prognostications. A golden red dawn broke the day wide open. Some Queens-villians watched the sky with trepidation and recited the old saying, "Red sun at night, sailor's delight. Red sun in morning, sailors take warning," but most just got busy, trusting the blue in the sky to hold true. Birdsong fluted on the morning breeze, and a faint air of excitement thrummed through the village. Work always came before play, though, so Jaymie skipped next door and let herself into the bed-and-breakfast kitchen, beginning a fresh batch of morning glory muffins.

Anna, looking wan, came into the kitchen from the hall to the family's quarters carrying Tabitha, her little girl. Jaymie chucked the child's chin, then studied Anna. "I probably shouldn't say this, but you don't really look very well," she said, pulling a chair out for her friend and pushing her to sit down.

Just a month ago, Anna had learned that she was pregnant, a calamity of sorts, given that she and Clive, her Jamaican-born husband, were trying to make a go of the bed-and-breakfast into which she had sunk her entire inheritance. She was not a natural-born innkeeper and not much of a cook, so it seemed an odd business to undertake, from Jaymie's view, but that had been the Joneses' choice to make. Trouble was, the smell of almost all food now made Anna sick first thing in the morning, and running a bed-and-breakfast meant a lot of cooking *first thing in the morning*. Jaymie was happy to help, though it was a major commitment to be there every single morning that there were guests at the Shady Rest. Going to Canada for a few days the week before to visit her grandmother had been touch and go up until the last minute, when they were sure there were no guests booked at the B&B.

"So, how are you feeling?" Jaymie asked.

"Not so great. I had this with Tabby. It's just typical morning sickness. If I can get past the first trimester, it'll get better, just as my memory is getting worse."

Jaymie laughed, and made breakfast. Anna held herself together long enough to serve, and then they had a coffee together, decaf for the expectant mom.

"So Clive won't be here, I suppose," Jaymie said, dandling Tabby on her lap.

"No, it's not a holiday in Canada. He's working today."

"Do you think you'll feel up to bringing Tabby to the Fourth celebrations? Don't worry about dinner; we've got lots for everyone."

Anna brightened. "Really? You know my little girl, she loooves a party. I don't know if we'll stay for the fireworks, though. It might be a little late for my little Tabby-cat," she said, leaning over and brushing back her daughter's wild hair, a riot of curls. Anna's fair, freckled complexion and Clive's dark good looks had blended in Tabitha. Her skin was a beautiful mocha color, and her curly hair was dark with red tints.

"Party!" Tabby said, waving her hands around in the air.

"Yes, party," Jaymie chuckled, setting Tabby down. The little girl retrieved her fairy wings—she never went anywhere without fairy wings—and flitted around the kitchen. Interested in an outsider's take, Jaymie brought Anna up to speed on her ongoing trouble with Kathy Cooper as Tabitha sat down in the corner to play tea party—her new favorite game—with her dolls.

Anna said, "I met her one day when I took some papers to Craig Cooper's office. He's been organizing the bed-and-breakfast accounts."

"Kathy works for him."

"She works for him?" Anna frowned and shook her head. "I didn't know that. She wasn't working while I was there. She was in kind of a hurry, just leaving, actually. They seem really tight, as a couple, you know? It's nice. I saw them kissing," she said, with a grin. "They didn't know it, but I could see them through the front window before I came in. When the door chime sounded, they jumped apart! I guess they figured afternoon delight wasn't very professional looking."

Jaymie said, "I wish I saw that side of her. If I knew what it was I did to Kathy, I'd correct it. I'm determined to make this better. I can't believe I let it go all this time."

"You'll make it up. No one could stay mad at you, Jaymie," Anna said.

Jaymie returned home, showered and dressed carefully in shorts and a cute red, white and blue T-shirt, both new. The downside of spending the winter writing a cookbook—and testing recipes—was that her clothes from the previous summer were a little too tight. Descending to the kitchen to pack for the day spent on the riverfront, she found that Becca was ahead of her, a surprise in and of itself, and was collecting things in the kitchen. She stood staring at the pile she had already mounded on the trestle table, but her expression was blank.

"What's up?" Jaymie asked.

Becca, dressed in white capris and a blue blouse with a red scarf as a belt, twiddled her fingers. "I've forgotten something, but I can't think what."

Jaymie regarded her sister for a long moment. Becca was the kind who was so organized, she had a list of all her lists, and that was not a joke. For her not only to have forgotten something, but to not have a list to remind her of what she had forgotten, was unheard of. Grabbing a step stool, Jaymie climbed up and reached into the top cupboard for her vintage plaid Thermos bottle. Just because it was July, that didn't mean she wouldn't have tea, even if she had to drink it out of a melamine mug.

All of a sudden, though, she turned and stumbled coming

down off the step stool as a thought struck her. "Becca! Are you . . . you really like this guy, Kevin, don't you?"

Her sister nodded. "I hope you like him, too," she replied, holding her younger sister's gaze.

"Do you *love* him?"

Becca shrugged, but colored a bit. Jaymie smiled. Well, that explained that. Only love could make Rebecca Leighton Burke disorganized. Jaymie didn't have anything more to say about it; she just began to pack the blanket—vintage, of course—and other necessities: sun block, first aid kit, antacids. A vintage Red Flyer wagon was the mode of carrying it all to the park. Nobody in town lived far enough away to drive.

She wondered, though, as she mechanically packed, why her stuffy and bossy older sister found it so easy to fall in love and make a commitment, while Jaymie was so cautious, so afraid to get hurt. Joel's defection still bothered her seven months later, even though she wouldn't take him back if he begged. In fact, she spent more time pondering Joel than thinking of Daniel. Not good.

But maybe it was natural. Seven months wasn't really *that* long to mourn a breakup, she supposed, especially since she would have married Joel if he had asked her. *And* she would have regretted it. Now she couldn't see him and Heidi, his new girlfriend, together without noticing all the things about him that drove her mad: his constant "corrections" of his better half's grammar and vivacity, his ego and his tendency to think he was right *all* the time.

Daniel Collins was cut from different cloth; he was patient and good-natured, smart without being egotistical, kind to animals and small children. He was a goldarned Eagle Scout of perfection. But she didn't love him. At least not yet.

She and Becca had lunch together and then coordinated with the others by phone to meet in Boardwalk Park to get a premium space from which to watch the sailboat race from Heartbreak Island, around Fawn Island downstream, and back. Jaymie took Hoppy, of course, because the little dog would enjoy the afternoon so much, but she would have to bring him back to the house before nightfall, since fireworks were not his favorite thing.

Once they arrived, they scanned the park but were the first of their group and so got to pick the spot. It was directly opposite the bottom point of heart-shaped Heartbreak Island. Already some of the sail craft were gathered, anchored at the mouth of the marina entrance. There was just enough breeze on the river that they might get in the race, which was fairly short and limited to smaller sail craft. It would be run in the east channel, closer to Johnsonville, Ontario; that channel was shallow enough that freighters could not use it.

While Becca walked down to the dock to wait for the ferry that would be bringing her new beau, Jaymie spread out the blanket on the grassy rise near, but not on, the walkway, and screwed Hoppy's tether into the ground. As she stood and shaded her eyes, she saw Daniel walking toward her, and her heart did a little skip. Maybe she cared for him more than she thought! Jaymie greeted Daniel with a hug and kiss, but was saved from too serious a greeting by the arrival of Dee and her husband, and Valetta and her extended family.

Valetta Nibley was a self-described spinster who owned her own house—a small cottage in the oldest section of town, near the Emporium—but she was rarely alone. Her widowed brother, Brock, and his two kids, and her sister-in-law, Violet—Valetta and Brock's brother had died

many years before, but both had maintained a strong relationship with his widow—were often with Valetta, leaning
on her for support and taking up most of her free time.

That's how Jaymie thought of it, but Valetta probably saw
it differently; it was her life, and they were her family. As
the two kids tore off to meet up with friends, Brock unfolded
a low card table and set his cooler beneath it. Daniel greeted
Hoppy, who loved him ardently in the way only a dog could,
then sat down on the blanket beside Jaymie.

"So, where is Becca's new guy?" he murmured, moving
a bit to pull a doggie toy out from under him. He tossed it
to Hoppy, who settled down to chew on it.

"Kevin is leaving his car in Johnsonville and coming on
the next ferry, so Becca walked down to meet him. Looks
like the two o'clock is on its way over now. He'll go back on
the last ferry."

The ferry between Johnsonville and Queensville stopped
at Heartbreak Island on each run, so it took its time, and
could not carry cars, just passengers. There were municipal
parking lots in both Johnsonville and Queensville for folks
to take the ferry back and forth. Jaymie's attention was
pulled away from the ferry, though, by a sight she did not
want to see, not today. Kathy Cooper, picnic basket and
blanket in hand, stood up on the walkway scanning the
crowd. When she saw Jaymie and their eyes met, she gave
a tight little smile and headed toward them.

Okay, think positive, Jaymie told herself. Maybe she was
going to try to be nice.

But Kathy ignored her and spread her blanket on the
walkway, directly in front of Jaymie's party. It was not only
deliberately rude, it was dumb. The walkway was understood to be off limits. Folks had to have an easy way to stroll

from one area to another, and the paved walk, by common consent, was left unblocked by chairs or blankets.

Valetta just shrugged. Kathy greeted *her* pleasantly and smiled at the others while ignoring Jaymie. Daniel appeared startled. She had told him about her and Kathy's feud, but he likely hadn't realized the depth of it. She was going to take the high road and ignore Kathy's provocation. It was a lovely day, and she would not let it be spoiled.

That was the mantra she repeated to herself over and over, even as every little thing the woman did bugged her. Kathy edged her picnic basket closer to Jaymie's blanket until it was sitting partially on it. She left the park for a few minutes and returned with a lawn chair, which she plunked down directly in front of Jaymie, so her view would be of Kathy's butt when the race started. She tossed a cookie to a squirrel, "accidentally" throwing most of the crumbs on Jaymie.

Daniel got up to join Brock in throwing a Frisbee to Eva and William, Brock Nibley's kids, and Jaymie finally leaned over to her friend and muttered, "Valetta, if Kathy doesn't stop it, I am going to have to say something. Can't you see what she's doing?"

Valetta frowned. "I know, I know. Do you want me to talk to her?"

"Would you? I don't want a scene, but I don't want to steam about this all day."

Valetta got up and circled their group of blankets to bend over and talk to Kathy. The other woman shook her head, shrugged, then twisted in her seat, giving Jaymie a poisonous look. She got up and walked around her chair, standing on the edge of Jaymie's blanket, hands on her hips in a defiant stance.

Her plain face set in a grim expression, Kathy said, "So, you have to poison my friends' minds about me too, now, right? You have to try to turn everyone against me."

Valetta, twisting her bony hands together, said, "Kathy, that's not—"

"You just hate me *so* much," Kathy went on, ignoring their mutual friend.

"I don't know what you're talking about, Kathy," Jaymie said, standing up. "I don't *hate* you."

"Oh, come *on*. You hate that I'm the only one in this town who doesn't kiss your precious Leighton ass."

Jaymie, stunned, opened her mouth, but nothing came out. Daniel, seeing the confrontation, began to walk toward them.

"And now you're trying to hook a millionaire," the angry woman said loudly, gesturing toward Daniel. A nerve jumped in her forehead, and her whole body trembled.

"That's ridiculous," Jaymie retorted. She would *not* get angry, she just wouldn't! They had coexisted in the same small town for years with just a subversive feud that amounted to little more than nasty gossip and snide remarks, but now, for it to flare out into the open . . . what was going on?

"You're too flipping lazy to go out and get a job like everyone else, so you're chasing down the only rich guy available," Kathy taunted, her lips curled back from slightly buck teeth in an unpleasant sneer. She tossed her ponytail. "It's pathetic. You just want to stay home, play tea party and marry a millionaire."

"Kathy Cooper, you have no right to speak to me that way," Jaymie said, her cheeks flaming with a mortified blush that was spreading down to her neck. "You should really watch what you say to me, you know," Jaymie said, her voice trembling, "or you'll be sorry." How she'd be sorry, Jaymie didn't know, but she was humiliated and furious and had to say something.

Craig Cooper, his expression dark, strode toward them as Anna approached Jaymie's party hand in hand with her little daughter. The confluence of new arrivals broke up the argument. Craig angrily whipped his wife's blanket off the ground and folded up her chair. He grabbed her arm, talked to her in low tones, and moved a ways away, setting up their spot off the walkway, just down from Jaymie's group.

"What was that all about?" Anna asked.

"That was one more incident proving Kathy Cooper's hatred of me," Jaymie said, watching the couple, who appeared to be arguing.

"Kathy Cooper?"

"Yeah, Kathy and Craig, her husband," she said, motioning toward the couple. "*You* know. At least Craig seems to have some good sense."

Anna looked toward the two and frowned, but as Valetta claimed Jaymie's attention, she spread a pretty pastel plaid blanket on the grass and set down their little wicker basket. It was one Jaymie had found for Anna, and she had filled it with children's melamine dishes and pastel vintage linens for the Joneses. Tabby then insisted on having her fairy wings attached, and she fluttered around while Hoppy barked at her.

As Valetta went back to her brother, Anna tugged on Jaymie's sleeve. "We need to talk," Anna said, shooting worried glances toward the Coopers.

"Okay. What's—oh, wait; there's Becca!"

Arm in arm, up the walkway from the docks, came Becca and her new fellow. Jaymie examined him from afar, wondering if this would be brother-in-law number three. Number one had remarried and now had a family, and number two had moved back to England, leaving Becca a poorer but wiser woman. This guy was older than Becca. He looked to be in his early fifties, with a trim gray beard and sunglasses, and he wore cargo shorts, a short sleeve shirt and a Tilley hat.

"Jaymie, this is Kevin Brevard. Kevin, this is my sister, Jaymie."

"Hello, Jaymie, so nice to meet you," he said, holding out his hand, then pulling Jaymie in for a hug. He smelled nice, like a bottle of allspice, and had a faint English accent.

They chatted for a while, and he gratefully shared her tea, doled out into melamine mugs. He didn't sit down on the ground. Instead, he had a walking stick that folded out into a stool, and he sat on that while Becca fussed around him, making sure he was comfortable. Tabby took to him immediately, and he picked her up to sit on his knee and told her a story while they waited for the sailboat race to begin.

Becca pulled Jaymie aside. "Well?" she said.

"Well what?" Jaymie said, with a deliberately blank look. When Becca made a sour face, Jaymie laughed. "Of *course* I like Kevin. He seems really nice."

"He is. And he's . . . kind." Becca chewed her lip while she watched Kevin and Daniel talk. Daniel was pointing into town, toward where his house was. "We went to see Grandma Leighton on the weekend, and she took to him so fast! You know how she can be; no one is good enough for you or me. But Kevin told her a joke about a parrot, a vicar and a barmaid, and she was howling with laughter. She took me aside and told me to marry him."

"That's a little fast, isn't it?" Jaymie said, watching her sister's face.

Becca had a round face, and right now an earnest but undecided expression, her mouth pulled down, her eyes squinted. She fiddled with her long string of red, white and blue beads. But at Jaymie's assertion, she nodded, and said, "Of course. *Too* fast." She turned to Jaymie. "What about you and Daniel? How is that going?"

"I like Daniel," Jaymie said, "but . . ." She trailed off as she saw Joel Anderson and his girlfriend, Heidi, walk over and first talk to Kathy and Craig Cooper, then move on to Valetta. Heidi, a pretty, slim blonde, bent over to talk to Brock's kids, then took his daughter, Eva, by the hand to some open grass and showed her how to do a cartwheel.

Becca followed Jaymie's line of sight, and her lips tightened. "You're not still pining after him, are you? Joel is a jerk."

"Why do you always do that?" Jaymie said, rounding on her sister. "Do you think I'll magically one day agree with you and hop away transformed?"

Becca put her hand on Jaymie's arm. "I'm sorry. I should know you have to get over this in your own time."

"I'm almost there, Becca, really. Just leave it alone."

"Okay, I just . . ." She trailed off and shrugged.

"No, I'm fine. I don't miss him, I don't want Joel back. I think I miss the naïveté I had, that my feelings were true and returned, that I had nothing to fear, that it was all real."

Becca nodded. "I get it. I've been there."

They rejoined the others, and Heidi skipped over to Jaymie and squealed, jumping up and down. She grabbed Jaymie's bare forearms in a tight grip. "I've been dying to talk to you! Guess what?" she asked, then continued, "I can't wait for you to guess. Joel and I are getting married this December! Isn't that great?"

✣ Four ✣

JAYMIE SAT ON the blanket watching, through the rail-
ings along the walkway, the brilliant sun sparkle off the
St. Clair. Sail craft from the marina were jockeying for
position at the harbor mouth, the starting point for the race,
anchoring until the official start time. Each sailor was likely
testing the wind, hoping it would stiffen and praying it
wouldn't die.

Daniel eyed her with concern, and that was irritating the
heck out of Jaymie. After Heidi's announcement, she had
done pretty well, she thought. She'd hugged her new friend
and congratulated Joel. She took a deep breath and let it out
slowly, intent on not alienating Daniel with her irritation at
his concern. But it reaffirmed that she was still a ways away
from being ready for something more serious with him,
despite his obvious interest.

The race, part of the week-long St. Clair Regatta, started,
and the boats sailed off in the stiffening breeze. Jaymie and

the others watched, but once they disappeared downriver, it would be an hour or more before they were back in sight.

"Want to go for a walk?" Jaymie asked, turning to Daniel. He took her arm, and they strolled off with Hoppy.

There was a carnival atmosphere in the riverside park, and they wove in and out among groups of picnickers. There were lots of folks dressed up, and a proliferation of Uncle Sams and Betsy Rosses. There was even one clever Statue of Liberty costume. *They really should have a costume competition*, Jaymie thought, pointing out to Daniel two Uncle Sams playing Frisbee. She giggled at the incongruous picture, as Hoppy jumped and quivered, wanting to join the game.

To deflect the inevitable conversation about Heidi and Joel, Jaymie told him, as they walked, about her troubles with Kathy, and how she really did not know what it was that had started the feud between them. He talked about his own high school days, how he was the techie nerd who took a lot of flack, which changed when he got into college and found friends with whom he could really bond. It had been a revelation to him, he said, that he didn't need to be friends with everyone, and that he would always find people who liked him just for himself.

Again Jaymie was reminded of Daniel's stellar qualities as a man and a friend. He was someone whose advice she should be seeking, she realized suddenly. She moved closer, and he put his arm around her. It felt right to be walking with him this way, and it was comfortable. "How do you think I should handle the trouble with Kathy?" she asked, looking up at his beaky profile. "If I had any clue what I did that upset her, I might be able to fix it, but she won't tell me!"

"I think you're on the right path. Just keep hold of your temper. I had an employee once who liked to push his coworkers to the brink. Then, when they blew up, he could act innocent, like they were the ones who had the problem, not him. She seems to be trying to irk you enough that you'll blow up."

"I never really thought of it that way. She's doing a good job," Jaymie said. They had reached the far end of Board-walk Park, where a large gazebo, built in the style of a Victorian bandstand—octagonal, with ornate gingerbread and a railing around it—provided a stage for local dignitar-ies and school bands. Jaymie and Becca had agreed that it would be too crowded and too noisy near the gazebo, prefer-ring the farther end of the boardwalk for their picnic ground. They were right, as the mass of people milled around listen-ing to the fife-and-drum corps of a local Revolutionary War reenactment society. She and Daniel listened for a moment, but when one of the fife players screeched an especially sharp note, she grimaced, and said, "Let's go back. What do you think of Becca's new boyfriend?"

Their conversation returned to Kevin as they strolled back, hand in hand; they agreed that he seemed to be a nice guy from their limited observation so far. When they got back to the others, Jaymie noticed that little Connor, Kathy's nephew, was nearby, sitting with his mom, Kylie Hofstadter, and an older man Jaymie assumed was the late Drew Walk-er's father, Andy. Craig was sitting with Kathy, but the two were not talking; instead, both appeared to be texting, while Kathy kept shooting unhappy glances at both her husband and her sister.

Once Jaymie sat down, Valetta tugged on her T-shirt.

"Look down there," she murmured to Jaymie, pointing down the walkway to a tall, shambling fellow in ripped shorts and enormous, unlaced work boots. "Johnny Stanko."

Jaymie kind of remembered him from high school.

Stanko was always a troublemaker who started fights, skipped classes and smoked in the washroom—and not just cigarettes. He was the local pothead, a grade or two ahead of her. Each grade had taken him a couple of years to complete, so he was older, probably in his late thirties by now. Hands shoved in his shorts pockets, gaze turned out to the river, he seemed to be just ambling with no goal in mind. But on his current course, he would inevitably meet with Craig Cooper, the object of years of his relentless bullying.

"And here we go," Jaymie whispered, as Stanko came up even with Craig and Kathy Cooper and stopped to stand and watch a freighter ease upriver in the shipping channel. "Surely he must know what he's doing? He can't have stopped there accidentally." There was a tension in Stanko's powerful shoulders that warned that he knew exactly who was behind him.

Kathy said something to Craig; he shook his head. She leaned over and said something more vehemently. He ignored her. She stood and walked over to the railing and tapped Stanko on the shoulder. When he saw her, he did a double take, then stepped back. So maybe he hadn't known who was sitting there. Jaymie watched, fascinated. Daniel asked her what was going on, but she just shook her head and said, "Wait. I'll tell you in a minute."

Valetta grabbed Jaymie's wrist. "Kathy's totally peeved; you can see it in the way she's standing, hands on her hips. I think she's going to rag him out."

"For all that stuff that happened between him and Craig back in high school?" Jaymie said. "Good grief, she really can hold a grudge and not just with me!"

It was like waiting for the fuse to burn down on a Roman candle, watching Kathy and Stanko together; Craig kept his distance, his wrinkled brow and frown evidence of his uncertainty. Stanko turned away, but Kathy grabbed his arm and shook it.

Isolated words from their confrontation began floating on the river breeze: *years ago*, *mean*, *old days*. Jaymie glanced over at Valetta, whose compressed lips indicated that she heard, too. Craig finally got involved, but not before Stanko shook his free fist at Kathy and pulled his arm out of her grip. Kathy's husband surged to his feet and approached, saying something to Stanko.

"Then you oughtta keep your old lady in check, Pooper," Stanko shouted, his booming voice now making every word audible. "If I had any guts at all, I'd whack the both of you!" He stormed off and headed down to the dockside.

Daniel, who had watched the whole scene, shook his head as Kathy and Craig went back to their blanket on the edge of the walkway. Gesturing toward Kathy, he said to Jaymie, "She may be one of those who you just can't reach. That guy, though . . . why would she push him like that? He looks like trouble."

She briefly explained about the Coopers' past association with Johnny Stanko, how the older guy had made Craig his personal punching bag for three years. "One thing Kathy is *not*, is a coward."

Valetta got up and walked away, and a few minutes later Jaymie saw her down on the dock with Johnny Stanko; the two were talking intently, then Valetta patted his shoulder and turned toward the steps up to Boardwalk Park. What on earth did those two have to talk about?

The sun climbed in the sky, and while Daniel played with Hoppy and Tabitha, Jaymie chatted with Kevin; he seemed like a very nice man. He told PG jokes and mildly amusing stories, and was fascinated by Jaymie's fondness for vintage kitchenware. He shared some stories of his mother's kitchen, in a small village in Dorset county in England, and relayed how sorry he was that he had missed the Tea with the Queen the month before. He'd be there next year, he said. He would love to have a part, but supposed it wouldn't be appropriate, since he wasn't really a Queensvillian.

"I'd very much enjoy playing Mr. Brown to the local Queen Victoria!" he said, and in his best Scottish accent, admittedly superior to most, added, "Och, aye, and wearin' a kilt . . . I've verra good legs, you know!"

Becca watched them chat and beamed with joy, which Jaymie found both sweet and a little unsettling. When her older sister had gotten married for the second time, it had been sudden, a spur-of-the-moment decision that she ended up regretting and that had left her climbing out of a deep pit of debt for years. Kevin seemed like a genuinely nice guy, but Jaymie hoped her sister wouldn't make any sudden decisions.

When the ball that Daniel was tossing to Tabitha landed close to Kathy and Craig, he strolled over to pick it up and engaged them in conversation. Jaymie watched uneasily while nominally listening to Kevin talk about his childhood and the year that the Christmas pudding blew up. She dutifully laughed, but then excused herself and got up, approaching to hear Daniel saying to Kathy, "You should give her a chance, you know, because she's a wonderful person."

Oh crap! Why did he feel the need to intervene? Kathy, of course, shot her a disgusted look, while Craig responded in a mumble to Daniel's comment. She stood a ways away, debating how to get Daniel's attention without ruining the day by engaging with Kathy again, when she saw Connor trot over to his aunt. Relieved that Daniel's intervention would be ended by Connor's arrival, she turned away, but was caught up short by the screech of Kathy's angry voice.

She turned back, and saw Kylie Hofstadter pulling her son away from Kathy as she stood and yelled after her sister, "Kylie, let him stay! It's up to him, isn't it?"

"You ruined that, Kath," Kylie yelled back, as Connor wriggled in his mother's grasp. "You ruined that when you told him Grandpa Andy doesn't want to see him."

Jaymie was reminded of the scene in the Emporium, and how Kathy had said to Connor that his grandfather didn't want him around.

Craig said to his wife, "Just leave it, Kathy. We'll sort it out tomorrow. Don't ruin the day."

Kathy broke down in tears, watching Connor with Kylie and Andy Walker. Craig awkwardly patted her shoulder, but she moved away from him, her shoulder hunched. "Andy Walker has been deliberately trying to alienate Connor from me for months now," she sobbed, anger and pain mingled in her voice. "You *know* that's true, Craig, you *know* it!" She looked up at her husband, watching his face as she said, "If Connor's going with us, then—" Craig put a finger to her mouth and pulled her away from the group. He spoke to her in a hushed tone.

Hands on her hips, she listened for a moment, but then shook her head and grabbed his arm, furiously talking in his face. He looked about to reply, but instead shrugged and pulled away from her, then strode off, shoulders hunched. Kathy watched him go, then sat down alone, pulling grass and tossing it onto the path. Jaymie was torn. There was so much pain evident in her slumped posture and obvious loneliness, but Jaymie was not going to approach her in public just to be rebuffed. If there was ever going to be a reconciliation between them, it was going to have to be in private where they could hash out their differences.

Jaymie joined Becca and Kevin, who stood at the railing above the river, arms linked, watching for the sailboats to reappear from Fawn Island. Some of their neighbors on Heartbreak Island had boats in the competition, and Jaymie grabbed her binoculars when she saw some sail craft appearing downriver. "That boat in the front is the *Heartbreak Kid*, out of the Heartbreak Island marina," she told Daniel, who joined her. "It belongs to Ruby and Garnet Redmond, a sister and brother team who sail competitively every summer. Here, look through the binoculars."

"They're raising the spinnaker!" Becca cried. "Go, Redmonds!"

Hundreds had surged to the walkway overlooking the St. Clair to watch the end of the race, and applause broke out at the swift use by the frontrunners of their blooming spinnaker sails, fuller sails that caught the wind dramatically as the boats sailed downwind. They made the river a garden of gaudy delights.

Jaymie jumped up and down. "I love this part of the race," she cried, and took the binoculars back. Through them she could see Ruby leaning way out over the water, providing much needed balance, while Garnet steered. It was tricky to raise the spinnaker in a race, and some boats were too close to each other to do it, but the *Heartbreak Kid* was out in front, followed by the *Sea Urchin*, and both had room to hoist the ballooning sails. The wind was right, and the added pull made both surge ahead, but the *Heartbreak Kid* sailed to a clear victory, the Redmonds' third win in a row.

"That was exciting!" Jaymie said.

"The Redmonds win again!" Valetta said. They discussed for a few minutes who would be put out by the third win, and who, among those who belonged to the sailing club on the island, would demand that the Redmonds be disqualified next year to give others a chance. The owners of the *Sea Urchin* were sure to be fuming.

Daniel listened for a while, and said, "Do you like to sail, Jaymie?"

"Only as a passenger."

Valetta raised her eyebrows and looked from one to the other. "Do *you* like sailing, Daniel?" she asked.

He shrugged. "Not much sailing where I'm from. Bakersfield is kinda deserty; more cowboy boots and rodeos than sailing and tea parties. And Phoenix, my company headquarters, is the same."

So why had he come to Queensville and bought Stowe House? That was still a mystery to Jaymie. He never had explained how he found Stowe House and why he wanted to live there.

As folks drifted away from the railing, Jaymie noticed Ella Douglas in her motorized wheelchair trundling down the walkway, accompanied by a man who must be her husband. Her guess was confirmed when Valetta went to talk to them and then beckoned Jaymie.

The tall, slightly stooped man, his head showing a faint corona of bristle where his receding hairline had encouraged him to shave it bald, smiled. He shoved his hand out to her, clasped hers in his and pumped vigorously. "Hey there, Jaymie. I'm Bob Douglas. My wife told me how you stuck up for her when *that* woman," he said, shooting an annoyed look at Kathy Cooper, who was moving her blanket yet again, "had the audacity to accuse her of running over her nephew on purpose."

Kathy looked over, as if she'd heard her name, and regarded Bob with a pinched expression. She shifted her gaze to stare at Ella.

Hoping Kathy wasn't going to make trouble and confront Ella, Jaymie said, "It's nothing." She turned to Ella. "I'm glad you came out for the festivities. I know you're not feeling well."

Ella shrugged, her knitted shawl slipping off her thin shoulders. Her husband retrieved it and tucked it in around her again as she pulled up the fluffy gray blanket that covered her thin legs. "It's a good day today," she said, with a faint smile. "Can't let life pass you by!"

Matt Laskan approached Kathy, shooting a curious look at Jaymie and the others on the walkway. "Where's Craig?" he asked Kathy.

"Gone to the office," she said, with a disgusted shake of her head. "Can you believe it? Work on the Fourth of July. You really need to pull your weight, Matt. Craig's been working a lot of weekends and holidays. I know you've been distracted, but really!"

Matt frowned, then shook his head. "He can't have gone to the office, or at least I hope not. Maybe he went home to work?"

She regarded him steadily, as if daring him to contradict her. "No, he *said* he was going in to the office."

Jaymie turned back to the Douglases, wondering if she should bring up knowing Ella was Eleanor Grimshaw, but decided against it. "Are you both staying to picnic and watch the fireworks?" she asked them.

Bob met his wife's eyes, then shrugged. "We're not sure," he said. "Depends on how she feels."

"If you want to stay but haven't brought dinner, you can join us," Jaymie said. She indicated the low table Brock had set up and the bowls and dishes that were being put out.

Ella looked undecided. "I don't know. My diet . . . I'm such a picky eater."

"I'm trying to do more homemade stuff," Bob said.

"He's even trying his hand at home preserving," Ella said with a proud smile.

"We've got lots of variety," Jaymie said. Just then, Becca lifted out the lime jelly mold and gave Jaymie a quizzical look as she peeled back the plastic wrap. Jaymie bit her lip to keep from laughing; it looked even worse in the light of day, an acid green nightmare.

"I made tomato cucumber salad," Valetta said. "And Violet and Dee both brought fried chicken."

"I made potato salad!" Jaymie added. She pointed to her bowl, the square-based vintage Depression glass bowl she had just bought and couldn't resist using. "I can tell you exactly what's in it, if you need to know."

Ella shrugged. "I don't eat tomatoes *or* potatoes. I think we'll probably go home anyway, at least for dinner. We might come back for the fireworks, if it doesn't get too cold. Or I'll send Bob back alone to watch."

"Oh, I wouldn't come back here without you, my dear," he said. "I wouldn't enjoy myself!"

Raised voices near them made Jaymie look toward Matt Laskan and Kathy Cooper. That woman was having a banner day when it came to arguments. She and Matt were standing face-to-face. "I don't care what you say, Craig and I are moving to Toledo," Kathy said. "I think I know slightly more about that than you do."

Matt gazed at her steadily. "I don't think *you* even really believe that anymore, Kathy."

"I have been planning this for too long to not do it," she said, her voice trembling with intensity.

Jaymie was riveted by the conversation, even though it was clearly private.

"Connor, Craig and I are moving to Toledo, and Laskan

Cooper is opening a branch office." There was a sob in her voice, and she darted a look over at Kylie. Her chin went up and she squared her shoulders. "That is that, and I won't back down on this, Matt. I know this company can afford it, and we're doing it."

"You are *not* doing it." Matt stared at her in puzzlement. "You're crazy, Kathy! You are just Craig's wife, not his damn boss!"

There were tears on Kathy's cheeks as she said with an ugly tone, "We're going, or *you'll* be the sorry one. You know what I mean, Matt. I'll *make* you sorry, and you know I can do it."

As Matt stormed off, Jaymie was left feeling disturbed and on edge. Kathy was so clearly unhappy, and if she could just reach out to her . . . but she was not going to go over there and risk another public harangue. She noticed that Kylie was watching her sister too and hoped that the two of them would find a way to solve their differences. The bond between sisters was far deeper, in her experience, than any between mere friends. She turned back to Becca, Daniel and Kevin with a lingering sense of sadness and a renewed determination to begin to fix her long-broken friendship with Kathy the very next day.

THE DOUGLASES DIDN'T stay to eat. There was far too much food, as was always true at every Fourth of July picnic Jaymie had ever been to. The one uneaten item was the weird green jelly mold that devolved into slime by the end of the meal, a victim of the heat, and had to be put out of its misery, dumped in the trash by a laughing Daniel.

But everything else was good, and despite the temptation to stretch out on the blanket after dinner for a nap, Daniel and Jaymie took Hoppy for a walk as the sun sank in the sky behind them. It took longer than expected because there were dozens of dogs, and of course Hoppy had to greet and sniff butts with each and every one of them, including a dachshund dressed as a hot dog and a border collie in an Uncle Sam outfit. Hoppy even had a play-scrap with Junk Junior, a bichon mix who was his best friend. When they got back, all of the dinner stuff had already been cleared away by Becca and Valetta, who had walked it back to their respective houses and the safety of refrigerators.

"I should have been here to help!" Jaymie protested.

"You had better things to do," Valetta said with a wink at Daniel, who grinned self-consciously.

Cushions and blankets for lounging were brought out of totes, while the fireworks display was readied on the island. Brock, Violet, Valetta and Kevin—who the three Nibleys roped in once they found out he was an excellent card player—played bridge on Brock's abbreviated card table, while Becca and Dee played dummy euchre on the top of a cooler. Jaymie and Daniel sat together. She petted Hoppy's head as the little dog draped himself across her lap.

Brock Nibley called Daniel over to referee and lend his expert opinion to a dispute he was having with Valetta over some computer issue, and Jaymie chose that moment to announce that she was taking Hoppy home before the fireworks and would refill the Thermos with tea at the same time. She walked through the village with Anna and little Tabitha, who was almost asleep after such an exciting day, tripping and lagging behind until her mom lifted her up to carry her while Jaymie carried their basket for Anna. Jaymie fed Hoppy and Denver, made a pot of tea and filled the Thermos, made sure the house was securely locked and walked back to the park, finding everyone just as she had left them, except that Kathy Cooper was now over sitting with and talking to her sister, Kylie, and Andy Walker.

The discussion looked civil, and Jaymie was relieved. There was something about the day's events that left her feeling more hopeful about being able to broach the distance between herself and her old friend. Was that crazy? She watched the three adults and tried to figure it out. Kathy was emotional, it was true, but right now, as she talked to Andy and Kylie, she had Connor on her lap, hugging him to her and resting her cheek on his towhead. Kylie was smiling; she reached out to touch her son but left him where he was, snuggled on his aunt's lap.

No one who loved a child that much could be impossible to reach.

Darkness fell, and the card games finished. The town considerately doused the lights over the walkway for the duration of the pyrotechnics every year, so when the lights went down, everyone settled in their spots to watch the show. Daniel reached out to her and took her hand in his as they lay back and watched the shower of brilliant fireworks over the river. She moved closer, into the crook of his arm, and rested her head on his shoulder.

A contentment stole into Jaymie's heart as she watched, and she knew that if she could just get past Joel's defection enough to be open to love, Daniel Collins would make a wonderful husband. *If* that's what she wanted. They'd only been going out for a month or so, and she had time before they took their relationship to any further depth. It was all speculative anyway.

People kept implying that Daniel was so interested in her and that she ought to jump at him. She didn't see it that way.

Marriage was not an experiment, and she didn't intend to do it twice. It wasn't Daniel who was pushing anyway; he had been nothing but patient and kind, not pressing her on the physical side of their relationship beyond a good-night kiss, which so far had been pleasant but not earth-shattering.

She had time.

A grand finale of pops and booms and crackles echoed off the riverbanks. They all stood, lit sparklers and sang "The Star Spangled Banner" as one last firework burst over the St. Clair, the red, white and blue shower reflected in the glassy surface below. Someone screamed, and someone else laughed and a dog began to howl. *Poor puppy*, Jaymie thought. Some dog owners had no sense. Dogs hated fireworks. But finally the last sparks floated to the water, and the crowd applauded. It was time to pack up and go.

Brock meticulously folded up his card table, as Violet, who would stay the night with Valetta, herded his weary, hopped-up, whiny kids down to where their car was parked. He and his children lived on a hobby farm outside of town, and thus the car was a necessity. Becca and Kevin laughed together as they folded their lawn chairs. Kevin had about half an hour before he had to be down to the dock for the last ferry back to Johnsonville.

"I have to go to the washroom," Jaymie said, folding her blanket and adding it to the pile in their little red wagon.

"The washroom? You're not going *here*, are you, in the park?" Becca said, wrinkling her brow, her pale face yellowish in the old-fashioned lights over the walkway.

"I sure am."

"It's a public washroom, Jaymie, and it's been busy all day here. It'll be disgusting!"

"Becca, I've had four cups of tea. I *need* to go! I should have gone at home when I took Hoppy back, but I didn't think about it. Besides, I don't have your delicate sensibilities about washroom cleanliness."

She strode off, but as she approached the cinder-block building, a square structure with both women's and men's washrooms as well as a public drinking fountain on each end, she heard a noise, and forlorn sobbing. Standing in the mud by the water fountain was Connor, Kathy Cooper's nephew. Jaymie approached, and bent over him. "Connor, are you okay? Where's your mommy?"

He stuck his hand in his mouth and shook his head, still making a moaning noise in the back of his throat. She couldn't make out what he was saying.

"Can I take you back to your Mommy? She must be here somewhere." She straightened and looked down to the grassy area where she had last seen Kylie Hofstadter and Andy Walker. There was just enough light from the public washroom lighting to allow her to see. She took Connor's hand to lead him away, toward the few people who were still folding chairs and blankets as they prepared to leave the park; maybe someone would know where Kylie was. But Connor tugged her back toward the washroom. "Is Mommy inside?" The boy shook his head. Jaymie stuck her head in the ladies' washroom anyway and hallooed, but there was not a soul inside. The crowd outside was thinning as well.

"Come on, Connor, your mom and grandpa must be looking for you. Let's go find them." She took his hand, but he again tugged her back to the washroom. "Are you trying to tell me she's here somewhere?"

He nodded. Darn preverbal boy; Tabitha, about the same age, would have been able to tell her. "Well, where is she?"

Connor *seemed* to understand, and he pointed to the washroom, or maybe *past* the washroom. Jaymie frowned. Was Kylie sick, vomiting behind the building, maybe? It wouldn't be the first time someone overindulged at a picnic or consumed a bad batch of mayonnaise-laden potato salad or had a touch of sunstroke.

"You stay right here, you understand?" Jaymie said. Connor nodded and sucked on his fist some more.

Jaymie, wishing she had brought a flashlight, poked her head around the back of the washroom, where it faced the river. There was a dark hump on the ground. "Kylie, are you okay?" She went over and tried to figure out what was where. "Kylie?" she said, putting her hand on the woman's shoulder. She wasn't breathing. "Damn, damn, *damn*!" Jaymie shrieked. She darted back around the washrooms, where Connor still stood.

A woman was approaching, heading to the washroom as well, and Jaymie called out to her, "Help me, please!"

"What's wrong?" the other woman said. "Are you okay?" She shone a light in Jaymie's eyes, blinding her momentarily. "What's up?" She shone the light down to the ground.

Jaymie recognized her; she was the African-American policewoman who had patrolled the Leighton's back alley during the trouble in May. "Officer Jenkins! I know you . . . remember me?"

The officer was blessedly calm and quick to respond. "I do," the young woman said, regarding her solemnly, her glance darting over to Connor. "You look awful, like you've seen a ghost. What's wrong?"

"This fellow's mom is . . . is sick . . . or something worse . . . behind the washroom. I don't know what to do!"

Becca approached. Jaymie pushed the boy toward her older sister and said, "Can you look after Connor? Kylie is sick. Or . . . something." She gave her sister a meaningful look, and then led the policewoman behind the washroom. Officer Jenkins already had her cell phone out, and as she shone her flashlight over the form, she was dialing a number quickly.

The light played over the woman on the ground as the officer rapidly spoke to someone on the other end of her call. One look was all it took, and Jaymie knew; this was not Kylie, and she was not merely ill. Kneeling in the soft, moist dirt, Jaymie gasped, "Kathy! It's Kathy Cooper!" She sobbed, covering her mouth with one shaking hand.

Kathy's eyes were open and staring, but blood coated her face and soaked the pale T-shirt she had on. Her arms were flung out, one fist tightly closed on some grayish hair or wool, or something like that. As the flashlight flickered, it sparkled off something shiny next to Kathy's bloody head; a broken glass bowl, one that Jaymie recognized, lay in the damp grass. It was Jaymie's square-based Depression glass bowl, broken into two glittering chunks.

❋ Five ❋

"KATHY, *KATHY*!" SHE couldn't believe it, *wouldn't* believe it. Kathy had to be just dazed. Jaymie grabbed her shoulders and tried to lift her up. The metallic odor of blood mingled with the sour smell of old mayonnaise from the glass bowl, and she felt lightheaded. "Kathy, say something," she sobbed.

"Stop it!" the off-duty policewoman said. "Step away from her, *now*!" She spoke rapidly into the cell phone again, while she shoved her flashlight into her shorts pocket, then grabbed Jaymie's T-shirt sleeve.

Jaymie staggered to her feet, shivering uncontrollably, as the policewoman pulled her away from the scene.

Officer Jenkins snapped her cell phone shut and took Jaymie by the shoulders. "There's nothing you can do for her now," she said, shaking Jaymie slightly. "She's gone. You need to wait right here until the team arrives."

A sob caught in Jaymie's throat. It couldn't be what it looked like, it just couldn't! She stumbled over to Becca, who stood several feet away.

"What the heck is going on?" Becca muttered, holding Connor to her leg with one hand. "Where's Kylie? And Kathy?"

Kevin and Daniel walked toward them, a look of deep concern on Daniel's face.

When Jaymie didn't answer, Becca peered at her in the shadowy gloom and asked, "Are you okay, sis?"

"I . . . I don't know." From a distance Jaymie heard a woman's frantic voice calling for Connor. She looked around, searching the grassy slope, where a few groups of people still lingered.

"Connor! There he is; my baby!" Kylie Hofstadter surged up the rise near the washroom, knelt and gathered her little boy up in her arms. "I was so worried about you, baby boy. Why did you wander off?" She hugged him hard, as Andy Walker followed up the hill and touched the boy's head, relief written on his tanned face.

"Auntie Kaffy," the boy said and began to cry, moaning sobs that cut through the misty stillness.

"What about Auntie Kathy?" Kylie asked, searching his face, stroking his head. "Where is she? Were you trying to find her?"

Jaymie watched the tableau, and then looked over at Bernice Jenkins, who stood guard near the corner of the washroom, her expression grim in the yellow light. In the distance the sound of a siren strengthened.

"Jaymie, what the hell is going on?" Becca asked, her voice tight with fear.

Jaymie realized that she was crying. Daniel put his arm

around her shoulders and echoed Becca's question. "What's going on?" he asked, as a cop car screamed to a halt on the street below the park.

"It's Kathy Cooper," Jaymie said, her words catching on a sob. "She's . . . she's *dead!*" She hadn't meant to say it so loud.

Kylie whirled. "What the frick are you talking about?" she asked. She handed Connor over to Andy Walker, who took the little boy a ways away, his face set and bleak. He had heard Jaymie too, probably.

Jaymie blinked, and couldn't find the words. She just shook her head. Kylie, appearing frightened, backed away, and retreated to Andy and Connor.

"I don't know what's going on," Daniel said, eyeing Jaymie with concern on his face. "But I think we ought to wait until we find more out before we say another word."

Jaymie shook her head. There was nothing more to find out; the horrible truth was that Kathy Cooper was dead. The only question was, who killed her, and why with Jaymie's glass bowl?

More police cars screamed up, sirens wailing. Uniformed officers pushed everyone back to the bottom of the hill, onto the grass by the street, and set up a perimeter. Jaymie watched it all from Daniel's protective embrace. But then a gray sedan arrived, and out of it stepped Detective Zachary Christian. He was the same detective who had been the investigator of the murder at the Leighton house in May. Even in the middle of the night, by the yellowish illumination of a bug light, he looked like he had stepped out of the pages of a romance novel; tall, dark haired, broad shouldered and good-looking.

He approached Bernice Jenkins, and she talked to him for a few minutes, gesturing eloquently, and finally pointing in Jaymie's direction. He straightened, swiveled and stared at her, a frown twisting his lips. She shrugged out of Daniel's embrace, and stood free of him, waiting. It only took a moment. Christian headed toward her.

"What the hell happened here?" he asked, as he strode toward her.

"I wish I knew," Jaymie said. The detective ordered the others to move away, and Jaymie repeated her story to him.

He gazed down at her. "You found another body. What are the odds, in this fly-speck town, that one woman would find two bodies?"

She shrugged, and the tears started again, even as she bit her lip, trying to quell them. "We used to be friends," she said, but it came out garbled, mingled with a sob.

"You and the dead woman?"

Jaymie nodded.

He looked off into the distance over her head for a long moment, then sighed. He called to some of the uniformed officers and made a twirling motion that took in all the people gathered on the rolling slope of grass. "Everyone here, to the station. Segregate as much as possible, especially these folks," he said, indicating Jaymie, Becca, Daniel and the others in their group, as well as Kylie and Andy. When Bernice approached, he said to her, "Call in Wolverhampton PD. We may need a few officers for canvassing the area. I want someone on the highway on both sides of town, and radio the ferry operator; I want the names of everyone on the last ferry. We have a killer, and I don't want to miss him or her. There were a thousand people or more in the park tonight, and every damned one of them needs to be interviewed."

A half hour later, in the familiar confines of an interview room at the Queensville police headquarters, Jaymie had a lot of time to think after the forensic team photographed then swabbed her hands and scraped her fingernails, with her permission. Her tears dried. Kathy Cooper was dead, and in a short while, Jaymie was going to have to tell Detective Christian that not only were she and the murdered woman enemies, her ex-friend had apparently been killed by a blow from one of Jaymie's new finds, the antique Depression glass bowl with her fingerprints smeared all over it.

The air-conditioning must have been working overtime, because she was getting cold. *Think, Jaymie, think*, she admonished herself. Who could have had access to the bowl? Who had killed Kathy Cooper? She closed her eyes, but all that came to her were the scene, and the figure. The first time she'd come around the corner, all she had seen had been a humped figure, and she'd thought maybe Kylie was sick. It was only when Bernice Jenkins, with her supersize flashlight, had accompanied her that she had seen more, had recognized Kathy, had seen . . . what? Besides her glass bowl cracked in two, what?

The area had been trampled all day. There were footprints . . . lots of footprints: tiny ones, medium-size ones, huge ones that were more deeply indented into the mud near the water fountain. Were they deeper because the person had stood there awhile, waiting? Or because the person was heavy? She didn't know. Something else had troubled her at the time, something . . .

The door opened and she blinked, dazed by the bright lights as she opened her eyes. Detective Christian looked down at her quizzically. "Were you sleeping?"

"No," she said. "I was thinking."

He shut the door behind him. "That's what my wife always said when she had her eyes closed."

Wife. So he was married? She looked down at his left hand, third finger. There was a groove where a ring might have once sat, but it wasn't there now. He caught her glance and looked down. "Three years later, and the shadow of a ring still lingers, right? Does that ever go away?"

"I don't know," she said, the inevitable blush rising to her cheek. "Detective, how did Kathy die?" she asked. "Was it the glass bowl that killed her?"

His eyebrows rose, and he sat down opposite her, at the bare white table that was bolted to the floor. "You saw the bowl?"

She nodded. "When Officer Jenkins played her flashlight around Kathy, I saw it." She had to do it, had to tell him now, or it would look like she was hiding something, which is what he had accused her of in the last case. "In fact, I recognized it; it is . . . was *my* bowl." She shuddered.

"Your bowl?"

"I brought it to the picnic with my homemade potato salad in it."

He drummed his fingers on the table and watched her, his expression impassive. Sighing, he said, "Why don't we start from the beginning."

"Good idea. Two days ago—"

"I'm talking about today."

"So am I," she said. "This all pertains, trust me. Two days ago—"

"Look, I need to just find out about today, then you can tell me about a week ago, or last year or 1995."

Little did he know that she just might have needed to go back to 1995 to tell him the *whole* story, but she wouldn't say that now. "I know you're probably in a hurry, but . . ." She trailed off and shook her head. "Okay, fine. Today."

Taking a deep breath, she related packing the bowl full of potato salad in the cooler.

"Why a glass bowl? Don't people use plastic? Or . . . what's that stuff called? . . . Tupperware?"

"You've seen my place. The bowl is my newest vintage find, and I like . . . I *liked* it. I always use my latest find a few times, just to get the feel of it, you know?" Tears gathered in her eyes. "Poor Kathy!" She covered her face with her hands, and her next words sounded oddly muffled. "God, I wish we hadn't fought. I wish I hadn't waited to try to make up with her. I wish—"

He leaned across the table, pulling her hands away from her face, and said, "Whoa, *whoa*! Wait a minute, you and the vic fought? When? Why?"

"That's what I was trying to tell you," she said. "Two days ago—"

He put up one hand and sat back, watching her, his dark gray eyes brooding under thick brows and hooded lids. Finally he sighed, scrubbed his hand through his dark hair and shook his head. "Okay, go on. Tell me from the beginning . . . *your* beginning."

So she told him, briefly, about her and Kathy's history, and then sped ahead to two days before and the confrontation at the Emporium. "So that's why I went to Craig's office to talk to him, and then to the feed store to catch up with her friend, Dani Brougham." She then told him about their day, and how Kathy had behaved at the July Fourth festivities.

"She was trying to egg me on into a fight, I could tell. And she got one. She said the most insane things . . . that I was chasing Daniel because he's rich and I'm lazy." Her indignation blossomed when she noted the smirk on his face. "I am *not* lazy. I work hard."

"Sorry, I'm not laughing. I have to say, though, the whole thing seems bizarre. She cut you off in high school and you still don't know why? And you haven't talked since, in a town this small?"

Jaymie shook her head, trying to figure out how to explain. "It's been awkward at times. But she made her feelings plain, and folks just didn't invite us to the same places. I don't know what happened back at Wolverhampton High, and now I probably never will." That awful thought made the whole thing worse, somehow. Sadness choked her. "She's gone. I was going to try to make up with her, but she's gone, and I'll never know why she hated me."

"You say she also had confrontations with other people today?"

She told him as much as she could remember about Johnny Stanko, Matt Laskan and about the trouble between Kathy and Kylie. She felt like a snitch, talking about Kylie, who had surely suffered enough since the death of her fiancé, but anything could be important to the investigation. She had learned that last time, when the slightest clue had told her who the real murderer was, and almost too late!

"Detective, was it . . . was it really my bowl that killed Kathy?" she asked again.

His eyes held no emotion and gave her no clue. "We won't know until the autopsy."

"Will you tell me when you find out? I just can't bear the thought that I brought . . ." Her voice broke. She cleared her throat and tried again. "That I supplied a murderer with a weapon!"

His expression softened. "I'll tell you, if I can, whether the murder was committed with the bowl," he said, his voice gentle. "It'll be the most unusual weapon I've ever seen, I'll tell you that, if it turns out to be what the killer used. I'm curious: Why didn't you miss the bowl after dinner? And who had the opportunity to take it?"

"Daniel and I went for a walk after we ate. I guess the bowl must have been taken then, before Becca and Valetta cleared all the stuff away, so they never noticed. You'll have to ask them. Maybe they'll remember something."

Detective Christian stood and tapped his notes together. "You can go home now. We'll want you to review your statement and sign it. You know the drill. If you think of anything more, you can add it in then." He opened the door for her, and said, "In the meantime, try not to worry about it. If someone is going to kill someone, they'll *find* a weapon. If it turns out to have been the bowl, it was likely just chance."

She left the interview room but got lost and ended up down a dead-end hall, which held a string of interview rooms, each with a glass window facing onto the hall. As she turned to head back the way she came, she saw Kylie through the glass window sitting alone, head cradled in one hand. Jaymie stopped and stared. *That poor girl.* Kylie had already lost her fiancé, and now she'd lost her sister. Some families just seemed to have more than their share of tragedy.

Jaymie headed back out to the main foyer and then out of the police station. Daniel, waiting beside his Jeep in the misty darkness, walked toward her, folding her into his embrace. "You okay?" he said, looking down at her face by the glow of the parking lot's overhead lights.

"Yeah. I just want to go home. Is Becca still here?"

"No, the rest of them are gone. I told Becca I'd wait for you and sent her and Kevin back to your place. He was supposed to go back to Johnsonville on the last ferry, but he missed it, of course. They wouldn't have let him go anyway,

I don't suppose. You're the last one. I guess that detective saved the best for last."

Jaymie looked up at him. "What do you mean?"

Daniel hugged her to him and walked her to the passenger side of the Jeep. "Nothing. Come on; I'm gonna drive you home. It's way after midnight and you must be beat."

❊ Six ❊

BECCA WAS WAITING up for her, and raced down the dim front hall, enfolding her in an embrace. "You okay?" she said, releasing her after a few moments.

Jaymie nodded and petted Hoppy, who bounced around her feet. "I'm all right. But let's not talk about Kathy tonight, okay?"

"That's all right. I do have something to talk to you about, though, sis," Becca said.

"First, I need tea," Jaymie said. They headed down the long central hall to the back kitchen, a room that took up the whole width of the house. There, she filled the kettle, pulled out the box of Tetley, bought at a Canadian grocery store, from the cupboard and dropped two tea bags in the old Brown Betty teapot. Becca knew enough not to talk until they each had a steaming cup and were sitting opposite each other at the work-worn trestle table. "What's up?"

"I put Kevin in Mom and Dad's old room," Becca said.

"Okay. Where else were you supposed to put him, a hammock strung from the rafters?"

"*And* I'm sleeping there with him."

Jaymie said, "Well, yeah. If you guys are at that stage of your relationship, then, of course."

Becca slumped and wiped her brow with mock relief. "I thought you were going to give me no end of trouble about that," she admitted.

Jaymie shook her head. "Becca, really? For crying out loud, when did I become this . . . this fuddy duddy that everyone has to tiptoe around? I'm thirty-two, not *eighty*-two."

Grinning, her older sister said, "Actually, Grandma Leighton is probably more easygoing than you are. You were always more straitlaced than I would have expected."

Irritated, Jaymie retorted, "Joel lived here, Becca, you *know* that. I'm assuming you know I'm not a virgin. Not that there's anything wrong with being a virgin."

Becca made a face, wrinkling her nose. "I tried not to think about you and Joel."

Jaymie well knew how her sister felt about her former boyfriend, and it was mutual. He thought she was an interfering busybody. "I'm not ten anymore, and I don't need my big sister worrying about me. And I'm *not* prim and proper, like some spinster aunt in a historical romance novel."

"Don't take it the wrong way," Becca said, reaching across the table and patting her hands. "I've always admired your aloofness. You're a really smart girl."

"Despite Joel," Jaymie said, with a sad smile, which faded immediately. The tragedy they'd experienced that night was too new, too raw, to be ignored, and Jaymie had questions. "Sis, when you and Valetta cleaned up the dinner dishes, did you notice my Depression glass bowl anywhere?"

Becca's mouth compressed. "That detective called me just before you came home and asked me the same thing." She shook her head. "I can't remember a *thing* about that bowl! Valetta and I were cleaning up, but there were a lot of people milling around. We were talking and laughing and . . ." Her eyes welled with tears and she put one hand to her cheek. "And to think . . . oh, Jaymie, was that what he killed her with?"

Funny how a murderer was always a *he*. Jaymie nodded. "*Someone* killed Kathy Cooper with my bowl. I saw it, Becca, the bowl, I mean . . . broken in half right near her bloody head." She shuddered, and a sob welled up in her throat.

Becca jumped up and came around the table and pulled Jaymie to her, holding her and rocking her. Surrendering for just a moment, Jaymie let the tears flow, tears for Kathy and her lost life and the friend Jaymie remembered from middle school. Memories flashed into her brain, of the silly games, the sleepovers, the whispered confidences. They should have been friends for life. Jaymie pulled away, grabbed a tissue from the box on the table, dried her eyes and blew her nose. "I'm all right."

"I know, hon, but you must be tired. Go to bed, Jaymie. You need sleep."

She followed Becca upstairs, said good night and went to bed, followed by a subdued Hoppy. Jaymie picked up her latest romance novel, a gripping story about a winsome waif's search for love—and a duke—in Regency England. Denver joined her, curling up at her feet, and Jaymie even lifted Hoppy up; he was a restless sleeper and so was seldom given the privilege of sleeping on her bed, but sadness made her want to be kind to someone or something. Finally, she drifted off, but awoke several times in the night, jarred to consciousness once by a sense that something was missing, and again by Hoppy's twitchy dreams.

It was a long night.

The morning started as it always did, with a quick cup of coffee, then a jaunt over to Anna's to make breakfast for the bed-and-breakfast guests. When she was finished, they sat down for a cup of coffee, as usual. Anna had heard about the murder from one of her guests, who had been in the park when the police arrived, and she was aghast to learn that Jaymie had found the body, and that it was Kathy Cooper.

"Oh, girlfriend! How awful for you," she said, watching Jaymie's face. "I feel so bad!"

Tears pricked the back of Jaymie's eyelids. "It was terrible." She shook off the dull ache in her heart. "You and Tabby were there when Becca and Valetta cleared the picnic dishes, right?"

Anna nodded. "I volunteered to help, but they wouldn't let me."

"After years of picnics, pie socials and heritage association dinners, they have it down to a science," Jaymie said. "You remember the bowl I showed you, the heavy glass one I brought the potato salad in?" Anna nodded. "Did you see anyone take it from the table before they cleared the dishes?"

Anna wrinkled her nose, her freckles scrunching up to play connect the dots on her cheeks. She shrugged. "I don't remember it at all. Why? Is it important?"

"Not if you don't remember. There's no real reason why you should."

Anna sat still for a moment, her mouth slightly open. "Do you mean . . . was that what they used? Oh, Jaymie! I'm so sorry."

"I know. It's worse, somehow, that she was killed with that bowl, something I loved, something I brought. I feel like I handed the killer a weapon and said, have at it."

"But you didn't, Jaymie."

"Please don't say anything to anyone else about the bowl. I'll get over it," she said, aiming a tremulous smile at Anna, who looked distraught. The last thing she wanted to do was stress out her pregnant friend. "Don't worry about me, Anna. Really."

Breakfast was only the beginning of the day at a bed-and-breakfast; Anna had a full house, and that required more laundry, bed changing and cleaning. Jaymie left her to go at the part of the job Anna enjoyed, with the promise that she would be back the next morning, as usual, to cook breakfast for Anna's guests.

Jaymie returned home and spent a half hour with Becca and Kevin talking over the events of the previous day and evening. Both reassured her, as the detective had, that if someone was set on killing Kathy, they would have found a weapon, even if the bowl hadn't been handy.

But . . . why the bowl? Jaymie couldn't help but think that the killer *had* to be someone who knew both that she and Kathy were "enemies," and that the Depression glass bowl with the potato salad was what Jaymie had brought to the picnic. That would limit the suspects to a reasonably small group. Kevin, however, pointed out that it may merely have been a case of a heavy and handy object. Soon after, they left. Kevin had to return to Canada on the ferry, and Becca wanted to walk him to the dock. She seemed happy, and Kevin was good to her. Jaymie hoped their budding love would fully flower.

Jaymie called Hoppy in and clipped his leash to his

collar. The little three-legged Yorkie-Poo was itching for a walk, and Jaymie needed to check in at the Emporium to see if any of the previous day's rental baskets had been returned. When possible, she asked that renters wash the melamine dishes they returned, but sometimes, if they were only in town for a day, they just couldn't do that, so she needed to get the dishes and wash them as quickly as possible.

Every fine day at eleven, Valetta would close her pharmacy/catalog order desk and have a cup of tea on the porch of the Emporium. Valetta Nibley had the sharpest eyes in Queensville and a long nose that sniffed out scandal and gossip as well as Hoppy sniffed out his canine enemies. If anyone had seen who lifted the bowl from Brock's table, she would have. Valetta was already on the porch steps in the July sunshine, sipping tea from a chipped mug that stated, "Pharmacists Do It OTC."

The Queensville Emporium was the oldest store in continuous usage for miles around. The storefront looked like it was still the 1800s, with painted wood columns supporting a pitched porch roof, big picture windows and a high false front. But in a determined bow to modernity, the front of the store was lined with boxes of colorful Water Weenies, hula hoops and water guns for purchase, and the big glass windows were plastered with ads ranging from houses for sale to babysitting services to cottages for rent on Heartbreak Island. Rose Tree Cottage was not advertised; the Leighton family's property was booked for the entire summer by returning guests from previous years, except for the two weeks when Jaymie and Becca's parents would use it. Jaymie had already been out to clean it four times, and she made a weekly trip there to check on the lawn, make sure the cottagers were happy and collect the rent.

Bill Waterman, the local handyman, had a ladder resting against the porch overhang and was taking down the red, white and blue bunting. His nephew, who was working with him for the summer, held the ladder. She waved at the handyman, then greeted her friend and sat on the step with Valetta, letting Hoppy sniff around the clumps of weedy grass surrounding the porch supports.

Valetta put her arm around Jaymie's shoulder, hugged her and released. She, like Becca and DeeDee Stubbs, was forty-seven or so, but only owned up to forty-two. She made no other attempt to cheat her age, though, letting her dark, thick hair gray at the temples and wearing increasingly strong glasses with bifocals that openly admitted to being bifocals. "You okay, kiddo?" she asked.

"I'm all right. Did the detective talk to you?"

"He sure did. I might have swooned, if I'd thought he would catch me. That is one handsome man."

Jaymie smiled, and it felt good. Valetta was quirky and humorous, but a fast friend of the *forever* type. She was full of contradictions: by turns she was a gossip who knew how to keep a secret, a cranky spinster (by her own accounting) who was a romantic at heart, and a woman who supposedly disliked children, while they flocked to her good-natured matter-of-factness.

"Did the handsome detective ask you about my bowl?"

Valetta set her empty tea mug on the wooden step. "He did . . . called me early this morning. First, he asked me if you had taken it away with you on your walk."

"He *didn't*!" Jaymie gasped. So she was a suspect, as she feared. How could he not suspect her, though, when it was her bowl, and she and Kathy had argued that very day and had, by her own admission, a long-standing enmity? "What did you say?"

"I said you did not have it, I could guarantee that, and he asked how I was so sure. I said, well, first, it would have been hard for you to conceal a bowl while walking arm in arm with your guy and wearing shorts and a T-shirt."

Foolishly, Jaymie felt her heart thump, and she wondered what the detective had thought when he'd heard that she and Daniel were commonly viewed as a couple. But that was silly, and she knew it. As attractive as she found the detective, and as intriguing as she had found him in their interaction during the murder investigation in May, he had made it clear she was a quaint small-town girl, in his eyes.

"Then I told him the truth: I know your bowl was on the table when you walked away because there was still salad in it, and I dished it out to a couple of other people."

"I wondered what had become of the rest of the salad. I figured you had just thrown it out."

"No, it was real good. Never waste good food. I dished some up to a guy in an Uncle Sam suit, and then . . ." She paused, chewing her cheek, a sign she was worried about something. She gazed down the road and squinted.

"What is it? What's wrong?"

Valetta pushed her glasses up on her nose and frowned. "I gave the bowl to Johnny Stanko to finish up the rest."

The memory of Stanko walking away, muttering that he ought to "whack" both Kathy and Craig came back to her. "Oh!"

"Now, I know what you're thinking, Jaymie, but I won't believe it," Valetta said, tears gathering in her eyes. "I won't believe he killed Kathy!"

"I didn't know you were close to him."

The other woman was still for a moment while the sounds of summer filled the silence: a lawn mower's steady thrum, children's voices at play and the *chirr* of an annoyed chipmunk. She waved as a car passed, and Hoppy trotted up to her on the top step, resting his chin on her knee. She scruffed under his chin, and he flopped on his back, exposing his belly. "I babysat Johnny when he was just a kid," she finally said as she petted the little dog's belly, smoothing the ruffled fur into a swirl on his pink tummy.

"I thought he had an older sister who died recently. Why didn't she babysit him?"

"She ran away from home when she was just fifteen or so. She didn't come back to Queensville until their parents died. There was some insurance money, and she bought that little house, while Johnny drank his share away."

"And now she's gone, too. Sad for him. Valetta, I hate to say it, but he said he ought to whack them both, Kathy and Craig. And then Kathy dies, *with* the bowl that he had in his hands!"

"I know, I know! I told that detective everything. God forgive me," she whispered, her head down. She was silent for a long moment, then raised her head and said, voice trembling, "But I will not believe Johnny killed Kathy Cooper." She looked Jaymie in the eye. "He has worked so hard to change his life: sobriety, peacekeeping, making up to folks for all he did when he was younger . . . that's all important to him now."

"Is that what you talked about when you followed him down to the dock?"

She nodded, gently moved Hoppy aside and stood up, stretching her lanky form. "I have to get back to work. I really hope they don't arrest Johnny." She looked down, meeting Jaymie's eyes. "He didn't do it, I would bet my life on it!" Valetta took friendship and loyalty seriously, but this time she was backing a dark horse.

"Did he bring the bowl back? If he did, then it's all right."

"I don't *know* if he did," Valetta said, groaning, swinging her empty mug on her finger. "That's the problem. If I knew he brought it back, then I could have told Detective Christian. But I don't remember seeing the bowl after that, and I know it wasn't on the table when Becca and I cleaned up." She shrugged and disappeared inside.

Jaymie retrieved the melamine that had been returned with the baskets from the day before, checked the reservation book for the weekend rentals, then walked home.

IT WAS AN old tradition to take food to the bereaved, and it was one that was observed rigidly by their Grandma Leighton, less so by their mom. Becca and Jaymie worked together and made some individual dinners for Craig, but Jaymie also wanted to take something to Kathy's mom, who at one time had been an integral part of Queensville society. Once she had belonged to the Lady's Guild, went to church regularly and for any dinner, civic or church-related, she and her husband could be counted on to provide the hams. Becca and Jaymie's mom always said that Hofstadter hams were the best in the county.

Everything changed when Kathy and Kylie's dad died. Without the strong hand of the patriarch, both the farm and the family unit seemed to disintegrate.

So Jaymie wanted to do something for Mrs. Hofstadter, who had, after all, lost a daughter. Jaymie may not have spent a lot of time at the farm, but everyone knew how kind the girls' mother was, and how unassuming. A casserole of macaroni and cheese was the answer; even though the weather was balmy, mac and cheese was always appropriate. After washing up the melamine from the baskets, Jaymie got to work.

As she grated the piles of cheddar and mozzarella for the dish, Jaymie wondered, where had the notion of food for those mourning a loss come from? Maybe Grandma Leighton would know, but if not, there was always her knowledgeable friend, Google. It would make a great chapter in *More Recipes from the Vintage Kitchen*, since it was a community tradition that dated back . . . well, she'd need to learn more about it.

While Becca took the individual dinners to Craig Cooper, Jaymie put the casserole on the seat of her van and took off to the Hofstadter farm, which was down an unpaved country lane a couple of miles out of Queensville. As she pulled up the driveway, she became increasingly uneasy at the derelict appearance of the property. Had the woman moved away, and Jaymie just hadn't heard? The once tidy lane, lined with cedars, was now also lined on the lawn side with junk: a broken washing machine tipped over, green garbage bags full and sagging, disintegrating cardboard boxes and paper litter everywhere. The front lawn grass was so long that it was bent over and tamped down by rain and wind.

It didn't get any better closer to the big red-brick house. A window on the second floor was broken and stuffed with what looked like a comforter and a piece of cardboard, and the front porch was full of more junk. The lane was so rutted that Jaymie decided to save her suspension and park her ancient van along the line of now ragged cedars. She did so, grabbed the casserole—still warm from the oven—and made her way toward the back door of the house. There was a battered pickup truck parked by the sidewalk that led to the back door, and the sound of voices raised in anger drifted to Jaymie. She paused out of sight and listened.

"Mom, we have to have a funeral."

It had to be Kylie speaking. There was a mumbled reply,

then Kylie said, "*I'll* do it, then. Craig is no freaking good. I don't even know if he cares. I gotta go. If I'm going to plan everything, then I'll have to get started."

Interesting. So by Kylie's reckoning, Kathy and Craig's marriage was not the happy little nest after all. It sounded like Kylie was preparing to leave, and Jaymie felt awkward lingering by the side of the house. If she was caught, it would look like exactly what it was: eavesdropping. Jaymie advanced around to the back door.

Kylie Hofstadter was standing at the open door with Connor, and Mrs. Hofstadter was standing in the mudroom. Kylie whirled around when she saw Jaymie. "What are *you* doing here?" she asked.

"Kylie Marie Hofstadter!" her mother said. "That's no way to greet someone!"

Strolling up the walk, awkwardly carrying the glass casserole dish, Jaymie considered her words carefully. "I'm so sorry about Kathy, Mrs. Hofstadter. I don't know if you remember me; I'm Jaymie Leighton, Alan and Joy Leighton's daughter? Kathy and I used to be friends. We . . . we had our issues, but I will never forget the fun we had as kids, and how close we once were."

"Right," Kylie said. She turned Connor around and sent him scooting toward the pickup with a pat on his bum, all the while glaring at Jaymie. "You have some nerve coming here like this." Her voice was tight with anger.

Jaymie, trying to ignore Kylie—whose opinion of her had, no doubt, been poisoned by Kathy—moved forward until she could better see Mrs. Hofstadter, who stood in the open door. The years had not been kind to the woman. Always portly but neat and tidy, she was now slatternly, with a dirty housedress on and feet clad in filthy slippers. The smell of organic waste drifted from the house; it was the scent of hopelessness. Paint was gone from the doorframes, and some of the wood looked like it was rotting out. Jaymie now understood why Kathy had tried to get her mother to sell the farm. If this kept up, the house would fall down around the woman's ears, and no one would ever know what happened to her.

"Mrs. Hofstadter," Jaymie said, holding out the casserole. "I just wanted to drop by and bring you this."

Kylie, who looked like she had been on the verge of leaving before, appeared rooted in place. She was a young woman, not more than twenty-five or -six, but there were dark circles under her eyes and her hair was a rat's nest. "She doesn't need your food—freakin' Leighton charity. Do you think we don't take care of our mom?" Her voice bubbled with anger and tears.

In the face of so much pain, Jaymie was silent, not trusting her voice to be steady. The tragedy of Kathy's death was at its most profound right here, right now.

Mrs. Hofstadter took the casserole. "Kylie, enough!" She turned to Jaymie and, water welling in her dull brown eyes, said, "I appreciate you thinking of me. Give my love to your grandma when you see her next. She was always real good to us. And to your mama, of course!"

"Mom and Grandma Leighton always said there were no better hams in the state than Hofstadter farm hams." It sounded inane in the midst of the family's tragedy.

"You should leave now," Kylie said, her hands balled into fists at her side.

"I'll come back another day for the empty casserole dish, Mrs. Hofstadter," Jaymie said, turning and walking away. It suddenly occurred to her that she had never thought to ask Mrs. Hofstadter why Kathy had turned against her, and, with Kylie there, there was no talking to her *this* time, but she had an excuse to come back—to pick up the casserole dish. She felt genuinely bad for the woman, who had lost so much, and wanted to help in any way she could. That, her grandmother would say, was what community was all about.

❧ Seven ❦

BECCA WAS ON the phone to her assistant in London, Ontario, when Jaymie got back to the house from the Hofstadter farm.

"I can't explain how the Old Imari platter got broken, Sabrina. We packed it as we always do, but we can't control how the courier treats it," Becca was saying, pacing the length of the kitchen. She caught Jaymie's attention and rolled her eyes. "Tell the customer that if she can photograph the broken item and send me the picture, I will either reimburse her, or send her another, as soon as I . . . no, wait, Sabrina, calm down! I *know* she's upset, and I'm sorry she chewed you out like that. You don't have to take that. Give her my cell number if she wants to yell at someone. Laurel is always difficult, and I won't take a hit on this. She's been known to try to get something for nothing. Failing the photo, she can *send* me the pieces, and I'll reimburse her for the platter *and* the mailing costs. I just need some proof that it's broken." She clicked the off button and grimaced to Jaymie.

"Problem?"

"Problem *customer*," Becca said. Rebecca Leighton Burke's business, RLB China Matching, provided china dishes in old and/or discontinued patterns to people all over the map, from Chilliwack to Chattanooga. "This woman claims the Old Imari platter I sent her was broken when it arrived. It could happen; shipping is never foolproof. But if she doesn't send me a picture or the pieces, am I supposed to just blindly believe her? That platter is worth five hundred dollars."

"It's insured, right?"

"Of course, but that's not the point. If Sabrina can't solve this, I might have to go back to London for a few days. Will you be okay, if I do?"

"I'll be fine. How did it go with Craig Cooper?"

"He wasn't home. I gather he was at the police station. His sister, Chloe, was there, though."

"I'd forgotten about Chloe!"

"She lives in Wolverhampton now, works at a hair-stylist's. She didn't seem too cut up that Kathy was gone."

"Did she dislike her?"

Becca shrugged, and Jaymie felt a moment of irritation. If she had been there, she would have wormed her way into the house and asked some questions about Kathy and Craig's relationship. "Well, what did she say?" Jaymie asked.

"Not much; she's staying with Craig to help plan the funeral, I guess."

"Well, I just saw Kylie Hofstadter out at the Hofstadter farm, and she claims *she's* organizing the funeral!"

"I was just dropping off food, for crying out loud, not conducting an inquisition." Becca already had her cell phone out and was scrolling down through her list of contacts. "I have to solve this platter problem," she said, her tone gruff. She moved out onto the summer porch, where she sat in one of the wicker chairs and made some calls.

So much for help with figuring out what had happened to Kathy! Jaymie had pictured talking to her older sister about what she'd heard from Valetta about Johnny Stanko and the bowl, and more about her troubling visit to the Hofstadter farm. Jaymie turned for comfort to the big box of cookbooks Becca had bought her the other day at the estate auction. She soon knew she was in trouble, because the stack of ones to discard was tiny, while the pile of ones she wanted to keep was so tall it toppled over on the trestle table.

The one that she had mined for the potato salad recipe (the one she hadn't ended up using!) was a gem; it was a thick, blue, cloth-bound book called *The Lilly Wallace New American Cook Book*, and it was far more entertaining than she would have thought, given the plain binding. Sea moss pudding. Brains à la king. Tomato orange aspic. Were these things really so prevalent in 1943, when the book was published? She'd have to talk to her Grandma Leighton about that!

Out on the lawn, Hoppy started to bark, and Jaymie figured it was Dipsy Poodle again. She loved to taunt Hoppy by meandering close to the fence, then shying nervously away when he got too close. Hoppy never gave up trying to win the pretty little poodle's attention, though. Jaymie kept perusing the cookbook and marked a page she wanted to show Rebecca about place-settings for china. A shadow fell across the page of her cookbook, and she looked up, annoyed. It was Detective Christian; she slapped the book closed.

"Your sister said to just come in," he said, gesturing

toward the summer porch, where Becca's voice still droned on.

"Sure, of course." She jumped up, unnerved by his sudden appearance when she was lost in recipe land. "Do you want coffee? Or tea?"

"It's July, and the middle of the day," he commented. "Though it's nice and cool in here."

"These old houses are well insulated. The deep summer porch is good for keeping the hot sun off the back wall, too. Folks used to sleep out on the summer porch on hot nights." But he wasn't there for a lesson in house construction from the 1800s. He had been in her kitchen before, and he'd commented that it looked like the kitchen of an eighty-year-old rather than a young woman. He clearly didn't know that retro was fashionable. "How about some lemonade? Then you can ask me what you want."

His eyebrows rose as he sat down at the trestle table. "Why do you think I'm here with questions?"

"Why else would you be here?" she asked. She got out two glasses and poured lemonade that she had made for their picnic the day before. She plunked one down in front of him, and some sloshed over the side. She got a paper towel and gave it to him.

He mopped up the lemonade, then took a long drink, sighing with appreciation. "It's good."

She sat down opposite him and waited. She always talked too much in his presence. Today, she would simply wait.

"More cookbooks?" he asked about the toppled stack that splayed across the shiny wood surface. He eyed her cookbook shelf, which was already jammed full.

She nodded. "Becca bought me a box of them at an estate sale."

"Why does anyone care about old cookbooks?"

She thought about it, not reacting to his bluntness, but to the actual question. "It's like stepping back in time, and a lot of us like to do that. Some folks join battle reenactment troops, some collect coins or stamps and some of us like to read cookbooks and try out old recipes. It takes me back to life in another era before fast food and packaged mixes. If you wanted a cake, you had to make it, not rely on Betty Crocker or Duncan Hines."

He nodded, holding her gaze.

She waited, but he didn't say anything, and finally, carefully keeping the irritation out of her voice, she said, "Detective, do you want to tell me why you're here, or are we going to play the silent game?"

He grinned, then quickly smothered the look. "Jaymie, can you think of any reason you would be mentioned when it comes to Kathy Cooper's murder?"

It was not what she expected, but then, she didn't really know what to expect. "I'm not sure what you mean."

He paused and stared into her eyes for a moment. "Your name keeps coming up when I ask around about Kathy Cooper's murder, and people who might have it in for her."

"I've already told you about our tiff, and the feud from high school."

He grimaced and swiped his hand through his tousled hair. "Fair enough. Is that it?"

"Yes."

"How many people knew about that?"

She shrugged. "Pretty much the whole town. In case you haven't noticed, gossip is a way of life here. I told you who else she fought with recently. That is it for my knowledge of Kathy Cooper."

"Okay. You asked me something last night, and I can tell

you now: as far as the medical examiner is concerned, your bowl was the weapon used to kill Kathy Cooper."

It was like a body blow; Jaymie's head swam, and her vision blurred. She put her head in her hands. "I figured as much," she mumbled. "That means whoever did it planned ahead, right?"

"You can understand, then, why I need to track the bowl."

"I've spoken to Valetta. She told me about giving the bowl to Johnny, and she also said she told you about it."

Becca came in from the summer porch that moment, with a look of concern on her face. "Why are you asking people if Jaymie had any reason to want to harm Kathy?" she asked the detective, her voice trembling with suppressed anger and fear.

"What are you talking about, Becca?" Jaymie asked, twisting to look at her older sister.

"I just got off the phone with DeeDee Stubbs," she said. "This guy has been all over town asking people if that old crap between you and Kathy was enough that you'd want to kill her. He's been asking about the quarrel you had at the picnic. I don't think you need to say another word to him, Jaymie."

Jaymie gazed steadily at the detective, a sick feeling wringing her stomach. Hoppy trotted into the kitchen and stood staring at him, too. He barked once, a warning, and growled, sensing the tension.

"I'm just doing my job," he said. "It is my task to investigate every aspect of this case, and, I'm sorry, Jaymie, but by your own admission, you and the victim did not get along."

"A teenage quarrel is no reason to kill someone," Becca said. "Otherwise this town would be decimated by half."

"Okay, but that 'teenage quarrel,'" he said, sketching quote marks in the air, "had flared up recently by all accounts. Two run-ins in the span of two days."

"You're done talking to him," Becca said, putting her hand on her sister's shoulder.

Jaymie shrugged it off. "No, I want this solved. He knows I didn't kill Kathy Cooper," she said, still holding the detective's gaze. She hoped what she was saying was true.

"Actually, I'm about done." He stood and straightened his suit jacket. "Thank you for the lemonade, ladies. I appreciate your time, Jaymie. If you think of anything else, we can talk when you come in to sign your statement."

"Wait! Have you asked Johnny Stanko what he did with the bowl?"

"Mr. Stanko is avoiding us," Christian said, with a rueful grimace. "In a town this small, you wouldn't think that was possible, but he's not home and hasn't been since the murder, as far as we can tell. He could be holed up inside his house, but he's not answering the door, and we don't have enough for a warrant. Yet." He held her gaze and said, with emphasis, "It would be best for him if he did talk to us, if he wants to clear his name."

Once he was gone, Becca sat down at the table, and Jaymie sat, too. "Do you think Johnny did it?" Becca asked, her voice trembling. "Why else would he be avoiding the cops?"

Jaymie shrugged. She was still reeling. Her bowl was the murder weapon. She was a suspect. "Valetta doesn't seem to think the guy is guilty, even though he's the last one who apparently had the bowl. She doesn't know what he did with it, though."

"Maybe he took off. If he did do it, wouldn't he have run? He always was impulsive, if I remember right. And he's been in trouble before."

"Do you remember his sister? Valetta told me she was older than him."

"Vaguely, but she was younger than we were, kind of in between Johnny and us in age. *She* was trouble, too . . . hung around a tough crowd, then took off. I moved away from Queensville myself, so I don't know what became of her."

"She came back. She owned a house here; that's why Johnny came back. He inherited the house when she died. Valetta told me all that." She thought back to the day before, the confrontation between Kathy and Johnny. Had there been enough anger there, enough vitriol for him to plot to kill her? He seemed so purposeless; was he even capable of that kind of planning? She knew so little, but she was intent on knowing more. She was not going to sit silently on a list of suspects and do nothing.

And whoever had killed Kathy needed to be caught. If she could help the police in any way, then she would.

The phone rang, and Becca answered it, then handed it over to Jaymie. It was Daniel.

"I was going to just drop in, but I didn't know if you were resting or whatever. Are you okay?"

She appreciated the concern she heard in his voice. Jaymie told him what she'd been doing and about the detective's visit. Becca was gesturing in the background, and Jaymie covered the receiver for a moment.

"What is it?"

"Why don't you ask him over for dinner?"

"Okay." Jaymie uncovered the phone receiver, and said, "Hey, Daniel, would you like to come here for dinner tonight? We're just doing hamburgers on the grill."

He agreed enthusiastically, and they hung up, deciding to talk later about the puzzling aspects of Kathy's death. Jaymie turned to Becca. "I'm going to invite Valetta and

Dee, too. I want to figure out what everyone knows about Kathy and if they have any ideas about who might have killed her."

"I only wanted you to invite Daniel over so I could get to know him better," Becca grumbled.

"I know," Jaymie said. "But you'll excuse me if I'm just a little more concerned with being a suspect in a murder case."

When Heidi Lockland phoned later to delicately probe about the murder, Jaymie invited her and Joel, too. May as well get used to them getting married, she thought, grimly. Daniel didn't like Joel much, but they were polite to each other in public. Jaymie called Anna and asked her to come over, but she wasn't feeling up to it.

Later, Becca stood at the counter peeling hard-boiled eggs for deviling, while Jaymie chopped vegetables for salad.

"You know," Becca said, looking over at her, "I don't want you to throw away a great guy like Daniel for the sake of Joel."

"I'm not throwing Daniel away. I like him, he likes me; I don't think there's anything serious yet. Just let it be, okay?" Jaymie said, aggravated. "Just because you get married on the second date, doesn't mean I will."

Becca froze, stared at her for a minute, then went back to work, the smell of boiled eggs filling the kitchen. Good thing Anna had decided against coming over. Eggs made her ill, right now.

"I'm sorry," Jaymie said, glancing over at her sister. "You *know* I didn't mean it. I just wish you wouldn't push so hard about Daniel."

"I'll stop. It's just . . ." She shook her head.

"What?"

"I don't want you to miss out, Jaymie."

"On what, marriage?"

She shrugged. "Marriage, kids, the whole thing."

Jaymie realized that Becca rarely talked about her inability to have kids. It was a tender spot, one that had only been spoken of twice that Jaymie could remember. "I know you mean it in the best way, Becca, but it has to be right. For me."

Becca reached over and gave her a quick hug. "Let's get this show on the road, since you've invited everyone we know over. What vintage junk do you want to use as serving pieces *this* time?"

Jaymie laughed. "I'll show you."

❧ Eight ❧

THE AIR COOLED as the sun sank behind the trees, glowing golden red and shooting brilliant shafts between leafy branches. Desultory conversation over dinner had sputtered out. There was no point in putting it off any longer. Jaymie had gathered everyone there for a reason. She looked around her circle of friends, and said, "So, does anyone here have any ideas regarding Kathy's death?"

Joel, sitting in one of the old Adirondack chairs with Heidi on his lap, said, "I didn't know her much. I saw her sometimes when I took stuff in to Craig, but that was about it."

Heidi cast a questioning look down at him, but said nothing.

DeeDee said, "My hubby can't stand Craig. He says he doesn't trust him. I don't know why. But he's never said anything about Kathy."

"How about *you*, though?" Jaymie asked.

"You can't cross-examine our friends, Jaymie," Becca protested.

"I'm just asking," Jaymie snapped back. She did wish sometimes that Becca wouldn't interfere. She was a lot like Joel, in many ways, but if Jaymie *told* Becca that, her sister would hit the roof.

"It's okay, Becca; Jaymie just wants to get to the bottom of things. Kathy was a good woman in some ways," Dee volunteered. "I was on a hospital fund-raising committee for Wolverhampton General with her. She worked hard . . . harder than most of the others."

"But what about her personally?" Jaymie pressed her advantage.

Sighing, Dee shrugged, and said, "I couldn't warm up to her. I know how much grief she caused you, Jaymie, and I just figured I didn't need her brand of drama in my life." She fiddled with the strap of her leather sandals, and muttered, "She seemed to have problems with a lot of people, even on the committee."

Valetta, usually one to stick up for anyone who was being criticized, quietly added, "Kathy was troubled. I worried about her a lot. You saw how she was yesterday; I thought she was going to blow her top when Johnny came along the Boardwalk path."

"Did anything happen when Daniel and I went for a walk? Or when I took Hoppy home?" Jaymie had already tried to pump Becca for information, but with Kevin there, she hadn't noticed a thing. Perhaps the others had been more observant.

A couple of them exchanged glances. There was silence for a long moment, broken only by the sound of a breeze rustling through the poplar trees, tossing the high branches. Valetta wrinkled her forehead in thought, and said, "Well, let's see. When Kylie and Andy arrived with Connor, Connor wanted to run to Kathy, but Kylie restrained him. I couldn't figure out why they sat there, with the whole park available. I mean, everyone knows Kylie has had trouble with her sister, but Kylie and Andy sat down right next to Kathy and Craig."

"It looked to me like Andy and Craig were in cahoots to try to get the sisters to get along," Dee said.

"Maybe," Becca said. "But still, Kylie kept Connor away from Kathy."

"Until later," Jaymie said. "When I came back from taking Hoppy home, Kathy, Kylie and Andy were all sitting together, and Connor was on Kathy's lap." She paused, then said, "Does anyone know about Kathy and Craig moving to Toledo to open a branch office of Laskan Cooper?" She looked around.

Joel cleared his throat, but shook his head when Jaymie looked toward him.

"Isn't anyone curious?" she probed.

"I think it was a plan that was in the works, but I didn't know they had decided on it for sure." Valetta shrugged. "I might be able to find out more."

"Why do you want to know any of this?" Daniel, who had been silent until that moment, eyed Jaymie with alarm. "You *are* going to let the cops take care of this one, aren't you? You almost got killed last time there was trouble, Jaymie."

"I agree with Daniel," Becca said. "Let the police do what they need to do."

Jaymie looked toward her sister with surprise, she who just hours before had been so contrary with Detective Christian. She decided to let it slide. "Okay. All right. Fine." No promises, though. She'd do what she wanted.

Conversation turned to other topics. Dee and Becca went inside to prepare a treat, butterscotch pecan cookies and Dee's homemade ice cream, served in vintage crystal champagne saucers that Jaymie liked to use for dessert. What was the point of nice things if you never used them?

When Jaymie strolled over to tempt Hoppy away from the fence, where he was whining at Dipsy Poodle, Heidi followed her, a troubled expression on her pale, pretty face.

"Jaymie, can I talk to you for a moment?" She plunked down in the grass and extended her tanned legs, leaning back on her hands.

Jaymie sat down by her, cross-legged, and snapped her fingers, trying to get Hoppy's attention. "What's up?" Heidi wasn't often so serious. Her perpetual expression seemed to be a sunny smile.

"I got to thinking about it, and . . . well, actually, Joel seems to think I wasn't sensitive to your feelings yesterday, the way I told you about us getting married."

That was Joel, censoring his girlfriend again. He needed to constantly "fix" the women in his life, critiquing their mannerisms and vocabularies, their ways of interacting with other people. Why had Jaymie put up with him for so long? And why, oh why, had she ever imagined she was in love with him? Every little detail she learned of his behavior toward Heidi was another step on the road to recovering from their failed relationship. "Don't you worry about that," Jaymie said, holding Heidi's gaze. "You were understandably happy and excited. Don't let anyone, least of all Joel, dampen that."

Tears welled in Heidi's eyes. She reached out and pulled Jaymie into an unexpected hug. "Thank you. You are just the sweetest . . . why did Joel ever leave you? I don't understand."

"Well, he had *you*," Jaymie pointed out, bluntly, pulling away. She had never intended to become Heidi's "bestest friend."

"Oh. Right."

Dee, her eyes wide with curiosity, brought them each a bowl of ice cream and a cookie, and Jaymie smiled up at her reassuringly. She trotted back to the group and whispered to Becca, then settled down to eat. Jaymie scooped up some of the ice cream with the cookie as Heidi delicately spooned some into her mouth, then set the dish aside. Hoppy trotted over and polished off her deserted dessert, cookie and all, while Dipsy barked from the other side of the fence.

"Heidi, if we're being honest, why do you put up with Joel?" Jaymie asked, setting her empty bowl down in the grass. "He can be a great guy, but he's so critical. Doesn't that drive you nuts?"

"But he's usually right," she said, drawing her knees up and hugging them. "I *can* be thoughtless. I never realized how screwed up my whole family was until I came to Queensville to live. My daddy treated me like I was the center of the universe, you know? When he wasn't working, that is. And he was usually working. But suddenly he'd notice me, and then it would be a lavish birthday party, and a cruise and new clothes. A pony that I was afraid of. A trip to Switzerland." She sighed and rested her chin on her knees. "I hate skiing."

Poor little rich girl. "There are good things about being wealthy, Heidi."

"I guess. I don't have to work."

"That wasn't actually one of the good things I was thinking of." They sat in silence for a moment, then Jaymie remembered something from the day before. "When you and Joel were coming along the path yesterday, you stopped and talked to Craig and Kathy. I didn't even know you knew them."

Heidi colored faintly, her cheeks tinged with pink, and looked away. "Um, well, Joel uses Craig at tax time, and . . ."

"Go on," Jaymie said, puzzled by Heidi's sudden reticence.

After a long pause, Heidi said, softly, "Kathy kind of made friends with me when I first came to Queensville and Joel and I got together. No one else would talk to me, but Kathy was really nice. They had us over to dinner and everything."

Jaymie didn't say anything. She was not going to hurt Heidi by saying that Kathy likely befriended her because she perceived her to be Jaymie's enemy. The girl's next words showed that such a comment was unnecessary.

Heidi said, "I *know* why she talked to me, why she went out of her way when no one else would give me the time of day, but Kathy had a nice side. I know you may not—"

"No, I get that. Really, I do. I only experienced one side of Kathy in the last few years, but we were friends once, and she was a nice girl."

"I feel so bad about what happened to her," Heidi said, with a sniffle. "I guess that's why I'm so emotional today. I just feel bad about . . . about still being happy."

Jaymie filed away the thought that Joel had made it seem like he didn't know Craig and Kathy beyond retaining Craig as an accountant, but they had been to the Coopers' home for dinner. That indicated a social relationship beyond what he was admitting to. "No matter what Joel says, Heidi, you are not insensitive. Don't ever let him make you doubt yourself." She paused, then went on, "You know, you might be able to help me."

"Really? How?"

Becca and Dee were still eyeing her and Heidi as they sat together talking, and even Valetta was watching them. Joel was too busy bending Daniel's ear about something to notice.

"Heidi, let's take Hoppy for an after-dinner walk."

They both jumped up, and Jaymie took their bowls into the kitchen and grabbed Hoppy's leash, and they took off down the walkway to the back gate. Once they were out on the lane, Jaymie introduced Heidi to Trip Findley, her elderly but fit neighbor, whose property was behind theirs on the same back lane. Just back from his evening stroll, he lingered and flirted a little with Heidi, who giggled, then Jaymie turned toward the river and they proceeded.

"So, what did Kathy say to you yesterday?" Jaymie asked.

"Well, she congratulated me on the engagement." She thought for a moment. "Nothing else, really."

Jaymie was disappointed. She wasn't sure what she was looking for; anything at all, she supposed, that would give her some indication of who else Kathy had angered lately, or threatened. Anything to point the investigation away from herself. The streets were quiet, the shops on Main were all closed and only a few folks strolled by on their evening walks. Mrs. Imogene Frump, working in her garden on her prizewinning roses, eyed them as they passed. Then, as Jaymie waved to her, she waved back and hobbled into her house as quickly as her arthritic hip and artificial knees would take her. Jaymie figured it would be all over the Queensville "telegraph system"—a string of geriatric gossips—that Jaymie Leighton had lost her mind and befriended the girl who'd stolen her boyfriend away.

The inhabited portion of the town dwindled as they approached the parkland that lined the river. It was time for some hard facts. "Heidi, because of the tension between Kathy and I and the public squabble we had yesterday and the fact that the weapon used to kill poor Kathy was my stupid bowl, I'm a suspect in her murder."

"Oh *no*!" Heidi exclaimed, turning toward her. "You wouldn't hurt a fly!"

"*I* know that, and *you* know that. All my friends know that. But it doesn't look good, so I want the police to find out who did it quickly." She paused, then added, "For her family's sake, too. I can't imagine how they feel right now."

"Poor Kylie is devastated."

"Do you know Kylie well?"

"Not really. But she must be, right?"

"What about Kathy? If you spent time with her, did she ever mention anything in relation to anyone who had threatened her, or with whom she had trouble?"

Heidi shrugged. "Maybe Joel will remember something."

Not likely. Joel was pretty self-absorbed and rarely noticed anything not relating to himself. So Heidi would not be a fount of helpful information. It was disappointing, but okay; the real reason Jaymie had wanted to go on this walk had been to have a look at the area again, to try to figure out if she had missed anything. Heidi wasn't the ideal companion, but no one else would have wanted to do this tonight, and Jaymie didn't want to wait.

Heidi shivered and rubbed her arms. "I should have brought a sweater."

A sweater? In July? "Do you want to go back?"

"Oh no! It's okay."

Heidi was thin, one of those girls with small bones and a petite frame. Not that Jaymie was gargantuan, but she was well rounded and curvy, especially after six months of testing recipes. Jaymie climbed the sloped grass to the railed path overlooking the river. A few sailboats were just heading into the marina for the evening.

They strolled down the walk, stopping often for Hoppy to examine every post of the railing, until they came to the very spot where Jaymie and Becca had been sitting. "Are you sure that when you stopped to talk, all Kathy said was congratulations on your engagement?"

Heidi frowned. "I think so. Let's see, Craig was talking to Joel, I talked to Kathy briefly . . . nope. Nothing else."

Jaymie sank into thought, recreating moments during the day, random comments that had puzzled her and still did. Something was nagging at her, some sound or sight that she hadn't processed yet. What was it? Something around the time she was looking for Connor's mom for him.

If she was going to figure out who did this and get herself off the hook—yes, the police had a better chance of figuring it out, but she hadn't done half bad the last time, when she had sniffed out the killer of Trevor Standish—then she needed to organize her thoughts and write down all the random bits and pieces of stuff to follow up on. The day before had been confusing and busy and upsetting, the ideal situation in which to get away with murder.

As Jaymie saw it, there were two possibilities: either the murder had been planned to take advantage of the crowd and the confusion, or it had been a spur-of-the-moment crime necessitated by something Kathy was either going to do or say. Of the two, the second seemed more likely, given that the killer could not count on finding a weapon like her heavy glass bowl handy.

As sad as it seemed, Kylie certainly had a motive, given that, from what Jaymie understood, Kathy intended to try to get custody of her nephew, Connor. That meant Andy

Walker had a motive, too. It would have been a lot harder to see his grandson if Connor were in Kathy's custody and they moved out of state. But there were other suspects. The husband was always a possibility, but as far as she knew, Craig and Kathy had a normal, imperfect but reasonably healthy marriage. She needed to find out more about that. Johnny Stanko was a great candidate; he had a hair-trigger temper, and had squabbled with Kathy just hours before her death. Valetta might not want to admit it, but he was also the last one who'd had the bowl . . . as far as she knew.

"How far are we going?" Heidi asked. She looked tired already, and cold.

Jaymie sighed. Heidi was not a great partner in crime fighting. Ideally, a coconspirator ought to be as curious as Jaymie was, and as energetic. That description fit more than one person in her circle of friends, but the absolute epitome of it was Valetta. She'd remember that the next time she wanted to snoop around. "I want to go as far as the public washroom." Hoppy eagerly tugged at the leash, wobbling on, nose to the ground. He had the energy and curiosity of a Jack Russell in the body of a Yorkie-Poo.

Twilight was gathering, but Jaymie could still see well enough. The crime-scene tape fluttered morosely from a post by the washroom and a nearby light standard, with a long strand of it wound around the railing by the river. Jaymie picked her way closer, examining the ground. She hoped Heidi wouldn't ask what she was looking for, because she had no clue. There were a lot of footprints, large, medium and tiny, and there was a deep line etched into the muddy ground. She had noticed an officer with a wheeled instrument, presumably measuring the crime scene, since he was calling out distances to a fellow officer who was sketching, so the line was likely just from the wheel of that tool.

She circled the washroom, watched by a wide-eyed Heidi, and nervously approached where Kathy had lain dead. Emotion welled up in her, and she experienced a sickening lurch of horror. What had Kathy felt? Had she faced some-one she knew, watching in puzzlement as they raised a glass bowl above her head? Or had a stranger approached from the shadows and hit her before she had time to react?

And why *was* Kathy behind the washroom? There was no indication that she had been dragged, so she must have gone there purposely. Or had someone she knew been lurking in the shadows and called out to her? Something was nagging at her yet again, something buried in her memory . . .

"Can we go back soon?" Heidi asked, her voice thin and reedy.

Jaymie looked up; the poor girl was shivering uncontrol-lably. Hoppy was still sniffing the area near the spot where Kathy had died, but Jaymie had no wish to examine the ground to see if there was blood mixed with the muck. "Sure, let's get back. Joel is probably wondering where you are."

"And Daniel will be wondering about you," Heidi said, happily scaling down the sloped embankment that acted almost like a levee for the St. Clair River.

Jaymie hoped not. She assumed Daniel would trust her ability to go for a walk in Queensville without getting into trouble.

They were silent on the way back, and Jaymie had too much time to think. Tears welled up in her eyes, tears for Craig and Mrs. Hofstadter and Kylie and Connor, but most of all for Kathy, whose life, no matter what anyone else thought of it, was precious to her. She had plans, ambitions, desires and seemingly years ahead of her.

When they were kids they had all played the game of

"What will I be when I grow up?" and though Jaymie's answer changed with her whims, Kathy always said the same thing: she was going to be a nurse. She wanted to help people. What had changed in her life? Had the child she lost soured her? Or had something else, a shadow from teenage-hood, darkened her outlook?

"Jaymie, are you crying?" Heidi asked.

Jaymie nodded, her mouth working. "I'm so sad for Kathy." She couldn't say more or her voice would break, and she held back the sob that formed in her throat as she kept walking. She felt Heidi's small hand clasp hers.

"It'll be all right, Jaymsie," Heidi said, using Joel's pet name for her and squeezing her hand. "It will. You don't think so now, but the police will figure out who killed her, and it will all turn out okay."

Jaymie squeezed Heidi's hand back and released. "Thank you, Heidi. I appreciate that."

"Did it help?"

"Sure."

Heidi skipped one hop. "Good. I've been working on being more supportive lately."

Jaymie stifled a sigh; that someone had to work on being supportive was a new one. But at least the girl was trying to improve. If every person did the same, the world would be a better place. Jaymie wished she had been as willing as Heidi to openly admit her imperfections and try to fix them. If she had, she and Kathy might have been able to patch up their problems, whatever they were.

As darkness closed in, they made it back to Jaymie's home and their friends. Valetta, Dee and Becca were finishing up the dishwashing while the guys still chatted outside, their voices low in the gloom. She unsnapped Hoppy's leash, and he lurched over to his food bowl by the stove and settled in for a good meal, crunching away while Denver materialized out of nowhere to stare at him as he ate. That feline intensity used to freak out poor Hoppy, but he was now immune to Denver's attempts to unnerve him.

Daniel appeared in the kitchen. "You're back," he said, putting his arm over her shoulders.

He was warm, and she appreciated his solid good nature. She leaned against him, and said, "Heidi and I went for a walk with Hoppy."

"Joel has some idea for a software application he says will revolutionize life for salespeople everywhere," he murmured.

Jaymie looked up in time to see Daniel roll his eyes. She chuckled. "Was he picking your brain?"

"Kinda. I got the feeling it was really a sales pitch, because he said whatever company developed it would make millions."

She laughed softly, longing to ask if Daniel had thought to say he already *made* millions, thank you very much, but that would be indelicate. Daniel never talked about money. That was one of the things she appreciated about him. He had loads of cash but drove a beat-up Jeep when he was in Queensville and didn't throw his money around. He had to go—something about a conference call with someone in Japan—so she walked him to the front door, experienced a rather nice kiss and said good night.

Dee, Joel and Heidi left. Becca was on the phone again with her assistant, so Valetta helped Jaymie with the last of the dishes, the crystal champagne saucers, standing by with a waffle-weave tea towel.

The low light over the kitchen sink glinted off Valetta's glasses. "You know, I know you didn't do it, Jaymie."

"I *hope* you know it!" Jaymie exclaimed, handing her older friend one of the champagne saucers to dry.

"Well, of course. That came out wrong. What I mean to say is, I know *you* didn't do it, so who did?"

"There were a lot of people who had run-ins with Kathy Cooper yesterday."

"But to kill someone? Over a run-in?"

"I know," Jaymie agreed. The kitchen was dim and peaceful, with just the drone of Becca's voice in the background. Hoppy was done with his meal and had curled up in his basket near the stove. Denver, happy now that everyone had gone, wound around her feet as she again dipped her hands into the hot soapy water in the Belfast sink. "The police are looking for Johnny Stanko."

"I know."

She glanced over at Valetta as she handed her friend another champagne saucer. "Do you know where he is?"

"I have an idea," Valetta admitted. She dried the crystal and set it on the table with the others.

Jaymie considered her next words carefully, and then said, "Maybe he ought to give himself up, or go in to talk to the cops, or something." She paused, but it had to be said. "Valetta, are you *so* sure he didn't lose his temper and kill Kathy?"

"I know people are going to think that. I suppose it's possible. He's been trying so hard to change, but everyone has their breaking point. Why would Kathy meet *him* behind the washroom, though, of all people?"

"I was wondering about that as Heidi and I walked along there tonight. So you think that Kathy went there purposely—like a planned meeting—and met her killer? That she was going there to talk to someone?"

"I do."

She eyed Valetta speculatively. "You have tomorrow off, right?"

"I do." Valetta waited, watching Jaymie's face, a look of hope in her eyes.

"Do you think we might be able to find Johnny Stanko if we gave it a shot tomorrow?"

"Yes," she said, with a sigh of relief. "I'm worried about him. I want him to go to the police, and I don't want it to turn into a bad situation. I was going to go alone, but I'd love company."

"Tomorrow, then."

"Come on over after you're done at the Shady Rest."

❖ Nine ❖

WITH A FLURRY of warnings to Jaymie to stay out of trouble, Becca left on the ferry the next morning. She wasn't taking her car because she was meeting Kevin in Johnsonville, and he was driving her to London. They were all going to meet on Heartbreak Island on Sunday to do some needed work on Rose Tree Cottage before their next renters arrived.

Jaymie and Hoppy had walked Becca down to the dock, and she threaded her way back through the village toward Valetta's. Valetta Nibley's cottage was in the old section of town, as were those of many of the "founding villagers," the homes of families who had been in Queensville for generations. Mrs. Trelawney Bellwood, who played Queen Victoria in the Tea with the Queen Heritage Society fundraising event every May during Victoria Day weekend, was in her back garden, which bordered a lane named after her husband's family, when Jaymie walked Hoppy past her property.

Roary, Mrs. Bellwood's pug, rushed the fence, yapping and snuffling and making a huge racket for a pug. This was a game Hoppy and Roary played, so Hoppy lunged at the fence too and they pretended to hate each other. Hoppy wobbled and lunged, while Roary yapped with asthmatic snuffles between each string of hoarse barklets. Put together, the two played amicably, but put a fence between them and they acted like tiny maniacs.

Mrs. Bellwood, who had only been visible as a rounded, madras plaid bottom wedged between her shed and the fence, straightened, hand to her back, and hobbled toward the chain-link fence, her face red. Her hands were shielded by garden gloves and she had a fistful of berry-laden vines. "How are you this morning, Jaymie? I hear you were out walking with that Lockland girl yesterday evening."

It was surprising that Mrs. Imogene Frump's information had made it all the way to her mortal enemy, Mrs. Bellwood, but they had connections in common among the ladies of the village. "So you and Mrs. Frump have been talking?" Jaymie said, teasing her elderly friend.

"Nonsense," Mrs. Bellwood said. "I don't know what you're talking about. Imogene and I have nothing to say to each other. Trip Findley was on his walk this morning and stopped to talk to me."

So that explained it. "Heidi is a nice girl," Jaymie said, pulling Hoppy back from the fence to give Roary time to recover from his fit. The pug sneezed, snuffled and wheezed, then flopped on his back and rolled in the sun-warmed grass. "She and Joel are getting married, and I thought I'd tell her a little about the village. She's been here a while, but hasn't really met anyone."

People had shut Heidi out of village life for months because she had "stolen" Jaymie's beau, but it was time the foolishness stopped. Jaymie was determined to right the wrong that had been done to the young woman. Yes, Heidi had "stolen" Joel, in one sense, but he was not a necklace left out to tempt a thief; he was a man, and if it hadn't been Heidi, it would have been someone else, Jaymie had decided. It was his way out of a relationship he was no longer invested in.

"One of those modern girls: fake tans, fake white teeth, fake *everything*," the old woman grumbled.

"So, you're ripping out the deadly nightshade?" Jaymie said, to change the subject.

Mrs. Bellwood waved the clump of weedy vines toward her potting shed. "It's growing up behind the shed, and I didn't even know it! Don't want Roary to get a mouthful. My boy will eat anything, even the deadly stuff."

"Is it dangerous for pets?" Given its name, Jaymie realized, that was probably so.

"It *is*. Millie Dickons's cat ate some last summer and died," she said baldly. "Started drooling all over her, swatted her with his claws, and then he was gone. They found a quarter pound of deadly nightshade berries in that greedy cat's stomach!"

"Wow, I didn't know that. I'll have to make sure there's none growing up in the trumpet vine. I don't think Denver or Hoppy would go for it, but you never know. I have to go now . . . meeting Valetta this morning." Jaymie tugged on Hoppy's leash.

"You tell her I'm waiting for that recipe she promised me for cranberry chutney!" the woman said, waving the handful of weeds.

"Okay, I'll let her know." She gave Hoppy another tug, and he obediently trotted back to the path.

They headed on down to Valetta's cottage, which was tucked at the other end of Bellwood Lane. It was a frame cottage with a front porch that stretched the width of the house, and was painted olive green with darker green trim. Jaymie thought the color was ugly, but Valetta was proud of her handiwork, so she never criticized. Becca claimed the color was modern and fit the Arts and Crafts–influenced style of the house. Valetta met her at the gate, and the women exchanged hellos.

"So, where do you think Johnny is?" Jaymie asked.

Valetta, dressed in a pair of black shorts, a black T-shirt and sunglasses, closed the gate behind her and darted her gaze up and down the street, as if looking for detectives lurking behind trees. "Follow me."

So, it was somewhere they could walk to, Jaymie surmised. However, after twenty minutes of walking in circles, down drive lanes, along the main street, into the newer section of town and then back to the old, Jaymie finally said, "Valetta, can we get there on foot or what? I don't know if you noticed, but we're now walking past Jewel's Junk for the second time." She waved to Jewel Dandridge, the proprietor of the junk shop that Jaymie frequented and sometimes looked after. Junk Junior, Jewel's bichon mix, barked at Hoppy from the wooden deck outside the shop; Hoppy yapped back and tugged at his leash, longing to go over and sniff butts with the other dog, his best canine buddy. Jewel watched them from her spot in the window of the shop.

"I'm just wandering in case anyone is following us," Valetta mumbled.

Well, that explained Valetta's version of undercover spy wear, shades and all. Jaymie glanced around at the quiet streets and lanes. The tourists who were in town were likely still lingering over coffee and beignets at the Queensville

Inn's coffee shop. A police officer would have shown up as clearly as a tattoo on a church lady.

"Okay," Valetta said, after a final look around. "I think it's safe."

Now they set off at a blistering pace, Valetta's long legs taking strides that Jaymie had to trot to keep up with. She dashed down a parking alley behind a row of Queen Anne–style homes, then cut down a sloped side street toward the neighborhood near the docks. There, the houses were a little rickety, slightly off kilter, some neat and rimmed in gardens, some decrepit and looking the worse for wear. She followed Valetta to the end of the street as even Hoppy began to tire, and stood beside her friend, staring at a small frame cottage that was painted a funky shade of lavender.

"This is Johnny Stanko's house?"

Valetta nodded and squinted at it through her sunglasses.

"And you think he's here, even though the police haven't been able to get him to come to the door?"

Valetta nodded again, looked both ways, and headed up the gravel laneway, past the house, to the overgrown back-yard, where a slanted stoop sagged wearily against the back. A screen door stood open, though the inside door was closed, and an array of cigarette butts and paper coffee cups littered the lengthy grass around the porch. Weeds squeezed through the porch boards, and weed vines—mostly bind-weed and nightshade—climbed the uprights that held the roof of the tiny porch. Jaymie kept Hoppy back from the nightshade, mindful of Mrs. Bellwood's warning, and waited while Valetta carefully climbed the rickety steps to the back door.

She pounded on it and called out, "Johnny, it's Valetta. Let me in!" When there was no answer, she pounded again and said, loudly, "I'm not leaving, so you'd better let me in."

She rattled the doorknob, but the door was jerked out of her hand and Johnny Stanko stood in the open doorway, bleary-eyed, staring moodily at her.

Pushing past him, she motioned Jaymie to follow, saying, "Shut the door after us. I want to talk to you, Johnny."

This wasn't what Jaymie had expected, but she followed. The house was musty and smelled of cigarette smoke, but it wasn't filthy, like she had expected. She followed her friend into the kitchen, a small gray room lined in dirty white cupboards stained with a yellow overlay of nicotine. Johnny, dressed only in shorts, his huge feet bare and slapping the gray linoleum like swim fins, padded over to the sink, got a mug down from the cupboard and spooned instant coffee into it from a jar. He ran the hot water, filled his mug and drank the "brew" down in a couple of gulps.

"Coffee?" he asked, holding up his mug.

"No, we're not here on a social call," Valetta snapped, hands on her hips. She had taken off her sunglasses and donned her usual thick, clear glasses. "Have you been here since the murder of Kathy Cooper?"

He warily shrugged, his gaze sliding away to settle on the old Arborite dinette set.

"A shrug is not an answer. Johnny, I know the police have been here knocking on your door and that you haven't answered. Why?"

Hoppy busily sniffed around Stanko's bare feet, but the man didn't move. He watched Valetta like she might lunge and bite him, but otherwise didn't say a word. Jaymie watched him in turn, wondering if he was the one who had murdered Kathy. Valetta glanced around the kitchen, her gaze pausing on the pie plate full of cigarette butts, and asked, "Do you have any food here?"

"You hungry?" He turned and padded into the next room,

and Valetta and Jaymie followed. "I got Cheetos, and Slim Jims and some corn chips left," he said, rustling through some shopping bags on the sofa.

Valetta, her charm bracelet jingling on her bony wrist, grabbed the man's shoulder. "Johnny, what did you do with the heavy glass bowl I gave you at the picnic, the one that had the potato salad in it? What did you do with it after you finished the salad?"

"I didn't kill Kathy Cooper with it, if that's what they're saying," he growled.

So he had heard about the murder weapon? How? Jaymie wondered.

"So what *did* you do with it? I told you to bring it back."

"And I did. I . . ." He trailed off, and his gaze slid sideways, then he continued, saying, "I put it back on the table."

Jaymie would have staked her life on the fact that Johnny Stanko was lying, and if he was, why? What had he really done with the bowl? "Are you sure?" she asked, examining his expression.

He glared at her. "Don't you believe me?"

"You've got to tell the police that, Johnny," Valetta commanded. "Promise me you'll go to the station and tell them."

"Yeah, okay."

"Good. Do it today."

Jaymie glanced at Valetta in surprise. Did her normally skeptical friend really think Stanko was a) telling the truth, and b) going to actually go to the police?

"You know, I was standing at the railing trying to work up the guts to apologize to Craig for all the crappy things I did to him in school, the swirlies, the pantsings, the noogies, the name-calling. And then that witch, Kathy, lit into me like I was some slug she was going to squash. She got me upset." His rumbling voice had a defeated whine to it.

"But you did the right thing, Johnny, you walked away," Valetta said. "I told you how proud I was of you."

Of course, he hadn't walked away until after he had threatened them, Jaymie thought, remembering his comment about whacking them both.

He nodded, looking like he was going to cry. "You've been real good to me, Val, not like most people in this town."

"I promised your sister I'd look after you if you came back to Queensville."

He nodded, tears welling in his eyes. "Poor Tammy! I miss her."

"I have to go," Jaymie said, uneasily. "Hoppy has to piddle." It was far too possible that they were standing in the home of a murderer, but Valetta seemed to have a blind spot where Stanko was concerned, so she was not about to say it.

"Okay, I have to go, too." Valetta put both hands on Stanko's broad shoulders and shook him. "Go to the cops, Johnny. I know you're scared, and I know you think they're out to get you, but that's not true. You need to go tell them everything so they can eliminate you as a suspect."

He looked sullen and unconvinced, which would be natural enough if he was really guilty of Kathy's murder.

Jaymie and Valetta walked back toward Jaymie's house in silence. Jaymie wished she could find a way to probe Valetta about Stanko's criminal past, but she was so protective of him! "Do you really think he's going to go to the police?"

Valetta shook her head. "I wish I could be sure. I'll check in on him later."

She headed home, and Jaymie let Hoppy into the backyard, while she checked the answering machine; there was a message from the police asking her to drop in to the station. Oops! She was supposed to go and sign her statement.

After an early lunch, Jaymie took Becca's car—it was a smoother ride than her rattletrap van—and headed out to the highway, where the new chrome-and-glass police department was. It shouldn't take long to simply sign a statement, she figured; then she'd go on with her afternoon. She had to work at the Emporium the next day, so any errands had to be done now.

But it seemed it wasn't going to be so simple. Instead of being given her statement to sign at the reception desk, she was escorted back to an interview room and deposited there. When she asked what she was waiting for, the officer said that Detective Christian had a couple more questions for her. She was given a clipboard with some departmental paper, in case she wanted to write an amendment to her statement with things she had forgotten about the time surrounding the murder.

Should she tell them where Johnny Stanko was? As much as she wanted to, it seemed like a betrayal of Valetta's trust. She tapped the pen on the paper and thought. She had lots of questions but no real new information.

The detective finally came in and sat down opposite her, but was reading a paper while he did so. He finally looked up. "Hello, Ms. Leighton. How are you today?"

Detective Christian had retreated from *Jaymie* to *Ms. Leighton*. Her stomach twisted into a queasy knot as she got a bad feeling about the interview. "I'm fine."

"We asked you to come in today to answer a few more questions about July Fourth and the murder of Kathy Cooper."

"Uh, no, I came in today to sign my statement."

"And to answer a few more questions."

"Okay. I've tried to think about anything more I know, but nothing is coming to mind."

He scanned down a sheet he had in his hand and looked back up. "You told us you had a run-in with the victim a few hours before her murder, is that correct?"

"Yes."

"But according to one witness, you've omitted a fairly important bit of information." His gray eyes were cold. "We have a signed statement that you warned the victim."

"I beg your pardon?"

"Do you recall saying to the victim that she had better shut her mouth, or you would make her sorry?"

Jaymie opened her mouth, but nothing came out. What exactly had she said, and who would have told the police about it? "I *might* have said . . . I don't know, something like that. Who told you about that?"

"That doesn't matter. Did you say it? You must have been very angry; the victim had just insulted you in front of the man you're dating and implied that you were only dating him for his money. So how angry *were* you?"

"This is ridiculous," Jaymie said, her cheeks flaming. "Yes, Kathy insulted me in front of Daniel, and it irritated me. It was rude! *And* untrue. And I said something, but I don't think it was quite *that* ominous." Who would have told the police? Who had the most to gain from making her look bad?

He sat and watched her.

It came to her in that moment that it had to be Craig Cooper who'd told the police what she said, making it sound much worse than it was. He had just been approaching, and must have heard her. She thought for a moment, her temper cooling, then said, "I told Kathy she shouldn't say such nasty things to me or she'd be sorry. I don't know what I meant, but I have never in my life even hit another person, much less murdered someone. Would you like me to add that to my statement?"

"If you would. Exactly how you remember it, please."
He glanced up near the ceiling.

They must be on video. She had seen enough cop shows
to know about that. Restraining her urge to poke her tongue
out at the camera, she read her statement through, made the
amendment and signed it, then stood. If she was going to
tell them about Johnny Stanko, she should do it now.

"Anything you want to add?"

She hesitated. "No." It wasn't turning in Johnny Stanko
that would have bothered her, but the betrayal of the trust
Valetta put in her. She'd give him some time to go to the
police, then press Valetta, make her see that Stanko may well
have snapped and killed Kathy. It made her uneasy to leave
him free, but she would give him twenty-four hours. "No,
I'm done. If I think of anything else, I'll let you know."

She headed away from the police station and directly to
Craig and Kathy's home, a modern rambler in the newer
section of Queensville. She may not have spent time with
them socially, but she did know exactly where they lived,
and, grieving widower or not, she was going to tell Craig to
stop trying to implicate her. If that's indeed what he was
doing, was it to turn investigators away from examining his
relationship with his wife? Why would he have killed her?
It had always appeared to be Craig and Kathy against the
world. Jaymie knocked on the door.

A woman about Jaymie's age opened the door. She was
slim, with tri-colored, asymmetrical razor-cut hair, the bold
slash of pink on one side a startling contrast to the white
and black streaks of the rest of it. She wore a ripped long
T-shirt and skinny jeans. "Yeah?" she said, staring at Jaymie
curiously.

"Uh, is Craig home?"

"No. Who are you?"

"Jaymie Leighton. I think you might have met my sister, Rebecca Leighton Burke, yesterday when she brought some food over?"

"Your sister? She's a lot older than you, yeah?"

This must be Chloe Cooper, Craig's sister, the hairdresser from Wolverhampton. Jaymie was curious about why Chloe disliked Kathy so much that even Becca caught on. Maybe this was an opportunity to find out. "She had to go back to Canada, but she asked me to drop in and see if Craig needed anything, any help with arrangements, any errands run. He *has* to be suffering. And you, too! You must miss your sister-in-law."

Chloe laughed. "That's funny, me missing Kathy. Wanna know the truth?"

Jaymie waited; was Chloe going to trash her late sister-in-law?

"I'm bored out of my mind. I'm staying here to help Craig, but then he screws off and leaves me alone. You want to come in?" She stepped back and held the door open.

"Sure." Jaymie entered, and Chloe slammed the door behind her. "Uh, does anyone know when the service is going to be, Chloe?"

"The cops haven't released the body to the funeral home yet, so it's anyone's guess. If they hold on to her too long, Craig's gonna have a memorial service, and then the funeral will be private."

Jaymie followed her through the living room into the sunny kitchen and took a seat at the breakfast bar. She glanced around, imagining Kathy in this clean, bright house. The kitchen was decorated in white and yellow, cheery and modern, with white appliances, bare white countertops and blond wood cabinets. It was about as different from the Leighton kitchen as could be imagined.

Chloe offered her coffee and babbled about how she was missing work at the hair salon in Wolverhampton, but how she was going back in a few days. "You need a new hairstyle," Chloe said, bluntly, plopping a mug in front of Jaymie without asking if she wanted milk or sugar.

"I what?"

"You need a new hairstyle. And highlights, at least. You're what . . . late thirties?"

"Early thirties," Jaymie said.

"That's what I mean; you look older than you should. Your hair's mousy. You need a hipper hairstyle."

Like hers? "I don't think—"

"Come in to A Tressful Time and I'll give you a new do."

"Sure," Jaymie said, knowing she never would.

"Hey, that detective guy is a hottie, right?" Chloe said, leaning toward Jaymie over the breakfast bar with a wicked smile. "You've met him, right? The one who is questioning everyone? I felt like confessing just to have him grill me *gooood*!"

Startled, Jaymie said, "Confessing? You didn't do it, though."

"Of course not. I wasn't anywhere near here. I was with some friends down at Cedar Point," she said, naming the amusement park in Sandusky, Ohio. "But I'd love that guy, that Detective Zack, to lock me up and have his way with me over the interrogation table." She stuck her hands out and mimicked handcuffs on her slim wrists.

"Sandusky . . . is that near Toledo?"

"Not really. Why?"

"I heard that Kathy and Craig were thinking of moving to Toledo. Is that true?"

"Nah. I heard something about that a while ago, but I think they'd given up on the idea."

There was a knock at the front door, and Chloe bounded out of the room toward the sound. Jaymie heard voices as Craig's sister talked to someone. The phone rang; after a few rings the machine clicked on, and Kathy's voice filled the kitchen: "Hi. We can't come to the phone right now. Leave a message after the beep." It was so weird to hear her voice, knowing that she was gone.

Jaymie barely listened to the message, something about an appointment Kathy had missed at the Payne Institute— the unfortunately named local medical school—as she heard voices rise in the living room. She slipped off her stool and moved toward the door.

"You tell your effing brother that I want his effing lawyer off my back." Kylie Hofstadter's strident voice was filled with anger. "Kathy's dead, and she'll never get her hands on my son now, so they can just screw off."

❧ Ten ❧

THE ANGER IN Kylie Hofstadter's voice was chilling. Jaymie didn't know whether to stay where she was or go to Chloe's defense.

"You get the hell away from here, Kylie," Chloe said.

"I have a right to be here. I'm getting something that Kathy had and wouldn't give back."

Jaymie moved to the living room just in time to see Kylie barge past Chloe and head up the stairs. Chloe was following, screeching at Kylie to get out or she would call the cops.

"Hey, hey! Let's talk about this," Jaymie said, emerging from her spot near the kitchen door.

"What are *you* doing here?" Kylie asked, pausing in her ascent and looking down at Jaymie. "First Mom's place, and now Craig's? You stalking us?"

Chloe glanced over at Jaymie with a frown. "She said she came to see if we needed any help with arrangements."

"Help? Hah! She's a suspect in Kathy's murder, you know."

Sighing in exasperation, Jaymie said, "I am not really a suspect, any more than anyone else who was there is. No more than *you* are! Listen, I was trying to make amends with Kathy, and now I just want to get to the bottom of things. I'm really sorry about your sister's death, Kylie." She watched the other woman's face squint, and had a feeling she was trying to force back tears. Kylie sat down on the steps as Chloe uneasily glanced back and forth between Kylie and Jaymie.

"I know you were in a custody fight with Kathy over Connor, but still . . . it must have been a shock to lose your sister that way."

Kylie drew in a long breath and covered her face, leaning against the banister. "We were coming to terms that very day," Kylie said, her lank brown hair falling in her face. "She said things had changed. She said she knew she wouldn't get Connor, and she was glad I was getting my act together."

If that was true, it explained why Kathy had been sitting with Kylie, Connor and Andy Walker when Jaymie came back from taking Hoppy home. But what had happened to change Kathy's mind from just a while before, when she had stated so positively to Matt Laskan that she, Connor and Craig were moving to Toledo? "What had changed?"

"I don't know. I asked, but she wouldn't say."

There was something there, something elusive that Jaymie was going to have to figure out later.

Chloe had been hovering nearby, but she now said, "Just get what you have to get. I don't really care." She turned away and headed back to the kitchen.

Jaymie approached the stairs and looked up at Kylie through the painted wood railing. "I'm so sorry," she said, searching the younger woman's expression. "I really am."

"Why? You and my sister were enemies. You hated her. Why would you be sorry she's dead?"

"But I *didn't* hate her. I never even really knew her as an adult."

Kylie's expression hardened, the tears drying on her pale cheeks. "I'll never believe that. Kathy had her faults, but she didn't imagine things. You were a bitch to her in high school, and you took every opportunity to try to make her look bad, like that episode with Ella Douglas in the Emporium, making it seem like Kathy was being mean to a helpless invalid."

Jaymie shook her head, frustrated. "I didn't . . . look, you were too young back then to know anything about what happened in high school. I still don't understand it myself."

Kylie gave her a withering look and stood, heading up the stairs. "Kathy was right; you'll always be little Miss Goody Two-shoes Leighton, who can do no wrong in this town," she threw over her shoulder.

Jaymie stood for a moment in the quietude of the chilly living room: a white leather sofa nobody sat on, a bland modern art piece over the sofa, pale gray carpet, pale cream walls. It was Kathy's home, the nest she'd created for herself. No family photos adorned the surfaces, no signs of her life or personal interests at all. Becca always said Jaymie was addicted to clutter, and maybe that was so, because this uncluttered, seemingly serene room, made her sad. She shivered and headed back to the sunny kitchen.

"I'll go now," she said to Chloe. "I'm so sorry about that scene with Kylie."

"It doesn't take much to set off those sisters," Chloe said, looking up from her hair-styling magazine.

"You didn't get along with Kathy, I take it?"

"Who did? She called me a spoiled, selfish little brat on their wedding day, and it's gone downhill from there."

That unfortunately sounded just like what Kathy had sometimes said to and about Jaymie. In the past, Kathy's anger toward Jaymie had manifested itself in irrational outbursts and dirt-slinging on social networking sites and through the town's gossip network, but there had never been anything said that explained her animosity. She appeared to have had a problem with a lot of people, but who was angry enough at her to kill her?

"Chloe, did you ever hear anyone threaten Kathy?"

Chloe looked up again from her magazine and wrinkled her brow. "Threaten her? No, duh! I would have told the cops if I had. But she sure was mad at a lot of people; last week she was foaming at the mouth about Matt, Craig's partner. Matt's a nice guy—and hot, for an old dude—but Kathy said something about him living a double life."

"What did she mean?"

"Do you think I know?" she said, with a scornful expression. She looked back down to her magazine.

A double life. Jaymie remembered the sense she'd had that Kathy was threatening Matt Laskan at the picnic. What had she known about him that might be unsavory, or even illegal? Did it have to do with business, or his personal life? She'd have to look into it, because she didn't think the guy was even on the police detective's radar. "Nothing else?"

The young woman shrugged, not looking up from her magazine.

"How is your brother doing? He must miss Kathy terribly. I mean, she was his wife."

She shrugged again and frowned. "I guess."

Jaymie waited, but Chloe was reading her magazine. She was done talking. "Okay. I'll let myself out." She headed for the front door, but paused and waited to see if Chloe would follow. She trod loudly to the front door, opened and closed it, then scooted back and slipped up the stairs, curious about what was taking Kylie so long.

She tiptoed down the carpeted hall, listening to the sound of Kylie shuffling through something. Peeking around the corner, she could see that the room was used for storage, with boxes lining one wall. Kylie had her back to the door and was rooting around in a closet. She gasped and stopped suddenly and clutched something to her chest. Then she started crying great gusty sobs.

Torn as to what to do, Jaymie stayed stock-still for a long moment, then crept away, feeling like a total jerk. In any other circumstance she would have offered comfort, but Kylie had already shown how little she liked or trusted Jaymie. Intruding on her in her moment of sorrow would have just made it worse. She began to slink down the stairs, but then paused, hand on the railing.

No. No! She pounded her fist on the railing. This was how her feud with Kathy had become so overblown. Jaymie hadn't handled it properly in the beginning, hadn't demanded answers. She needed to be more confrontational. She headed back up the stairs. Kylie's sobbing had calmed, and she was holding something to her chest and rocking back and forth.

"Are you going to be okay, Kylie?" Jaymie said softly.

The younger woman whirled, a photo album clutched to her chest. "What are *you* still doing here?" she asked, her face twisted in anguish.

Jaymie sat down cross-legged on the beige carpet and gently took the photo album, opening it and glancing through. It was full of photos of a girl and a baby in the yard behind the Hofstadter farmhouse. The baby became a child as the other dark-haired girl grew to slender adolescence. Jaymie stared down at a photo of an eleven-year-old Kathy staring defiantly into the camera from her seat in the V of an old maple tree. *Oh, Kathy, we used to be friends,* Jaymie thought. *How did it get so weird?*

The answer was easy; they never solved anything because they never talked things out. Instead, Jaymie ignored the problem, hoping it would go away. It hadn't; it hardened, turned to stone and then was put on the back burner when they all went away to college. "Your sister was the best friend I ever had," she said. "The closest. We told each other secrets."

"If that's true, why did you treat her like crap?" Kylie replied, her voice trembling with emotion.

Jaymie glanced up, puzzled. "When did I ever treat her like crap?"

"Oh, come on! You know, *that's* what drove Kathy crazy the most," Kylie said, shaking her finger in Jaymie's face. "You just denied it all ever happened. You kept acting like the innocent injured party, and everyone took your side! Kathy felt like an outsider in Queensville, and it was all because of you!"

Nausea welled up in Jaymie's stomach. She was getting close to an answer; she felt it. Did she want to know? Had she said something, done something, that she didn't even remember to cause half a lifetime of animosity? "Kylie, pretend you're explaining this all to someone who has no clue what you're talking about. What did I ever do or say to Kathy to make her so angry that she didn't speak to me, other than to berate me?"

Kylie rolled her eyes and snatched the photo album back. "You know what you said." She stood up and put the photo album in a fabric shopping bag.

"But I *don't*," Jaymie cried, leaping to her feet, frustrated. "Kylie, *please*, I'm begging you, tell me?"

The young woman stopped. Jaymie could hear footsteps

in the hall. She was about to be busted by Chloe for not leaving the house when she said she was, but she didn't care.

Kylie stared at her for a moment, then said, her voice trembling, "You told everyone at Wolverhampton High that our home smelled, and that *we* smelled. Like pigs. You said it, and laughed. You told Hank Barlow, the guy Kathy had a crush on, and he spread it around to all the guys, like you knew he would. Kathy was crazy over Hank, and you ruined it. He never talked to her again. In fact, he made oinking sounds in the hall when he saw her."

A line of boys, all oinking as Kathy passed, a bright red flush on her pale face. Kathy pushing Jaymie away, her body bowed by misery, her shoulders hunched in on herself. Jaymie remembered that, but she knew darn well she had nothing to do with it. "I never *ever* said such a . . . such an evil thing, Kylie, you have to believe me," she said, her voice choked by a sob. Tears welled up in her eyes. "I could *never* say something so mean in my life!"

Kylie shook her head and strode past her to the hall. Jaymie followed and saw Chloe, who was just coming toward the storage room.

"What's going on?" Chloe asked. "I thought you were gone?" She glared at Jaymie.

"I'm going now." She turned to Kylie in the dim hallway, where sunlight never penetrated, and reached out, lightly touching her bare arm. "I hope someday you can believe me. I would *never* have said anything like that about Kathy. We were best friends, and I loved her."

The other woman searched Jaymie's face, but her expression was doubtful.

Jaymie felt the need to repeat it. "I'm so sorry that someone spread that vile rumor, but I never, *ever* said it." She paused and turned to the other young woman. "I'd like to talk to Craig, Chloe, if you could let him know?"

She walked down the stairs and out the front door, holding on to her emotions until she got to the car and climbed in. Then she broke down, weeping, her forehead resting on the steering wheel. All these years it was someone's terrible lies that had kept Kathy and Jaymie apart. How could Kathy believe she'd say something so awful? They had been the best of friends from kindergarten on. And how could Kathy hold on to that pain for so many years without even trying to clear the air?

Jaymie was not blameless, though; when Kathy had first started ignoring her, she tried to break down her friend's walls, but she quit too soon, hurt by her former friend's rudeness. Give her time, everyone had said, but "time" had stretched into years, and it was never resolved. It was over now, and there was nothing she could do to change the past. She stared out the window of Becca's Lexus. Kylie, her face still pale with sadness, exited the house carrying the bag with the photo album. She cast Jaymie a quick look, but didn't wave. She got into her truck and zoomed off.

Finding Kathy's murderer would help everyone find solace. They couldn't bring her back, but they could catch whoever had ended her life so violently. The police were likely to do that, and soon, she hoped, but Jaymie had some unanswered questions of her own. Starting with: what did Kathy have on Matt Laskan, and was it enough for him to kill her to conceal it? There was no way to tell the police what she suspected about Matt. The conversation she had overheard was so vague. How would she frame an uneasy sense that Kathy had been threatening Matt at the picnic with some knowledge that Jaymie didn't even have a reference point to understand?

Joel knew more than he was saying about Laskan Cooper

and his acquaintance with the principal parties, she was positive of that. She backed out of the laneway and headed toward Heidi's side-split ranch in the new section of town. In the darkest days of the winter, when Joel's defection had been a new, raw wound that she thought would never heal, she had driven past Heidi's house many times, noting the transition from Christmas wreath to Valentine's hearts to St. Patty's Day shamrocks adorning the front door. The girl liked to celebrate every occasion, and now it had red, white and blue bunting framing the cream door, and a proud flag fluttering on a standard hooked to a flag mount beside it.

She pushed the bell and waited, taking deep, cleansing breaths. Heidi came to the door, and her pale face flushed a bright pink. "Jaymie!" she squealed. "How nice, you just dropping in like we're best friends. Come on in!"

Jaymie followed Heidi to the living room. She might have owned the house for less than a year, but it looked like she had done a lot. It was a 1960s ranch-style home formerly owned by the couple who'd built it, but who had moved to a new condo development in Wolverhampton. It had gone from sixties kitsch—Jaymie knew this because she and DeeDee had attended the garage sale where the couple and their kids had disposed of a lot of junk that Dee had bought and promptly sold on eBay—to its current state of mid-century modern opulence.

"Wow," Jaymie said, turning around and gazing at the white shag carpeting, a red Eames sofa and, surrounding the slate fireplace, a red accent wall. "You've done a lot of work. And an honest-to-goodness Eames sofa?"

Heidi made a face. "A copy. I couldn't find what I wanted, so I had to make do. Come on, sit. Can I get you coffee? Please? It's the one thing I do well. My friend Bernie is coming over, so I want to make a pot anyway."

"I don't want to interrupt you and your . . . friend." Jaymie furiously pondered . . . Bernie? She didn't know any guy in the village with that name. Someone from New York, maybe? "I really came to talk to Joel. Is he around?"

"No," Heidi said, heading back toward the kitchen. "He's off on one of his sales jaunts. I'll be back in a minute. Just let me get the coffee on."

"I don't want to interfere," Jaymie called out.

Heidi poked her head back in around the doorframe and smiled. "Don't be silly. Sit! I'll be back in a sec."

Jaymie wandered the room for a moment, exploring Heidi's unique and simple décor. If she did it all herself, the girl was a genius, melding mid-century modern vintage pieces with newer items. The mantel, one long, beautifully grained slab of wood set directly in the stone, was topped by a large canvas of what looked like one of the romance comics of the sixties. The mantel also held some white pieces—a vase, some figures—and one red porcelain heart tipped on its side.

She sat down on the sofa, finding it more comfortable than it looked, and saw that the journal open on the oval coffee table was a bridal magazine. Heidi would make a beautiful bride; Jaymie just hoped she knew what she was getting into with Joel. And she was pleased she could think that with no stabbing ache in her heart. She took another deep breath and relaxed.

A knock at the door was followed by a woman poking her head in and hollering, "Heidi, you here? I've got something for you!"

Jaymie stood, feeling awkward, as a young black woman in jeans and a pink, scoop-necked T-shirt, entered and looked at her.

"Jaymie Leighton!" she exclaimed. "How are you since . . . since the other night?"

It was Officer Jenkins! "I'm . . . okay, I guess."

The woman nodded, and Heidi entered with a white tray laden with a red coffee pot. "Bernie!" she cried. "I didn't hear you ring."

Bernie . . . aha! Bernice Jenkins.

"I knocked. I found something I know you want," she said, racing back to the door and opening it. "Look!" She started to pull a plain wood cabinet inside.

"Let me help you," Jaymie said. She and the police-woman dragged the piece into the living room.

"Oh, Bernie, it's gorgeous!" Heidi said, hopping and clapping in genuine enthusiasm. "Did you find it at that auction in Wolverhampton?"

"I did. And it was a steal!"

"Uh, what exactly is it?" Jaymie asked, as the two women looked the piece over.

"It's a martini bar!" Heidi said, opening one door to show glass shelves inside. "Isn't it cool? Oh . . . Jaymie . . . you've met Bernie?"

"We did meet."

"On the job," the woman said. "Even before the other night. Jaymie very nicely brought me a cup of coffee while I was doing watch duty in her back alley in May."

"I appreciated knowing someone was there, believe me," Jaymie said. "And I was so glad to see you the other night when I . . . when I found poor Kathy. But how did *you* two meet?"

"At Jewel's Junk," Heidi said. "Let's sit. I made coffee."

They sat and talked for a while, first about the teak-and-glass martini bar—both women were mid-century modern enthusiasts, it turned out—and then about Heidi and Joel's wedding in December. "I always wanted to be a winter bride," Heidi said, clasping her hands in front of her.

"So, will you be getting married here in town?" Jaymie asked. "Or going back to New York?"

"Oh, here. This is home, now."

"How about your family? Will they be coming to Queensville, then? It'll be neat to have Locklands back in Queensville. The Heritage Society will make a big fuss. Homer Lockland is kind of a hometown hero, the local boy who made good in the big city."

"Weeeell, actually, I don't know how much of my family will come," Heidi said, her gaze slipping away to the martini bar.

Bernie stayed mum, examining her magenta nails. Jaymie looked from one to the other, feeling like there was something she was missing. "Why? Your mother and father will want to see their daughter get married, won't they?"

"I haven't actually told them yet," Heidi murmured.

"But she should," Bernie added, watching her friend with concern. "They have a right to know, Heidi."

"Does Joel know you haven't told them yet?" Jaymie asked.

She shook her head, tears welling up in her blue eyes. "How can I tell him that? He'll be so hurt. But when I do tell my parents, they might cut me off. Then what will I do?"

She explained to Jaymie what Bernie apparently already knew: she had bought the home using her trust fund money, but still received an allowance that could be cut off if her parents disapproved of her behavior. Heidi was apparently afraid that getting engaged to an almost-penniless pharmaceutical sales rep would be considered bad behavior by her wealthy and snobbish parents. They talked for a while longer, but Jaymie remained defeated on what she really wanted, which was to talk to Joel about Matt Laskan.

Conversation inevitably turned to the murder of Kathy

Cooper. Jaymie told them what she had just discovered about the genesis of her and Kathy's "feud," and about her own innocence. "All this time, one conversation could have solved it, and now it's too late."

"But you didn't know," Heidi said, her hand on Jaymie's arm.

"So, if you didn't say what you were accused of saying, then someone else claimed you did. Maybe they wanted to sabotage your friendship with Kathy, or just make you look bad," Bernie said, leaning forward and holding Jaymie's gaze. "Did anyone have it in for you in high school?"

Jaymie thought back. She was popular in school, but not by any means the *most* popular girl. When Kathy deserted her, she had started hanging out with a couple of other girls, but never with the same bond of friendship. "Not that I know of." She vividly remembered the sense of hurt and betrayal when Kathy turned on her. That's the moment she'd begun to distrust other relationships, something that had tainted her emotional response to her first couple of boyfriends.

And Joel. Like a bolt of lightning, the similarity hit her: when Joel deserted her, she had retreated into that same suspicious shell. Whoa . . . that was something she needed to think about, her response to a sense of betrayal, and how it was perhaps making her wary of Daniel. She knew she was keeping him at arm's length, in a sense. And was that why Joel always said that she seemed so self-sufficient that she never needed anyone else? That had been his major complaint about her, and until now she had passed it off as nonsense, but what man didn't want to feel needed?

"Maybe someone wanted you to hang around with them, so they managed to separate you and Kathy," Bernie added.

She considered it. "I can't think of anyone who would

have deliberately sabotaged our friendship. What I *really* want to know is, who had it in for Kathy now?"

Bernice's dark eyes shuttered and she withdrew. "I can't really talk about the case, you know."

"No, of course not," Jaymie murmured, curiosity tugging at her like an impatient two-year-old.

Heidi, who had been looking back and forth between the two of them, rose, and said, "I'm going to refill the coffee pot, girls!"

When she was gone, Jaymie said, "Bernie, I know you can't tell me anything about the investigation. The detective has already been around to my place, and we talked, though, so I'm pretty much up to date."

Bernie's eyes widened. "He talked to you about it all? So it's true . . . Detective Hotstuff *does* like you!"

Jaymie sat back, mouth open. This she had not expected. "Me? Uh, are you talking about Detective Christian?"

Bernie grimaced and fell back against the sofa seat. "You didn't know about the rumors, huh?"

"I'm confused." And blushing again. Did she want to know what Bernie meant? Or would it complicate her life too much?

"I've said too much," the woman said, jumping up as Heidi came back, her eyes bright with curiosity. "Please, Jaymie, don't tell anyone what I said." She turned to her friend. "Look, Heidi, I've got to go. I'm working graveyard tonight, and I need some sleep. I think I'm already running on too little," she added, ruefully, giving Jaymie a quick glance.

"Wait! Let me pay you for the bar. It's perfect, by the way! Exactly what I was looking for." Heidi made out a check, and as she signed her name with a flourish, she said, "Bernie, Jaymie knows all about old kitchens, and you're looking to find stuff for yours, dishes and the like. You two should talk."

"I'd love to help, if I can," Jaymie said, feeling the blush gradually ebb from her cheeks.

"I just might take you up on that," the policewoman said, heading toward the door. "Catch you on the flip side!"

❖ Eleven ❖

As Heidi closed the door behind her friend, she cried, "Did I overhear her right when I eavesdropped? Did she say that Detective Yummers has the hots for you?"

Jaymie sighed. In a town as small as Queensville, she supposed it was inevitable that a guy as good-looking as Detective Christian would have dozens of women swooning over him and giving him silly nicknames. When she'd first seen him, she'd sworn he was right out of the pages of one of her favorite romance novels. "No, that is *not* what she said, and she's mistaken anyway."

"Well, spill!" Heidi said, dragging Jaymie back to sit down. "What did she mean, then?"

"She meant that he likes me. *Likes* can mean a lot of things, Heidi, and in his case, I'm afraid I amuse him. It's just a rumor anyway. Rumors are lies that people enjoy spreading around, if you ask me."

"Okay, all right, it's best if you keep thinking that way anyway," she said, with a wise little wink and nod. "He might be good for a roll in the hay, but Daniel Collins is the marrying kind."

Jaymie closed her eyes and counted to ten, took a deep breath, then opened them again. "Heidi, you said something about you and Joel going over to the Coopers' place for dinner. Was anyone else there?"

She nodded. "Matt Laskan and his girlfriend, Lily. She's a nice girl, real pretty."

So Matt Laskan had a girlfriend. That and his business partnership with Craig were two fertile areas to expose something unsavory that could possibly hurt someone. But if the supposed secret was business-related, Kathy would not have been keeping it to herself and using it as leverage for blackmail, would she? She'd have told her husband if it affected their livelihood.

Something personal, then? What could make Matt so angry he'd kill Kathy to keep her from spreading it around? And what would she have been able to find out about his personal life?

"Are Lily and Matt getting married?" That seemed to be the kind of thing Heidi would be interested to know.

Heidi frowned and sipped her coffee. Cocking her head to one side, she said, "I don't know, but they seemed real close, you know? She's a nice woman with a great job."

"What does she do?"

"She's a town councilor in Wolverhampton, the youngest woman ever to do that, I think. That's what Matt said anyway. She's real smart. She has a double degree in social work and law, and folks around here think she should run for . . . something or other at the state senate. Is that what we have, a senate?"

Jaymie nodded absently. If there was anything sordid in Matt Laskan's life, it could certainly hurt his girlfriend's chances in a senatorial race, but even beyond that, if his girlfriend didn't know about it, it could end the relationship. "How did Craig and Kathy's relationship seem to you? I heard something about them moving, leaving town?"

"I heard about that. It was supposed to be a secret; I don't know why." She frowned and thought about Jaymie's question. "They got along, I guess."

"You don't sound sure."

Heidi shrugged. "I don't know. It's hard to judge relationships from the outside, don't you think?"

"I suppose that's true. Why did Joel say he didn't know Craig and Kathy well when you went to their place for dinner?"

Heidi shrugged. "I don't know. That surprised me, too."

"And you didn't ask him about it?"

She looked startled. "Why would I do that?"

And that explained a lot about why Joel had thrown Jaymie over for the sweet and trusting Heidi. They chatted for a while longer, and Heidi showed her the bridal magazine and what dress she was considering, then Jaymie finished her coffee and left.

She had a lot to do at home, so she returned, worked on research for her second cookbook for a while, then sat back at her desk. It was hard to work on *More Recipes from the Vintage Kitchen* when she didn't know the fate of book one. She had researched the publishing process, trying to find out what to expect. But though she could find lots on the Internet about how to sell a novel, there was little information on how to approach a publisher with a cookbook: what they wanted to see, how long to wait, or even if she should be approaching more than one publisher at a time. She was so afraid of stepping on her own toes that she was nervous to the point of inertia.

She gave up in disgust. Her mind kept returning to the awful murder of her childhood friend. She grabbed a clipboard and some lined paper and descended to the kitchen, then made a pot of tea and took a cup and the cordless phone outside to sit in the shade of the trumpet vines that climbed all over the garage.

Who had killed Kathy Cooper? Jaymie wanted to know for several reasons, not the least of which was that she herself was a suspect. Take the emotion out of it and think logically, she admonished herself. First, who might have *wanted* to do it? She made a list: Craig Cooper, Kylie Hofstadter, Matt Laskan, Johnny Stanko. Anyone else? She tapped her pencil against the board, then jotted down another name: Andy Walker. In the Emporium, Kathy had told Connor his grandpa didn't want him, which was clearly not true. And at the picnic, Kathy had loudly said that Andy Walker had been trying to alienate Connor from her for months. The whole family was in turmoil, and the center of the hurricane was Kathy. Jaymie didn't know Andy Walker, but people had committed murder for less important reasons than keeping a beloved grandson in their lives.

Should she add Ella Douglas? After the confrontation in the Emporium, perhaps. But it just didn't feel like a big enough deal, from Ella/Eleanor's viewpoint, to make her kill Kathy. And a woman in a wheelchair? Ella looked as weak as a kitten. Could she even lift the heavy glass bowl, much less wield it as a weapon? However . . . maybe Ella's husband was pissed off enough at Kathy's behavior to take matters into his own hands. Jaymie needed to examine every possibility, and Bob was certainly a possibility. She added his name to the list.

From here, then, she needed to figure out how much she knew about where each one of them was at the time of the crime. The phone rang; it was Jaymie's mom.

"Honey, what's this I hear about Kathy Hofstadter being murdered?"

"Cooper is her married name, Mom. Kathy Cooper. Have you been talking to Becca?"

"No, Mimi Watson called to ask when we were coming up, and she told me about it. I had to hear it from a neighbor, not from my own daughter, who found that poor child! Your dad is frantic with worry."

That was most likely an exaggeration. Her mom projected all her worried feelings onto her husband, and if one listened to her, one would think he was a nervous wreck, when he was likely out golfing.

"It's awful, just awful!" she continued. "I knew you and she weren't close after high school, but . . . anyway, is it true that you found her?"

The local gossip machine even worked between Queensville and Boca Raton! Jaymie told her mother what was going on, but omitted any mention that she was a suspect.

"That's so sad! I'll send flowers. How is Martha doing?"

"Martha?"

"Kathy and Kylie's mother! Jaymie, you *know* who I mean."

"Sorry, Mom. I always called her Mrs. Hofstadter. I don't know how she is. I went there briefly, to drop off a casserole, but Kylie was there, and she was none too pleased to see me."

"Poor girl. Poor *Martha*! Will you tell her for me that when we come up, I'll visit her? I always liked Kathy, you know, and Martha, too."

Jaymie was silent for a long moment. "Why? *Why* did

you like Kathy, Mom? I'm not trying to be smart, I really want to know."

Her mom sighed, then said, "I felt sorry for her. Her father was really tough on those girls, you know, especially Kathy, as the oldest. And on poor Martha. But Kathy wanted to do something in life. She wanted to make a difference. She was going to be a nurse. If she hadn't married Craig Cooper, I think she would have done it."

There was a subtle criticism there concerning Jaymie's own lack of direction, but this was not the time to address it. "I think she might have been considering doing something about it now," Jaymie said, reminded of the call from the Payne Institute to the Coopers' home.

Talking to her mom reminded Jaymie of all the sterling qualities Kathy had possessed, and it made the loss more devastating and the split that had occurred between them more tragic, especially since it had been based on a lie. The Kathy who died was a woman she didn't even know, but one who would leave a hole in the lives of those who loved her, no matter how tumultuous their relationship appeared to be to Jaymie. As she signed off with her mom, Jaymie was more determined than ever that whoever killed Kathy would not get away with it.

THE NEXT MORNING—It was Saturday, a busy day at the bed-and-breakfast—Jaymie popped over to the Shady Rest with the egg-based breakfast casserole she had put together the night before for Anna; all it needed was baking in the oven. Anna could then cut it into big squares and serve it with bacon or sausage, fresh fruit, cereal, muffins and lots of coffee and orange juice. Clive was there for the weekend, and he had promised to do scrambled eggs, if anyone preferred them. "It's almost like a bread pudding," she told Anna at the front door, handing her the casserole with the baking directions taped on the foil. "Or French toast in a pan. Serve it with that Michigan maple syrup, and let them dig in!"

She then changed into capris and a cotton blouse and walked Hoppy to the Emporium in time to meet Valetta, who was opening the store. Jaymie took Hoppy over to play with Junk Junior at Jewel's shop, and began her day, filling in for the Klausners, who were enjoying a rare day off together. The first few hours were taken up with the normal procedures: opening mail, restocking shelves, dusting and cleaning in places the Klausners couldn't—and shouldn't—get to, which meant crawling under counters and getting up on a six-foot ladder to dust the tops of hundred-year-old shelves. At eleven, since there were no customers in the store, she took a tea break with Valetta on the porch. She told her friend what she had learned at the Cooper home and at Heidi and Joel's.

"I never said it, Valetta, really!" she said, about Kylie's assertion that Jaymie had started the quarrel between them in high school with cruel words that would haunt Kathy for years.

"I know that, kiddo," Valetta said, her eyes glinting behind her thick glasses. "You don't have a mean bone in your body. You *couldn't* say something like that!"

Jaymie got teary-eyed at that and sipped her cooling tea. She wasn't so sure her good friend's faith in her niceness as a kid was deserved, given the mean nickname she had made up for Craig Cooper. But she had been horrified when it spread, and had regretted it for the next two years of high school that she shared with the slightly older Craig. The blazing sun's heat burned the dew off as it climbed and chased away shadows.

Chloe Cooper, her previous day's torn T-shirt traded in for a retro sundress, strolled past on her way to Jewel's Junk; she stopped to talk with them for a few minutes. "I heard Jewel Dandridge has some fifties handbags and sunglasses," she said as she adjusted her cat's-eye jeweled vintage glasses. "I collect handbags."

"How is Craig doing, Chloe?" Valetta asked.

"Okay, I guess. He goes out walking a lot, alone. He's kinda moody. But he'll be okay. I never thought Kathy was good for him—pardon me for speaking ill of the dead."

"What do you mean?" Jaymie asked.

"Craig got past all that crap in high school, you know? The bullying, the names. But Kathy! Man, she was a piece of work. She never got over *any* of it. Sometimes Craig did crap to humor her, but nothing was ever enough for her. She wanted her "enemies" to suffer. She always said living well is the best revenge, but I had a feeling she'd have liked other kinds of revenge better."

Jaymie remembered that when Johnny Stanko was near them on the boardwalk path, Kathy had kept talking to Craig, probably urging him to confront his former bully, and when her husband kept shaking his head, she jumped up to confront him herself. Maybe Chloe was right about Craig.

"I felt sorry for Kathy," Valetta said. "Not being able to have a child . . . I think that affected her."

"Yeah, life sucks and then you die," Chloe said with brutal frankness. "But in the meantime you don't need to take the crappy stuff in life so to heart that you make everyone around you miserable." She walked on to Jewel's shop.

Valetta and Jaymie were silent for a long minute.

"I think she's got a point," Jaymie said. "Look how many people Kathy was quarreling with: Kylie, Andy Walker, Johnny, me. And even Matt Laskan; you saw them arguing, didn't you?"

She nodded. "Hey, I did find something out," Valetta said. "Brock told me that Craig and Kathy were looking at commercial listings in Toledo. They asked if he could hook them up with a reliable real estate agent there." Valetta's brother, Brock, was a real estate agent specializing in farm properties, but he also sold homes and some commercial properties. In small-town Michigan, no agent could afford to specialize too much.

"So they really were going to move to Toledo and start a branch office of Laskan Cooper."

"Ah, but listen to this: that was five or six months ago, just after Christmas. A few weeks ago, Craig called him and told him to forget about it. I guess Brock kept sending commercial listings from Toledo to his e-mail. Craig said he and Kathy had decided to stay in Queensville for the time being."

"Not according to Kathy," Jaymie said. She had been adamant that they were moving, and taking Connor with them. Why had Craig canceled the hunt, when Kathy was still dead set on moving? Had he known she wasn't going to be around to keep the pressure on?

Something had changed by later that day, something dramatic, because according to Kylie, Kathy had told her that she knew she wasn't going to be able to take custody of Connor after all, so she was glad Kylie was getting her act together. What did Kathy learn or figure out that changed everything?

It was all so confusing.

Jaymie and Valetta went back to work. There were lots of tourists in town but only a few ventured into the

Emporium, and then mostly because of the historic façade. Not many tourists wanted to buy Rice Krispies or a gallon of milk. Most of the serious shoppers were townies, and many of them said the same thing over and over. Jaymie got just a little tired of hearing, *So, another murder; remind me not to hang around* you *too much, Jaymie.* There was the usual litany of questions from the curious: What did she know? Who did she think did it? Was she upset, or happy that Kathy was dead? That last one horrified her, and she almost bit one person's head off when they said much the same thing.

"What do *you* think?" she barked. "Kathy and I were friends growing up, no matter what happened after."

Bob Douglas, who was in the store picking up something for his wife, came up to the counter after the chagrined customer slunk away. "Hey, Jaymie, take it easy, now," he said, putting one cool, bony hand on her wrist. "Folks are just curious, you know, and most people don't even think about what they're saying."

She eyed him appreciatively and nodded, taking a deep breath. "You're right. Thank you. I shouldn't have snapped, but I'm so sad about it all myself, and to hear people imply that I'd be happy . . . it just horrifies me."

"I know. Anyone looking at you would know you are an honest-to-goodness nice person. Of *course* you're sad! But I've been through misfortune, and I know people can be so thoughtless sometimes."

She had heard that his first wife died tragically: a car accident, or something, folks said. "You're right, of course. How is Ella doing?"

He looked worried. "Not so good. This is new medication," he said, holding up the paper pharmacy bag he had just gotten from Valetta. "I sure hope it helps. I'm trying to get in contact with the Mayo Clinic. They're number one in the world at treating problems with the endocrine system."

Valetta approached. "Bob, there's an endocrinologist in Port Huron. Do you want his phone number? It couldn't hurt to have him run some tests. Will your insurance cover it?"

"*If* we have a referral," he said, with a grimace. "But if we can't get that, I'll make an appointment anyway. If the guy is good, it'll be worth paying for it out of our savings. I don't think I can stand to see my girl suffer any more pain!" His voice broke and he cleared his throat.

Valetta bustled off to get him the phone number, and Jaymie watched him swallow his emotions. "I know you heard about Kathy Cooper's run-in with your wife here earlier this week. How did you feel about it?"

"I was mad! How dare she?" His pale face colored with a crimson flush starting in his neck and creeping upward, a vein throbbing above his right eye. "Ella has taken so much crap from doctors who don't believe she's really sick and her own family, who say she's delusional, and then that angry young woman had the gall to tell her she was bullying that poor little boy? Ella has paid and paid for her past behavior. I know she was a bully in high school. She told me all about it."

"Really? I would have thought she would have wanted to forget those days." Ella had been the new girl and, as such, ostracized in the tight small-town community of Wolverhampton High. It had made her prickly and difficult, if Jaymie remembered right.

"We talk about everything! She changed once she left this town. I have only ever known her as the sweet and wonderful woman she is now, the one who helped me heal from losing my dear first wife. The little boy, Connor, is the one I felt sorry for in the middle of that sad spectacle here in the store, made the center of Kathy Cooper's paranoid fantasies." He stopped and shook his head. "I'm really sorry that she was murdered; that shouldn't happen to anyone. But you have to wonder: How many people did she make angry? How many other folks did she attack like that?"

"Good point, Bob," Valetta said, handing him a slip of paper with the doctor's name and number.

Once he left, Jaymie thought over what he'd said while she reorganized her melamine picnic display. She took out the book that had the advance bookings for the picnic baskets and noted that Craig had picked one up for the July Fourth picnic, the Lover's Lane basket, but hadn't returned it yet. That was to be expected; how could he think about something like that while grieving for his wife? It worked to her advantage, since it would give her a good excuse to follow up with him. She could say she was dropping by to pick it up from him to save him the trouble. And just maybe she could get the answers to some of her questions.

Craig Cooper seemed to have known weeks ago that he had no intention of moving to Toledo, and yet Kathy had still thought they were, going by her conversation with Matt Laskan. She was *counting* on it. But then later that day she told Kylie she knew she wouldn't be getting custody of Connor. Were the two statements somehow tied together? Or had something else been going on?

They got busy, and the afternoon flew by. It was getting late, the brilliant, super-heated sun blazing down on Queensville from a slanted angle and overlaying everything with a rich golden glow. Jaymie began to haul the stuff on the porch back into the store in preparation for closing. First the big box of beach balls and the other box of Water Weenies. Then the assorted cartons of flags and kites, badminton sets, gardening paraphernalia. She was hauling the last box inside when she heard a siren not far away.

"What's that?" Valetta called from the back, where she was shutting down her pharmacy and catalog counters.

"I don't know." Jaymie stepped back out onto the porch and listened. More sirens. "Something big," she said to Valetta, who had come to the door.

"You follow the sound while I lock up," Valetta said, giving Jaymie a shove.

Jaymie dashed back in, grabbed her purse from the hook behind the counter and headed to the door. "Tell Jewel I'll be back for Hoppy in a few minutes," she called out over her shoulder, already skipping down the steps. It sounded like the sirens were heading down to the river. "I hope it's not a drowning!" Jaymie muttered as she trotted toward the wailing sirens. But the riverside was calm. The siren sound was from past the riverside, beyond the docks. She picked up her pace and headed toward Johnny Stanko's neighborhood.

A crowd was gathering, even as the police were trying to push them back. They had Stanko's house surrounded, and a sergeant used a bullhorn, saying, "Come on out, Stanko. We know you're in there, and we know you have a gun. Come on out, and no one will get hurt!"

The tension ratcheted up as neighbors gathered in worried knots, whispering to each other. A cop began to push them back, and one couple hustled their young child away. Jaymie tried to find out from a cluster of neighbors what was going on, but no one seemed to know anything. They had all just heard sirens and gathered to watch.

One shot rang out, and police descended on the house, breaking a window and tossing a tear gas container in. They waited just seconds before three of them fastened gas masks over their faces and broke down the front door with a battering ram.

Valetta, gasping for air, hobbled up to Jaymie and stood on one foot, pulling her shoe off and emptying a pebble out of it before putting it back on. "What's going on?" she cried, hopping around.

"I don't know, but it doesn't look good," Jaymie replied. She wasn't going to tell Valetta about the gunshot.

❧ Twelve ❧

VALETTA CLUTCHED JAYMIE'S arm, trembling with worry. Moments later an officer wearing a tear gas mask led a handcuffed Johnny Stanko out of the house. He was doubled over and retching, barefoot and wearing only jean cutoffs, his dirty blond hair falling over his eyes.

"Johnny!" Valetta cried.

He stumbled, and the officer righted him. Valetta started toward him, but a police officer stepped in front of her and grabbed her arm, not hard, but enough to stop her. "I'm sorry, ma'am, but I can't let you do that."

She wrenched her arm from his grip, stiffened her spine and said, "I'm only going to talk to him." She shouldered her way past a couple of people standing around gawking. Jaymie followed in her wake. "Johnny," Valetta called out. His head snapped up. "Johnny, don't say anything to the police, okay? I'll get you a lawyer. Don't say *anything*. You don't have to talk to them!"

He nodded, and was led away. She watched them go, eyeing the police with a stern gaze.

Jaymie, who had followed her, said, "Valetta, if you think he's innocent, why don't you want him talking to the police?" That was quite a change from the day before when she wanted him to go to the police and tell them his side of the story.

Her expression set in stubborn rebellion, she said, "Because I don't want them bullying him into confessing. He's such an easy target. This is different than if he'd gone in voluntarily. Idiot!" She stamped her foot. "Why didn't he listen to me?"

They started together back to the Emporium to make sure Valetta hadn't missed locking up anything in her haste to find out what the sirens were about, and so that Jaymie could get Hoppy. "Do you think they'll do that, try to pin it on him? They only want to find out who did it."

"But if they figure that's Johnny, their lives suddenly got easier."

"We don't even know that's why they picked him up."

"Even you know better than that, Jaymie. What I want to know is, who tipped them off that he was in his house?"

Valetta was so worried that Jaymie just didn't want to let her handle it all alone. She put her arm over her friend's shoulders as Hoppy bounced around them, yapping. "Come on over to my place. You can call the lawyer from there, and we'll talk about it. I have so many jumbled ideas, and I need someone to bounce them off."

Valetta agreed. They returned to the Leighton house, and Jaymie made dinner while her friend tracked down a lawyer who agreed to go to the police station and intervene for Johnny Stanko. Valetta guaranteed the lawyer's fees. Jaymie didn't say anything, but knowing how much lawyers cost, she thought that Valetta must really believe in Stanko's innocence if she was willing to do that for him. A public defender would have been the sensible alternative, but Valetta claimed that she knew the public defender in Wolverhampton, and she wouldn't let him defend a gerbil accused of attacking a giraffe.

After dinner and after Valetta was allowed to briefly speak with Johnny on the phone, they sat in the backyard with tea and the animals. Surly Denver sat on Valetta's lap and endured being stroked and petted for an hour as they talked about the murder and its aftermath. "What I can't figure out is, who turned him in? Johnny said he hadn't been out of the house at all, and I sure didn't tell anyone he was there." She glanced over at Jaymie.

"Neither did I, Valetta. Really."

Her friend nodded. "I know you wouldn't have, but—"

"But you wondered. It's okay. If you believe Johnny is innocent, let's think of who else could have done it. I've been trying to create a timeline for everybody who was there, but it's difficult." Jaymie ran back inside, got some paper and a clipboard and plopped back down in the old wood Adirondack chair. "These are the folks I've thought of who might have had reason to kill Kathy Cooper, but there are a lot of things I don't know yet." As she wrote each name, she said it out loud: "Kylie, Andy Walker, Craig, Matt Laskan, Ella and Bob Douglas."

"Ella and Bob?" Valetta said, adjusting her glasses and leaning toward Jaymie to gaze at the list. "Why them?"

"Well, Kathy had that run-in with Ella at the Emporium, and Bob said he was really angry about it."

"Okay. Weak, but just barely possible."

A house finch twittered happily at the neighbor's feeder until Dipsy barked at it and sent it fluttering away. "Let's start with Kylie: motive, means and opportunity." She jotted those words down with a dash after each one. "Motive is easy; Kathy had been trying to get custody of Connor, and if she'd been trying to do that, she must have been trying to make a case that Kylie is an unfit mother."

"That's just sad. A year ago, maybe even a few months ago, I might have agreed, but Kylie has really been making an effort," Valetta said. "Andy Walker has been helpful, too. I think they're good for each other, because both miss Drew, and both want what's best for Connor."

"Good for each other," Jaymie mused. "Interesting. Anyway, Kylie has to have been very angry at Kathy over the whole custody thing. And Kylie and Andy were in the park; *that* we know." She paused. "How did Connor get away from them? I wonder. They were looking for him that night. Where were *they*?" She looked off at the setting sun, red gold and hanging low in the sky, disappearing behind the line of poplars. "If they were in on the murder together, they could have parked Connor somewhere, done the deed, and when they came back, Connor was gone."

Valetta grimaced. "Isn't it too much of a coincidence that you then find Connor near Kathy? How did *that* happen?"

"I know. It's weird. They have to stay on the possibility list, either separately or together. They could have picked up the bowl, I suppose. By the way, what do you make of Johnny insisting that he put the bowl back down on our table?"

Valetta shook her head. "The problem with Johnny is, he's so used to getting in trouble, he seems to lie by instinct."

Jaymie privately thought, *That is exactly what a murderer would do*, but she wasn't going to say that to Valetta. Johnny Stanko was very much on her list of suspects. "On to Matt Laskan," she said. She related to her friend what she had overheard between Matt and Kathy at the picnic, how she seemed to be threatening him with some secret, and what Jaymie had learned about his high-profile girlfriend. "I don't know where he was; I can't even be sure he was in the park when Kathy died. Until I know, he has to stay on the list of suspects."

Valetta looked thoughtful. "I may know friends of his. Let me see if they know what he was doing on July Fourth after he left the picnic."

"And *I'm* going to try to find out what secret he's hiding. Not sure how I'm going to do it, but I will." She sighed. "We really don't know a lot, do we?" But maybe they did know more than she thought. Dani Brougham had said that Kathy told her she was going to get revenge on all her enemies; who were her enemies? Besides Jaymie. She definitely needed to talk to Dani again.

"And we can't forget about the standard reason to kill someone," Valetta said, suddenly. "Who did she leave money to? Who benefited? Was there an insurance policy on her?"

Jaymie's stomach dropped. How could she have forgotten to think of that motive? Wasn't money at the bottom of most murders? "How do we find out?"

"Leave that up to me," Valetta said.

"I'm going to follow up with Kathy's friend Dani, Craig and with Mrs. Hofstadter. Mom and Grandma both said they felt sorry for Kathy and her mom. I didn't realize their dad was so hard on Kathy especially."

Valetta stuck her long legs out in front of her. "I still can't figure out who would have told Kathy about what you supposedly said back in high school. Why? Why would anyone want to hurt you both like that?"

"I don't get it, either." Jaymie stretched out in the Adirondack chair and looked up at the sky, now shading to a lovely cobalt. Both were quiet for a long minute, soaking in the peace of a Queensville evening, robins singing their evening song, a dog woofing in the distance. But Jaymie couldn't stop thinking about what Kathy's death meant to her: no more chances to make up their quarrel. One day it seemed as if you had all the time in the world to settle problems, and the next, all that time had evaporated into nothing. "Who would say something so awful, period? I mean, that's really hurtful, no matter what way you look at that. It would take someone really mean to say it."

She thought of Johnny Stanko at that moment and how he'd said he wanted to apologize to Craig for all the mean things he did and said back in high school. But as far as she knew, he wasn't even aware Kathy existed back then. As far as she *knew. Hmmm.* "Johnny knew Craig, but I don't think he knew Kathy back in school, did he?"

"Well, I wasn't there," Valetta replied. "But I don't think so. He was older than you girls, remember."

"Craig was only a year ahead of Kathy and me, though," Jaymie reminded her friend. "And he sure knew Craig."

"They had classes together. Johnny was older, but had been left back so many times, he and Craig were in the same grade."

Jaymie glanced over at the bed-and-breakfast; Anna was out on her deck with Tabby, and she waved to them.

"Jaymie, I have something to tell you!" Anna called. "Something I forgot! Wait a minute; I'll come over." She descended the deck stairs and went down the backyard and through Jaymie's gate, letting Tabby down the minute the gate was safely closed behind them. The little girl immediately found Hoppy and the two began a rousing game of tag.

Jaymie got Anna a chair and a cup of chamomile tea to settle her icky stomach. "What's up?" she asked.

Anna turned a little pink and looked down at her mug.
"I can't believe I forgot to tell you this; it's really important,
but lately I just can't seem to remember anything!"

"Mommy brain," Valetta said with a sympathetic smile.

"I guess," Anna said.

"So what did you forget to tell me?" Jaymie asked, thinking it was probably a request for more help, maybe with the
cleaning and laundry now, in addition to the cooking. Anna
was in over her head with the bed-and-breakfast, and it was
only a matter of time before she figured it out and admitted it.

"You remember when I told you I went to Craig's office
and caught him and his wife kissing?"

Jaymie smiled sadly. "Yeah. I feel so bad for Craig. If he
and Kathy truly had a good relationship, he must be just lost
right now. In fact, his sister said he's always gone, out walking alone." Dipsy, next door, started yapping in response to
Tabby and Hoppy's game. She jumped at the fence until
Mimi came out and got her. Mimi waved at Jaymie, who
waved back.

"Oh, I wouldn't be so sure he's walking *or* alone," Anna
said, and she frowned darkly. "When you pointed out Kathy
to me on July Fourth, I realized that the woman I caught
him kissing in his office was *not* his wife!"

"What?" Jaymie and Valetta chorused together.

"What do you mean, not his wife?" Jaymie said, sitting
up in her chair.

Anna glanced over at Tabby, who was now lying in the
grass with Hoppy. Denver was ready to pounce, his hind end
wiggling in anticipation, but Tabby leaped up and ran in
circles and Denver dashed off to glare at the world from under
the holly bushes.

"What do you mean? Tell me!" Jaymie whispered, leaning

toward her friend. Valetta had moved to the edge of her seat, too.

"It wasn't Kathy Cooper I saw that morning at the Laskan Cooper office kissing Craig."

"Well? Who was it?"

"I don't know."

Jaymie sat back in her seat and glanced at Valetta. "Did you know anything about Craig cheating on Kathy?" she asked her friend, the town's gossip center.

"I didn't."

"And I'd swear his own sister didn't, either," Jaymie commented.

"Chloe Cooper? I go to her to get my hair done," Anna said.

"This changes a lot," Jaymie said. "And it possibly explains why Craig canceled the move to Toledo." But was it a motive for murder? Was he getting ready to kill Kathy, or just to tell her their marriage was over? There were a lot of new questions that needed mulling now.

"Anna, I'm trying to think of who all had access to the Depression glass bowl," Jaymie said. "Did you see anyone with it?"

She glanced over at Valetta, and then said, "You mean other than that big guy? The guy wearing the cutoffs?"

Johnny Stanko. "Did you see him with the bowl?"

"Well, yes." Anna hesitated. "I heard he was just arrested."

Valetta remained tight-lipped and silent.

"Did you see him bring the bowl back at any point?"

"No. No one brought the bowl back, I'm almost sure of it. I was sitting there the whole time while Becca and Dee were cleaning up."

Tears formed in Valetta's eyes. "Johnny didn't do it. I'll swear on a stack of bibles."

Jaymie was silent. Valetta might not want to admit it, but there was no proof he *didn't* do it, and lots of reason to think he might have. He had lied about at least one thing: Jaymie was reasonably sure he'd never brought the bowl back, or someone would have seen him do it. You couldn't miss him in a crowd, with his big bozo feet and large, muscular frame.

"I'd better get Tabby to bed," Anna said, noticing her little girl dozing in the grass with Hoppy curled up against her.

After they were gone, Valetta said that she had better go home, too. She had some early calls to make the next day and wanted to meet with Johnny's lawyer.

Jaymie called Becca and brought her up to date with everything that had happened, including the real reason Kathy hated her, and Johnny Stanko's arrest.

"I know Valetta doesn't believe it, but Stanko is a definite possibility. He does have anger issues," Becca said, agreeing with Jaymie on that.

"And he's the last person anyone saw with the bowl. I don't believe at all that he brought it back to the table, as he says he did."

"I'd remember if he did," Becca said. She reaffirmed that she and Kevin would meet Jaymie at Rose Tree Cottage the next morning, since they had some work to do on it between renters, but said she might be going back to London for a couple more days. Kevin had a friend of his coming in from England, and he wanted them to have dinner so he could introduce him to Becca.

"That's okay," Jaymie said. "I'll see you tomorrow, then." She filled the sink and put in the mugs and their dinner dishes.

The phone rang. It was Daniel, and he sounded tired.

"What's up?" Jaymie asked. She hadn't seen him much

at all lately, and when she had talked to him in the last couple of days, he was preoccupied.

"Trouble at the office. I have to fly back to Phoenix. I've been on conference calls for most of the day, but they need me there."

"How long will you be gone?"

"At least a week."

"Okay," she said, setting the washed dishes in the drainer and grabbing a tea towel. He was silent on the other end. "Daniel? You there?"

"Sure. I'll miss you, Jaymie. Will you miss me?"

"Of course I will."

"Promise me you won't go trying to investigate or anything? Or at least wait until I get back?"

She was startled. "Uh, I can't promise that."

"Please, Jaymie. I'll worry about you."

She rolled her eyes. "Johnny Stanko was arrested, you know."

"Really? For murder?"

"I'm assuming."

"Good," he said. "The police must have a good reason for taking him into custody."

"E-mail or call me from Phoenix," she said, and they said good-bye.

As she got ready for bed, she wondered again why Daniel had bought Stowe House, so far from his corporate offices in Phoenix, and from his family in the same city. She'd have to ask him, because it really made no sense.

She read for a while, trying to concentrate on her historical romance novel, but questions kept popping into her brain: How far along had Kathy's plans to get custody of Connor been? If Craig really was having an affair, as seemed certain, how did he feel about the Connor situation? She slipped out of bed, got her pad of paper and started writing down her questions.

Bob had said that Ella's family believed she was delusional; was that true? Did she feel threatened by Kathy's behavior, enough to take matters into her own hands? How strong or weak was she *really*? And how mobile? She paused and thought: Was it possible that Ella Douglas was faking some of her disability? Making herself seem weaker than she was? She wouldn't be the first person to fake an illness to get sympathy.

Matt Laskan: What was his secret, the one Kathy had been holding over his head? Was it bad enough to require a murder to conceal it?

Kylie and Kathy appeared to be on the verge of making up. How was that possible when Kathy had been so adamant about getting custody of Connor? Was that tied in with Craig's secret affair at all? Had Kathy become aware of it, perhaps?

Jaymie set the notebook aside and read for a while, finishing with a torrid love scene between the waif and the duke, a handsome and desirable Adonis. Finally Jaymie turned the light off and drifted to sleep, slipping, eventually, into a lovely dream of a summer day in the woods. A man was with her. He followed her. They played hide-and-go-seek; she turned a corner, and he caught her to him in a strong embrace. He whispered that he wanted her, that he adored her, that there was no one in the world like her.

She knew he was going to kiss her, and she even thought they might do something else. Shivering with physical desire, she put her head back, and he kissed her throat, pulling her to him hard. *"Zachary,"* she whispered.

"It's not Zachary. It's Craig," he murmured.

She was jarred awake. Craig? Why was *he* in her dream? That was an even bigger question than why she thought her dream lover was Detective Zachary Christian and not Daniel. She turned on the light and seized her notebook and scribbled quickly: Why did Matt Laskan say that Craig *can't have gone to the office* that day in the park? If Craig was not working and lied about it, where was he? With his mistress, or plotting to kill his wife?

❧ Thirteen ❧

IT WAS SUNDAY. Since Clive was at the bed-and-breakfast and could manage the eggs for the guests, Jaymie was able to get going early, so she took Hoppy and went out to Heartbreak Island by the first ferry, at 8:00 a.m. Rose Tree Cottage was vacant until the next morning, and this was her golden opportunity to make sure it was clean and the gardening was done. Kevin and Becca would meet her there at lunch.

As she approached, she was struck, as always, by how pretty the cottage was; set in a grove of pines, wood cladding silvered with time, wine-red roses climbing vigorously up trellises against the walls, it was peaceful. Slanting early morning sun peeped through the trees to play across the terra cotta colored roof tiles. As Hoppy bounced around, Jaymie got right down to work, mowing the small patch of grass with the push mower and then sweeping the grass cuttings off the stone path. The back lawn could wait another week. She put the mower away in the shed and sat down on the front step of the long, covered porch for a breather.

Heartbreak Island was rustic, and the roads were not paved. Every cottage on her road was surrounded by groves of pine trees that swayed and whispered in the breeze that swept up the river. Jaymie thought back to many years before, when she was thirteen. That summer, Kathy had stayed with Jaymie's family for a week in Rose Tree Cottage. They'd had a great time fishing, water-skiing, sailing in a friend's skiff and just generally goofing off. They'd spend all day together, only coming back at night for dinner and a campfire. Something Kathy said then came back to Jaymie. Why, she asked, didn't the family live in the cottage? If it belonged to her, she'd never want to leave.

Tears welled in Jaymie's eyes. If only some jerk hadn't decided to ruin their friendship, maybe there would have been many more weekends and holidays together at the cottage. But the anonymous jerk was not the only one responsible, and she had to remember that. She and Kathy had both played their part. With her thoughts taking such a melancholy turn, she was glad to see Kevin and Becca approach, hand in hand.

The rest of the day was spent cleaning the cottage, making a few small repairs and assessing the need for a new sump pump. Kevin was quite handy with a tool kit and tinkered with it, but he was concerned that the flooding of their leaching bed was a bigger problem than just their erratic sump pump. The couple asked her about how the police investigation was going, and she went through the dramatic arrest of Johnny again, for Kevin's sake, and told them what she had learned about Craig having an affair. They talked about it for a while, but there was a lot to do and not much time, so they parted a few hours later, Kevin and Becca to take the ferry back to Canada, and Jaymie and Hoppy to go back to Queensville, Jaymie having gotten no further in her theories concerning the murder.

It had been a long day, and Jaymie was tired, so there were no more troublesome dreams that night. She awoke refreshed and determined to figure out what had really happened to Kathy Cooper, whether Johnny was the killer or not. It was easy to write off Valetta's belief in him as mistaken loyalty, but maybe her friend was right and the cops were wrong.

After making and serving breakfast at Anna's—Clive had, of course, gone back to Toronto the evening before—Jaymie sat down in the bed-and-breakfast kitchen with a cup of coffee and a muffin. Tabby, in the corner of the sunny kitchen, played tea party at her little table and chairs. She had her odd assortment of dolls at the table, including a stuffed tiger known as Mr. Stripes, and a hand-sewn clown, Pushy. She also had many of the children's dishes Jaymie had found for her at various estate sales and thrift stores, bowls and plates and cups of all sizes.

"Tabby, why don't you give Mr. Stripes the bowl?" Jaymie asked. "Kitties like to drink out of bowls."

"Clowns like bowls, too," she said, with a prim nod of her head, as she had Pushy lapping up pretend tea.

"Oh, *do* they, now?" Jaymie said.

"She's got her own ideas, that's for sure," Anna said, smiling at her little girl's intense demeanor. "Look, Jaymie, I didn't want to say it the night before last in front of Valetta—she appears to have strong feelings about that Stanko fellow's innocence—but he just seems like the kind who could snap and do something to Kathy Cooper."

"I know; I think that, too. I can't ignore the possibility

that he's guilty. But what if she's right? I can't rule out
Kathy's hubby, his business partner or her own sister."

"Especially since Craig was cheating on Kathy. That's
the oldest reason in the world. Especially if Kathy was a
part owner of Laskan Cooper."

Jaymie's eyes widened. "I never thought of that! How
awkward would that be for Craig, if his wife owned part of
the business and he wanted to divorce her? Brilliant idea!"

"Thank you," Anna said, standing and curtseying. "Now,
shoo! I have cleaning to do."

"Wait, one more thing . . . what did Craig's girlfriend
look like?"

Anna thought. "She was gorgeous: blonde, tall, stacked.
The kind of woman who makes the rest of us feel inade-
quate. But she had nice eyes, too. They smiled, even though
she was clearly embarrassed to be caught." She nodded.
"Now, go! I have work to do."

Jaymie's first stop was the Emporium. She had a box full
of clean dishes and linens to make up the baskets for the
next weekend's rentals. Mr. Klausner, reading the paper,
magnifying glass held out between him and the *Wolverhampton Howler*, nodded to her but went right back to his
reading. Jaymie unpacked the box, restocking the shelves
for the basket rentals, and then checked the rental book.
Craig's name leaped out at her again, along with the lack of
a check mark in the *Return* column. As she made up that
day's rental baskets and phoned over to the Queensville Inn
to confirm the food hamper to go with it, she pondered the
conundrum of Craig's basket. He certainly had not rented
the picnic basket for him and Kathy that day, so who had he
shared the dinner with, his mistress? Time for some hard
questions. Craig would be her first order of business.

Valetta motioned for her to come back to her pharmacy window before she left, so Jaymie wove between the aisles back to her white-coated friend.

"How are you doing?" she asked Valetta, knowing how troubled she was by Johnny's arrest.

"I'm good." Valetta glanced around, pushed her glasses up onto her nose more securely, and said, "Look, I talked to my brother after church yesterday morning. It turns out that Brock knows the insurance agent for Kathy and Craig. They had policies on each other. That's not so strange, I guess, but listen to this: Craig contacted the insurance company two days after her murder to find out about the policy's payment schedule!"

"Wow, that's pretty quick for a grieving widower," Jaymie mused, leaning on the pharmacy-window shelf. "But we already know he's not so grieving. Any idea who the mistress could be?" She gave Valetta the description Anna had given her that morning. Her friend knew everyone in her capacity as pharmacist and catalog clerk.

"I'll think about it. No one comes to mind. I got something else this morning, too. The lawyer I retained for Johnny is partners with the guy who was representing Kathy in her attempt to get custody of Connor."

"Really? Did you find anything out?"

"I did," Valetta said, her eyes shining behind her thick lenses. "Listen to this: Kathy called the lawyer on the third and said circumstances might have changed, and if they had, she might not want to go ahead with the custody suit."

"If we can establish that Kylie knew about that, then her main motive to kill Kathy just pretty much disappeared—poof!"

"I hope that's true," Valetta replied.

"It looked like they were all trying to get along, so maybe we can write Kylie off as a suspect."

"I feel so bad for Kylie. I hope she can just move on with her life now. She really seems to be trying to get her act together."

Jaymie leaned closer, and murmured, "Valetta, do you know anything about Matt Laskan? He's not from around here, is he?"

"I don't think so. He and Craig met in college. Matt is from Port Huron, if I remember right."

Jaymie thought for a long moment. "I have a friend who works in fact-checking at the newspaper in Port Huron. I'll bet she can track down his family."

"Why?"

"Why not? I'm looking at anything right now. It's hard to dig into someone's life. I need to find the path of least resistance when it comes to information gathering. His family might know if he has any terrible secrets, right?"

"You have a point! Anyway, I need to get back to work. One of my customers just phoned in her prescription and it's a doozy."

Jaymie didn't ask who the customer was, and Valetta wouldn't have told her if she had. The privacy of her pharmacy clients was everything to her. "I need to get going, too."

"Wait one more sec . . . I talked to Crawford Funerals to see if they knew when Kathy's service is, and they said Friday, even if the body hasn't been released to the family yet. Go with me?"

"I will. Becca will want to go, too. I'll tell her."

Jaymie went home. When she was in university in Canada, she made friends with fellow Michigander Wendi Carlyle; they had stayed in touch, and saw each other at least once a year when they went camping with a bunch of girl-friends. Wendi's position as a fact-checker at the Port Huron newspaper meant she would have contacts and capabilities Jaymie did not have. She called Wendi, giving as much detail as she could about Matt Laskan. Then Jaymie made a couple of other calls and headed out to discover what she could, determined to either confirm the police's suspicion of Stanko or figure out if there was a murderer out there getting away with it. As much as she believed Detective Christian was competent, he didn't know the people of Queensville the way she did. And one heard every day of wrongly convicted murderers spending their lives in prison before some random fact, forgetful witness or DNA sample set them free.

First stop, Laskan Cooper. This was not going to be easy or fun; there were no two ways about it. She parked Becca's Lexus in front of the converted cottage—she was heading out to Dani's farm after talking to Craig, so she drove—and took a deep breath. Now or never.

This time Matt Laskan was in, and he came to the reception room. "Hi, can I help you?" He recognized her a fraction of a second later and looked puzzled.

"I'm here to see Craig. It must be difficult for you guys, with no receptionist. Kathy used to work for you, didn't she?"

"Only part-time, and mostly on data entry. Not in the office proper; she worked from home. We have a college kid working for us this summer, but she called in lazy this morning. You can go on back. I don't think Craig is really working."

He turned away, but Jaymie wanted to take advantage of talking to Matt in person. "You know, I used to be friends with Kathy. She could be . . . difficult at times, but I'm so sorry for everyone who knew her and cared for her."

He turned back and watched her warily. "She was a good person. Not always easy to deal with, but still . . ." He shook his head.

"You and your girlfriend probably spent a lot of time with Craig and Kathy . . . how is she taking it, your girlfriend?"

He looked startled. "Uh, she barely knows Kathy. They didn't have a lot in common."

"Yeah, I heard she's a councilor in Wolverhampton. Is she really running for senate in the next election?"

He swallowed. "It's possible."

Jaymie smiled, her heart pounding, as she said, "Now that your little problem is out of the way?"

"What do you mean, my 'little problem?'" He sounded sincerely puzzled.

Craig came out that moment, locking his office door behind him, a sheaf of papers under his arm. He started when he saw Jaymie. "What do you want?"

"I . . . I came to ask about something."

Both men stood stock-still, waiting.

She should have been more prepared. *Dummy!* "Um . . . well, Craig, I was at the Emporium this morning and I see that you've rented a picnic basket, but you haven't returned it yet. I wasn't aware that you and Kathy were using one of our baskets."

"They weren't," Matt said. "He went in and rented it for me and Lily."

"Oh. So you and your girlfriend were at the Fourth celebration? How interesting. I don't remember seeing her. How long did she stay?"

"What is going on?" Craig said, moving toward Jaymie. "Why are you asking questions like that? You talked to my sister . . . What are you up to?"

"Nothing. I was just curious, you know, about the picnic basket. I was sitting right next to Kathy all afternoon, for crying out loud, so I knew *you* weren't there with her. You came back here to work, right?"

"Yeah . . . no . . ."

Matt looked over at his partner. "Kathy said you were coming back here, but—"

"No, no, I wasn't. She was wrong."

"I knew she must have been," Matt said. "Because I changed the alarm code and hadn't told you what it was yet. You couldn't have come *here*."

"I went home to work for a while. She just misunderstood, when I said I had to work." Craig's face flushed a bright, unbecoming red. "I have to go. I'm sure you were leaving?" he said to Jaymie, and went to the door, holding it open for her.

"I'll be right out, Craig," she said. She turned back to his business partner. "Mr. Laskan, may I speak to you for one moment?"

The other man nodded, curiosity on his face.

Craig looked distinctly put out. "What is this all about?" he asked, his eyes narrowed, door still held open.

"Why does it matter to you?" Jaymie asked him, noting his squinted eyes and firmed lips.

"I just want to know. This is *my* business, Matt is *my* partner. I have a right to know what you want to ask him."

"No, you don't." Anger flared in her gut, making her more daring. Craig's pale skin looked gray in the fluorescent office lighting, and a nerve twitched in his temple. She glared at him, and said, "You saw fit to help Kathy when she was making me the target of her anger. In May you took photos of my backyard when I had the . . . that trouble." She was referring to a fellow's tragic murder on her summer porch, and Craig taking pictures of her shed with crime tape wound around it. "You aided and abetted Kathy with all the harassment, the rumors, *years* of crap. And you know what? I have finally found out what it was all about, her hatred of me, and it was a lie."

He said nothing, just stood there looking at her steadily.

Tears welled in her eyes. "She was mad at me for something I never even said. You owe me, Craig," she said, poking her finger at him. He moved away, his brow furrowing. "You *owe* me," she continued, "because now I can't even make it up with Kathy. Did you even *once* tell her to work it out with me? Did you think I wouldn't know about the stupid rumors, the mockery? Or did you *want* me to know?" It felt so good to finally face someone about the years of anger. Why hadn't she had the nerve to be a loud girl and have it out in public with Kathy? Being afraid of seeming "not nice" had taken its toll.

He was stunned and let the door fall closed. Matt stared at her, too.

She was shaking, and she had to calm herself, letting the tears dry in her eyes, because she did not want to weep in front of them. "I'm really sorry, Craig. I'm sure this is a bad time for me to be talking like this, but I'm so angry that when I finally found out what this rift between us was all about, it was nothing. Absolutely nothing! Someone said that I said something awful, but I didn't. And now I can't tell her the truth." Tears welled yet again, but she was not going to cry. "All those wasted years. And you didn't help, ever! You egged her on."

He didn't lash out, like she expected. "I know," he said, sadness lacing his voice. "I failed everyone, most of all, Kathy. Recently I've realized how I let myself be caught up in the anger of the past, all those years ago, and I used

Kathy's fury against you—and against others—to help me vent. I . . . I wish I'd figured it out earlier. I was wasting my life."

She stared at him. He was serious. A thought occurred to her. "I know about the other woman, Craig," she said. "Is that what's made you think twice?"

His face bleached, and a nerve in his temple leaped.

"Another woman?" Matt said, jolted out of his stunned silence.

"Can we talk about this outside?" Craig said, turning to Jaymie. He headed to the door with Matt asking what was going on from behind them. Craig ignored his partner.

Jaymie followed Craig outside.

The man whirled, his face twisted with anger. "You've got nerve, coming to me with your sad story of persecution and . . . and your gossip! I don't know what the hell you think you're doing here, but you'd better just leave. Maybe Kathy was right about you after all; you're a Goody Two-shoes Leighton who thinks everyone owes you a curtsey or a bow and an apology for even living."

"That's a load of crap, Craig," Jaymie said, trying to subdue her quivering. She had brought on this wave of fury and couldn't now go back on it. "You're just trying to evade the truth, that you were cheating on Kathy." Her stomach felt sick. She hated conflict, and here she was confronting a man she had been "enemies" with for years.

But tears oozed from his cold gray eyes. He shook his head. "I won't talk to you about this," he said, and strode away.

He roared off in his Chevy, and Jaymie went back into the office. Matt was sitting at his desk, head in his hands. He looked up as she sat across from him.

"What's going on, Matt?" she asked.

"I don't know," he said, an echo of hopelessness in his voice.

"Kathy was convinced that you guys were going to open a branch office in Toledo, and she and Craig were going to manage it. But you guys were calling it off. What happened?"

He shrugged. "It was never the right time for it. I fought it from the beginning, but Kathy was determined. Craig finally came around to my way of thinking, but now I'm wondering why." He sat back in his chair and glanced over at a picture on his desk. He and a beautiful woman stood, arm in arm, clearly at some kind of official function.

"Is that Lily?"

He nodded.

"She's lovely." Jaymie paused, then tackled the matter uppermost in her mind. "Did you know Craig was cheating on Kathy?"

"I don't know it *now*," he said, glaring at her. "What, I'm supposed to believe you over my friend of twelve years? I don't think so."

She took another tack. "Matt, I heard Kathy threaten you with some kind of hold she had over you. What was that about?"

His expression hardened, his brown eyes hard and angry. "It was about nothing. She was delusional. Kathy Cooper had problems—*deep* problems—and she infected everyone she came near. I would think you'd know that better than anyone."

"But there seemed to be something there, something she knew. I won't say a word to anyone, I promise."

He shook his head. "No wonder you two butted heads. Look, there is nothing there, I swear it. I have nothing to hide. She was delusional, I told you. She misunderstood something private, and . . . never mind! I have work to do, so it would be best if you just left." He shuffled some papers together on his desk.

Jaymie watched him for a moment. He was worried about something, but he was not going to tell her what, despite his assertion that he had nothing to hide. "So you and your girlfriend were at the picnic on the Fourth. I hate to ask, but can I get the basket back sometime?"

"We didn't even use it. I gave her the basket and was supposed to meet her, but she ended up having to go to some official function in Wolverhampton."

"So you didn't stay and watch the fireworks?"

"Not my kind of thing."

"And you didn't go to the function in Wolverhampton?"

"She said not to bother. It was going to be boring, and she wouldn't be able to spend any time with me anyway."

No discernible alibi, Jaymie thought, afraid to push him harder. She watched his eyes. "So where is the basket?"

"Lily still has it. I'll make sure she returns it. Now, will you *please* go away? I have a ton of work to do!"

"Okay. All right." As she walked away, she heard a deep sigh and what sounded like a sob, but when she looked back, Matt appeared immersed in work.

❧ Fourteen ❧

JAYMIE LEFT AS puzzled, or more so, than she had been when she came. It was strange, an out-of-body experience, to behave that way. But it sure was empowering. It would have been nice if she had actually learned something.

But maybe she had. Matt Laskan had not been with his girlfriend, and had been home alone as far as Jaymie could tell, so he didn't have an alibi. Craig didn't want anyone to know about his affair, not even his partner, Matt. And Matt was definitely hiding something, the secret that Kathy had confronted him with and had been holding over his head; if there was no secret, as he claimed, why was he not open about what Kathy was getting at? Maybe it didn't have anything to do with anything, but she was curious. Hopefully her friend in Port Huron would come up with something.

Jaymie drove out to the country, following Valetta's instructions, until she came to a sign announcing she was at the lane to the Brougham Spangler Horse Farm. She pulled in and drove up the lane past a modern, low rambler-style home toward an enclave of barns, drive sheds and a horse ring with paddocks and fenced fields beyond. As she parked the Lexus and reentered the unfiltered, un-air-conditioned world, she thought what a mistake it had been to take Becca's luxurious car. She couldn't leave the windows open as she drove because Becca didn't like dust in her car, so the drive was performed locked in a luxurious, climate-controlled vault. She should have driven her rough-and-tumble van; she would have enjoyed the country air streaming in. It was a truly gorgeous July day, the sun shining, barn swallows diving and soaring overhead, finches singing.

A couple of big dogs—a border collie cross and a shepherd cross—bounded over to her, one barking, but they skidded to a halt at one *tcht!* from a woman over by the training ring. Jaymie walked over to watch the action in the ring, both dogs following, but silently; Dani had a foal at the end of a long leather line. She stood in the middle of the ring and had the horse at a trot, going around in a circle. Jaymie joined a slim woman who stood at the fence, one booted foot up on the bottom rail.

"Hey," the woman said, as a greeting.

"What's Dani doing?" Jaymie asked.

"She's on the last step of breaking a foal to halter." The woman glanced over at Jaymie and perhaps felt her puzzlement. "Horses don't naturally take to a halter and bridle, so it's best to start early, get them used to it long before they're ready for a saddle. This one's a new colt, Chester, and he looks good, so we want to train him up right and early. Emma Spangler," she finished, putting out her hand. "And you are . . . ?"

"Jaymie Leighton."

The other woman nodded. "I've heard of you. Dani said she ran into you at the feed store the day before Kathy was killed."

Jaymie nodded. "That's what I want to talk to Dani about."

"This has been real hard on her." She slanted a serious glance over at Jaymie. "You're not going to upset her, are you?"

"I'm hoping, as Kathy's friend, she can tell me about anything that was bothering Kathy lately, so I don't know," Jaymie said, honestly.

"Okay. I appreciate the truth."

They watched for a while. Dani was so wholly engaged in her task, she didn't even notice Jaymie until she finally relaxed and walked the foal, a pretty reddish brown animal, to the ring gate.

"That was beautiful," Emma said.

Dani came over, kissed Emma soundly and smiled broadly. "Isn't he perfection?" She petted the colt's white-blazed nose. "We've got ourselves a winner."

Jaymie felt the shock of the intimacy of that kiss, but didn't want to show it. Dani Brougham was gay. It didn't matter a jot, but what shocked her most was that Kathy must have known that, and yet Dani was her best friend. She hadn't thought Kathy would be tolerant, much less accepting, of the couple. It saddened her that she hadn't known *that* Kathy in adulthood, the one who was clearly a good and loyal friend.

Dani was watching her when she looked back up.

She knows I'm shocked, Jaymie thought, *but not why.* It was not the kind of thing she could explain, so she just moved on. "You were Kathy's best friend," she said. "I wanted to say how sorry I am about her death."

Dani nodded, her expression stoic. "I understand you found her."

"It was terrible," Jaymie said. "Can we go somewhere and talk?"

Dani nodded.

"I'll take Chester," Emma said gently, touching Dani's shoulder. "You two go on up to the house. There's coffee made and some carrot cake I just finished frosting."

Dani led the way to the back door and down into a rec room. She said she had to wash the ring dust off her, but told Jaymie to go ahead and have a seat while she headed upstairs.

The rec room was big, maybe twenty-five feet long, and cool. There was a fireplace in the corner, and there were comfortable couches and chairs in a seating area at one end. The walls were adorned with ribbons, framed photos and a shelf that held trophies dating all the way from the 1980s to earlier this same year. Most had Dani's name on them, but some had Emma's. There was a framed newspaper clipping with a photo of a grinning youngster in pigtails holding up a ribbon. Under it, it said, "Danielle Brougham, age twelve, and her half-Arabian, Leon, bring home a first in the Michigan Youth Equitation Trials."

Passion: Dani had found hers early, but Jaymie was a late bloomer in every sense of the word, and was just now discovering an ardor for vintage kitchenware and old recipes. It was a sad, sad thing that Kathy, who had shown an early enthusiasm for health care and helping others, had not been able to follow through. Perhaps if she had lived, she still might have.

Jaymie sat on the sofa and thought about what she wanted to discuss with Dani. She wanted to know what Dani thought of the relationships in Kathy's life, with her husband, sister and the grandfather of her nephew. And what about Matt Laskan? Did Dani know if there was anyone else who would want Kathy dead? But the woman was going to have questions about her own motives, and Jaymie had to be prepared for that.

Finally Dani came down the stairs with two mugs and some carrot cake on a plain wood tray. "I didn't know how you take your coffee, so I brought sugar and milk."

"Great." Jaymie fixed her coffee, and sat back, eyeing the generous hunks of carrot cake on a platter.

"Take a piece," Dani said, grabbing a sizable chunk and a napkin for herself.

Jaymie did, and took a bite, closing her eyes in ecstasy. "I have to get this recipe," she mumbled, enjoying the subtle spice flavor and the chopped pecans. "Yum!"

They finished their cake in silence; then, as Jaymie licked icing off her fingers, Dani said, "I'll get Emma to give you the recipe."

"How long have you two been together?"

"Seven years."

"How'd you meet?"

"Horse show. She was a barrel racer and was looking for a trainer for a new horse she was thinking of buying."

"How did you meet Kathy?" Jaymie asked.

"I came in to Laskan Cooper to have my accounts done. About five years ago, I guess. When Kathy found out I had horses, she wanted to know all about it, and she came out to ride. She was inexperienced, but she loved horses, you could tell. If she'd had more time, she could have become a good rider. We became friends."

"I've known her almost my whole life," Jaymie said.

"You're the last person I would have expected to see here," Dani said, her voice husky with emotions she was trying to defeat. "You and she didn't get along, exactly, from what I understand from Kylie."

"We were the best of friends, once."

"What happened?"

"What's sad is, I didn't know what happened to end our friendship until just a couple of days ago. Apparently someone at our high school thought it would be funny to tell her that I said something unforgivable about her." Jaymie hung her head, feeling the searing awfulness of the words that must have pierced Kathy to the core. "Something really awful and personal. Someone told her that I said, to a guy she liked, that she smelled like pigs, her family smelled like pigs and their whole house smelled like pigs. It went around the school as some kind of great joke, and the guy never talked to her again." Jaymie shook her head. "I could never say something like that. Never! But she apparently believed that I said it, without even asking me about it. She never told me why she was angry, so I couldn't tell her that I didn't . . . didn't say it." Jaymie shook her head and looked into Dani's eyes. "Why did she believe I'd say a thing like that?"

"You don't know?"

Jaymie thought about it, about the occasionally catty remarks she had made, thinking she was being funny, about her nickname for Craig Cooper, the one that had stuck and stung for all those years. "You know, maybe I do know why she believed it. I wasn't a terrible kid, but I did have my moments."

"It wasn't just that. Kathy was touchy sometimes about where she came from. She was probably a little ashamed, especially at that age. Maybe she even worried that it was true."

"That . . . that they s-stank? But it *wasn't* true," Jaymie said.

Dani shrugged. "I don't know; I'm just speculating. I didn't know her then. So what do you want from me?"

"You knew her better than I did, at least these last years," Jaymie said, rubbing at a spot of frosting on her thumb. "I want to find out who killed her. I just can't let go of it. And to do that—to find out who might have wanted to hurt her—I need to know more about her."

"But I understood there's been an arrest."

"A very good friend of mine—someone whose opinion matters to me and who I trust—doesn't believe Johnny Stanko killed Kathy," Jaymie said. "And God only knows there were lots of other people who won't be crying at her funeral. She was a polarizing figure."

"But I still don't get it. How can I help?"

"You knew her in a different way than anyone else. You were her best . . . pretty much her *only* friend. Did she confide in you? Was it that kind of friendship?"

The woman hesitated and stared into Jaymie's eyes, her own full of doubt. "Why should I tell you anything? Why should I believe your motives?"

Jaymie nodded. "Fair enough." She thought for a long minute. "I'll tell you what I feel; that's pretty much all I can do. I can't shake this . . . this sense of sadness over the whole thing. All the what-ifs come back to haunt me. What if Kathy had turned to whoever told her such a horrible lie back in high school and said there would be no way I could say such a thing? What if I'd pursued it harder, instead of feeling hurt and withdrawing? I wish she had believed in me and our friendship. Despite everything, I'd have thought she would have given me a chance to tell her the truth. Instead, I just never knew. I can't think why she didn't just *say* something to me."

"Kids are insecure. I know that better than anyone. Like

I said, she probably believed it because she was afraid it was true, and that's exactly why she couldn't confront you. Hearing it secondhand was bad enough, but face-to-face would have been so much worse."

"It sounds like you've had experience?"

Dani nodded. "I briefly had a girlfriend in high school—not a girlfriend in the sense of Emma, just a friend—but when the others noticed us hanging out together, she was teased so much she turned against me, said she never really liked me, that she only hung around me because she felt sorry for me. She said a lot of other crap, too." Her expression was impassive, but anger flared in her eyes. "It hurt so bad, I lost a whole year of school. I never spoke to her again. I had to transfer to another school finally, after I tried to commit suicide. It was a long time before I trusted anyone again."

"I'm so sorry," Jaymie said, gazing into her eyes, where the hurt still lingered. "Do you ever wonder what that friend feels today, if she's sorry for what she said?"

The other woman frowned and looked down into her coffee, swirling it around. "You know, I never really thought of it that way. She was a kid too, so afraid of being ostracized. I wish she'd had more guts, but . . ." She shrugged. "Teenagehood sucks."

"You're probably right about why Kathy believed the lie. But I can't leave it alone; I keep thinking what might have been if she hadn't died. On the Fourth, before I even found out the truth, I swore to myself that the very next day I was going to corner her and hash it all out." She met Dani's gaze. "Why did I wait? Could I have changed anything? I just don't know. The only thing I can do now is help the police get whoever did that to her and her family."

"And you don't think Stanko did it?"

"That's just it; I don't *know*, not for sure. He was a bully in high school, and he gave Craig Cooper a real hard time, but I don't think he even knew Kathy. He *seems* like the type, and I wince even saying that, but he has a short temper and a history of violence, and he threatened Kathy at the picnic. She was so gutsy." Jaymie shook her head and took a long gulp of coffee. "I would have backed down, but she didn't."

"Okay. I've been wracking my brain the last couple of days trying to think of who might have done it, but when Stanko was arrested I just . . ." Dani shrugged. "But I hate when people make snap judgments, and if he's not guilty, I don't want him to suffer."

"I have to be completely honest here. I do have another motive for figuring this out. Kathy was killed with my glass bowl." She hung her head a moment, shivering as the horror of the scene came vividly back to her. She looked up; Dani's expression was soft with sympathy, but she waited, silent. "I brought that bowl to the picnic, and someone used it to kill her. That makes me really mad," she said, through her teeth. "But it also makes me a suspect. If Stanko didn't do it, then we'll be back at square one. I want to know the truth, and I can't just leave it up to the cops. This is personal."

"How can I help?"

"I need to know about her life. Did she say anything lately about anyone she was afraid of? Did she tell you about any fights she'd had? About her and Craig's relationship? Her and Kylie? Connor's grandfather, Andy Walker?"

"Whoa, that's a lot. Give me a minute." She sat back in her chair and drank down some of her coffee, her gaze unfocused. "Well, she and Craig; something was bothering her about that the other day. I talked to her on the phone on the morning of the Fourth. She wanted Emma and me to come in for a picnic, but one of the horses was colicky, and we had to stick around and walk her. Emma told me to go ahead to Queensville if I wanted, but Matilda is my oldest horse; I didn't want to let the poor old girl down." She closed her eyes for a second, then opened them. "Instead, I let Kathy down. What if I could have changed things that day, turned events so it wouldn't have happened? I guess I feel like you do. I'll never know."

Jaymie reached out and touched her knee. "So let's see that whoever did this to her pays. What else did you talk about that morning?"

"She was upset. I'm not quite sure, but I had a feeling that . . . that she was afraid for her marriage."

Jaymie nodded. "I can believe that. I know it won't go any further than this, so I'll tell you something I've just learned: Craig was cheating on her. I have a witness to him kissing another woman."

Dani gasped, eyes wide with shock. "Bastard! He was the one thing she was sure of in life, she once told me. What an asshole! Pardon the language."

"Pardoned," Jaymie said.

"She told me that she took his phone by accident one morning a few days before the Fourth. She saw text messages on there that weren't right, and I think she saw a photo that upset her. She wouldn't tell me everything, but she was devastated about it."

"I wonder if that was what was going on at the Emporium on the second. She had a phone in her hand and was looking at it, and she said something like "What the heck?" and she was upset. Maybe that's why she lashed out at Ella about running over Connor's toes."

"Oh, and that's another thing. She e-mailed me that she was planning on going over to Ella's place and apologizing for biting her head off. She said . . ." Dani frowned and stared down into her cup. "What did she say? Something I meant to ask her about. Oh yeah. She said that she wanted to *help* Ella. Ella Douglas is that woman in a wheelchair, right?"

"Yeah. She has a degenerative disease or something, and she's having a lot of trouble right now. Kathy wanted to be a nurse. Maybe she was thinking of going back into it?"

"I don't know," Dani said, slowly. "I think she wanted to help her, specifically to make up for snapping at her in the store. I'm not sure, but that's the only thing I can think of."

"Ella Douglas was a girl we knew in high school. Back then she was a bit of a bully," Jaymie said.

"Kathy did say that, but then said something about Ella being in trouble, and that she wanted to reach out to her."

"That's nice," Jaymie mused. She was silent for a moment, letting the coolness of Dani's rec room wash through her. "Everything I hear makes me wish I had not put off making it up with her somehow. You were her best friend; you must know about her plan to adopt her nephew and move to Toledo?"

Dani nodded, her expression troubled. "Connor meant the world to Kathy; he was *everything* to her. She and Kylie had a rocky relationship after Kylie's fiancé died. I tried to tell her to let Kylie recover on her own terms, but Kathy was so worried about what Kylie's depression was doing to Connor."

"But Kylie was getting better, I've heard?"

"That's real recent. Kathy was worried about a relapse. You have to understand, at one point Kylie was suicidal. Kathy didn't trust her recovery."

"Kathy also thought that Andy Walker was trying to alienate Connor from her."

Dani's gaze sharpened. "You knew about that?"

"I overheard her talking . . . actually, *yelling* it at Craig while they had an argument on the Fourth. Did Andy do something specific to make her think he was trying to turn Connor against her?"

"I'm not sure. My impression, if you want the truth, is that Connor was getting good at manipulating them both in that way kids have, to get what he wanted. When he was with Kathy, he'd say he wanted Grandpa, but Kylie said when he was with Grandpa Andy, he said he wanted Aunt Kathy."

"How did the plan to get custody of Connor and move away from Queensville come about?"

"Kathy figured if she could prove to the judge that Kylie wasn't stable, she'd get temporary custody of Connor. Then if she could get him to Toledo, she hoped Kylie would give up and forget about it."

"That's not likely. Kylie really seems to love her kid."

"*Exactly* what I told Kathy," Dani said, slapping her thigh. "But she wouldn't listen to me."

"Well, it does seem that she was giving up on the idea, from what I saw and heard on the Fourth. She was sitting with Kylie and Andy later in the day, and it looked like she had made up her mind to stop trying to get custody of Connor." She was not about to share the info she had from the lawyer, that Kathy had already prepared to abandon the custody suit, for some unnamed reason. There was so much confusion around her intentions that Jaymie just didn't quite understand.

Jaymie thought back to the conversation she had overheard between Kathy and Craig, when Kathy had been complaining about Andy Walker; it had almost seemed like Kathy was testing her husband, trying to push him to some definite statement. She had said something like "If Connor is going with us," but he had hushed her up. "I don't know what changed her mind from earlier that day, when she still appeared intent on getting custody."

"That I couldn't tell you."

The door to the rec room opened and Emma Spangler bopped in, dropped a kiss on Dani's forehead and smiled over at Jaymie, perching on the arm of the chair Dani was sitting in, her arm looped casually over Dani's shoulders. Despite her casual demeanor, there was an aura of tension in the set of her shoulders.

"So?" she said. "You guys solved the world's problems yet?" Emma looked down at Dani and examined her face.

"Not yet, but we're working on it. I'm fine, Emma," she said, patting her girlfriend's hip. "You can go wash up. There's still coffee."

"I love your carrot cake," Jaymie said. "You should make it next year for our annual Tea with the Queen event!"

Emma stood and hesitated. "The Heritage Society is a lot of old ladies. I . . . I wouldn't want to shock any of them by joining in, and I won't change who I am or hide anything."

Dani's face held a look of tenderness as she took Emma's hand. "It took a lot for Emma to come out. I've been out a long time, but she's only been out a few years, and she's lost family from it."

"My parents are fine with us, thank God, but my brother . . . he hasn't spoken to me since."

"I'm sorry." Looking between them, Jaymie smiled. "I think you might be surprised at some of those old ladies, though. When my friends, Anna and Clive, bought the bed-and-breakfast next to me, Clive was a little worried. He's Jamaican, and Queensville's population is, as you know,

quite . . . well, very pale complected. But Mrs. Bellwood—
she plays Queen Victoria at the tea every year—said that
Clive, if he wanted and was willing to grow a beard and wear
a turban, could play the part of Queen Victoria's dear friend
and confidant Abdul Karim. Mrs. Bellwood really takes her
part seriously and has done a lot of Queen Victoria research.
She said Clive was so tall and handsome, that he would do
the part justice. Not all of the old ladies are narrow-minded
bigots. Gossips, yes; prejudiced . . . not necessarily."

"I'll think about contributing next year," Emma said.
"I'm going upstairs to wash and change. Can I get you two
anything else?"

"No, we're fine. Go ahead, Em," Dani said.

When she was gone, Jaymie said, "One other thing I've
been trying to find out . . . was Kathy a part owner of Laskan
Cooper?"

"I don't think so. Why?"

"Well . . . if she was, and if Craig was planning on leaving her, it could get messy."

Dani did the necessary logic, and her eyes widened at
the implication. "You don't really think Craig is capable of
killing Kathy, do you?"

"I don't know," Jaymie said, sighing in exasperation.
"*Someone* did it, and it was someone who knew how she
felt about me, because they took *my* bowl and hit her over
the head with it."

"I didn't think of it that way, as a purposeful thing, choos-
ing the bowl. So you think it was meant to point to you?"

Jaymie said, "It could have been chance, I suppose."

"But you don't really believe that."

"No, I don't. I think someone knew that was my bowl,
and also knew I'd had a public argument with Kathy. Someone wanted me to look guilty. I doubt if they planned it

ahead, though, because they couldn't know I'd argue with Kathy in front of everyone, nor that we'd be sitting close together, nor that I would bring a heavy glass bowl to the picnic. So whoever did it was smart and willing to take chances."

"I wish I could help, but I've told you everything I can think of."

"And I appreciate it. Do you know Matt Laskan very well?"

"No, not at all."

"Well, I guess that's it, then," Jaymie said.

❈ Fifteen ❈

JAYMIE FINISHED HER coffee and excused herself, saying she was going on to Mrs. Hofstadter's farm to talk to her. She didn't really expect to find anything out from the woman; the visit was just to check in with her and express her mother and grandmother's sorrow for the loss of Kathy. Dani invited her to come out to their farm again under better circumstances to ride, if she wanted, and to bring a friend, and she and Emma both said if they thought of anything, they'd call Jaymie.

Back on the highway, heading toward the Hofstadter farm, Jaymie thought over her conversation with Dani Brougham. It was news that Kathy had planned to drop in on Ella and Bob Douglas the morning of the Fourth. If Jaymie could find a reason, she'd visit Ella and ask her about it. Despite Kathy's seemingly good intentions, had the two fought? Ella had been a bully in high school. Given Kathy's sensitivity toward bullying, had she upbraided the invalid for her past behavior? Ella wasn't high on her list of suspects, but it was worth a visit to check into it.

The Hofstadter farmhouse looked the same as it had on her last visit: desolate. Jaymie parked and took a moment to look around the yard and outbuildings. The barn was sagging alarmingly to one side, and there were huge gaps in the walls; you could actually see daylight right through it. But worse than the decrepitude of the barn was the amount of garbage everywhere. Stacked in front of the drive shed were what looked like old moldy mattresses rotted out by the hot summer sun, springs and a dozen or so sets of headboards and footboards. Several rusty vehicles—tires off, one burned out, one even had been spray painted with graffiti-like scrawls—sat in the circular drive. She had an eerie sense she was being watched, but Jaymie guessed that was from the cats who stretched out everywhere, on the hoods of the cars and up in the haymow. The door to the haymow was long gone, and Jaymie could see a variety of ginger and tabby cats lounging in the open space where the July sun warmed the barn's wood floor.

There were dozens of partially filled bowls and trays outside the back door, some with kitty kibble in them. As Jaymie made her way to the back door, one cat leisurely followed and rubbed against her ankle. The ginger tom rubbed and purred huskily; she bent down to pet him, scruffing him under his chin until his purr was as loud as a motorboat.

"That's Killian," Mrs. Hofstadter said.

She stood in the open door, a dirty apron on over her housedress. Stockings sagged down her ankles, and her bare legs showed bites, probably flea bites, Jaymie guessed.

"He knows you're the one made the macaroni and cheese," the woman continued, swiping back wisps of gray hair that escaped from an untidy bun. "Too much for just me, so I shared."

"That's okay, Mrs. Hofstadter. I'm glad the cats enjoyed it." She approached, and again, from the open door, wafted the smell of decay and mold. She was overwhelmed with sadness that this woman, once a member of Queensville society, or at least on the fringes of it, should now be so isolated and clearly having significant problems, hoarding being just one of them. "I just came to pick up the casserole dish."

"Oh . . . I . . . I don't know where it is," the woman said, her gaze sliding away from Jaymie.

"Can I come in? I can find it, I'm sure."

There was a long pause. "All right," she replied, but she was clearly reluctant to let a virtual stranger into her house.

Jaymie was not about to let that stop her, and eased past her through the mudroom into the kitchen. Her breath caught in her throat. It wasn't just the smell—decay and mold—but the mounds and stacks of junk everywhere. There were a table and four chairs, but the set was buried under papers: newspapers, advertising flyers and mail. There were dozens of shopping bags full of stuff, most of it new. Some of it was cleaning supplies, multiples of powder cleanser, detergent, dish soap, spray cleaner and sponges.

Jaymie glanced around and spotted her glass casserole dish sitting atop a stack of advertising flyers. The food had been scraped out of the dish, but it was still dirty. "There it is!" she said. "How about I just clean it here and take it with me. Is that okay?" She was uneasy about the woman. How could she live in this wreck? Did she even have access to clean bathroom facilities? How could her daughters let her live this way? She picked up the casserole dish.

"That's not your dish!" Mrs. Hofstadter said.

"Yes it is!" Jaymie said. "I recognize it. It's one I bought at the church bazaar last fall. Look . . . it still has some of the mac and cheese in the corners."

"No, I . . ." The woman shook her head and mumbled.

Jaymie watched her; she looked confused, her sagging cheeks threaded with broken capillary veins, puffing out with each breath. "Mrs. Hofstadter?"

"Oh, go ahead, take it!" she snapped, waving her hand.

The woman appeared worried, and cast her glance around the room, as if memorizing everything else she owned. Her heart pounding, Jaymie wondered: Was this what she was going to be like? Becca called her a hoarder. Forty years from now, would she be closeted in her home in Queensville, surrounded by so much junk she couldn't move? She loved buying stuff, she enjoyed new acquisitions and found it difficult to get rid of anything. But no . . . this was not her future. There was something else going on here beyond merely liking to acquire stuff.

Gently, she said, "I'm just going to wash it up, Mrs. H. Is that okay?" She moved toward the sink and began piling the dirty dishes to one side. "Have you had anything to eat today?"

The older woman shook her head. "I . . . I don't remember. With Kathy gone, I just don't know."

"I'm so sorry about Kathy. My mom and grandma both wanted me to express how awful they feel, and how much they know you'll miss her."

"She was the one who kept me organized."

Jaymie had some time, certainly enough to help Mrs. Hofstadter. She cleared a chair near the counter and made the older woman sit; then, while talking about the town, and upcoming events, she filled the basin with hot water and dish soap. At least the woman's utilities were all working.

Then she cleared the dish drainer of clean dishes, stacking them in the cupboard, and piled dirty ones in the suds to soak. She bustled around, not asking, but clearing space at the kitchen table while she talked.

It looked like someone had tried to do the same recently, because the stacks of stuff on the table were newish, papers from just the week before. Mrs. Hofstadter talked a little, telling Jaymie that Kathy used to come see her every day to make sure she was all right and had enough to eat.

The fridge was surprisingly clean, but there were signs that the latest food had been purchased was July third, one day before Kathy's death. Jaymie fought back tears, realizing anew what a hole that woman's passing would leave in many people's lives, especially that of her mother. She made a big pot of tea and moved Mrs. Hofstadter over to the table to drink some. She found some bread in the freezer and made her some toast too, with jam. "Kathy was a good woman," Jaymie said, her voice trembling. "I wish we had stayed friends."

Mrs. Hofstadter pursed her lips and shook her head. "My poor Kathy was so sad about that. She came home one day and said she wouldn't be going to your place anymore. I was surprised. I called your mom, but Joy didn't know what had gone wrong, either."

"You called my mom about it?" That was something she hadn't known.

"She said we'd have to let you girls work it out, but you never did. Kathy got closer to her sister after that. She always loved Kylie so much, looked after her. When Drew died, Kathy took care of her. Practically moved in here to help Kylie and me and little Connor. That's when she took out the policy."

"I beg your pardon?"

"The insurance policy. Kathy took out a big one—a

million dollars, I think—for Kylie and Connor. In case anything happened to her, you know."

Jaymie was stunned. A life insurance policy to benefit
Kylie and Connor? From being eased off the list of suspects,
Kylie had popped right back onto it.

Mrs. Hofstadter continued, becoming more lucid and
settled as she ate her toast and drank her tea. "Kathy worried
about them so much. But Connor will have enough money
to do whatever he wants now, if Kylie manages things right.
He can go to school, even become a doctor. That was Kathy's
dream, you know, to become a doctor or nurse. But we
couldn't afford to send her to medical school. Maybe Connor
will do it."

With a million bucks? That was possible. But it sure
would be interesting to know about the actual policy, and if
the payoff was Kylie's to do whatever she wanted with, or
if it was to be kept in trust for Connor until he reached a
certain age.

Yes, it sure would be good to know.

WHEN SHE GOT back home, there were several messages
on the answering machine, but she didn't have time to listen
to all of them. A knock at the back door sent Hoppy into a
barking frenzy. "Why can't I train you like Emma Spangler
has her dogs trained? Come on in!" she called out, hanging
the phone up without retrieving her messages.

And in walked Detective Christian in yet another dark
suit. "Ms. Leighton," he said, nodding.

"Hi!" she replied. "What's up?"

"That's what I'd like to know. You've been talking to
people, Ms. Leighton." He circled her kitchen, picking up
items, looking them over and setting them back down.

"I didn't know I wasn't allowed to talk to people anymore," she said, her tone acid, but feeling a chill of apprehension. She quickly reviewed what she had been discussing and with whom that morning. Anything that the police should know about? Any bone of gossip she could throw him to keep him from looking at her with that fishy-eyed, suspicious stare?

"Why are you talking to people, Ms. Leighton?"

She sighed and rolled her eyes. "Are you going to go all mysterioso detective on me?" she demanded. "Remember my first name? It's Jaymie. You can call me that, you know. Anyway, me? Mostly, I've been trying to solve the riddle of why Kathy Cooper stopped talking to me in high school."

"And?"

"It was all a misunderstanding."

"I don't think that's all you've been doing. You've been digging around in the dirt, haven't you? Asking questions, getting people riled up. That's *my* job."

She bit her lip and stayed silent, watching him.

"You *know* we've arrested Johnny Stanko for the murder of Kathy Cooper. Don't you think he's guilty? Do you have any other suspects in mind that you, based on your long detecting career, think might be more viable?"

Okay, if he was going to be Mister Sarcastic Detective, she had a few questions of her own for him. Watching him as he prowled her kitchen, followed by an unhappy Hoppy, she said, "Speaking of misunderstandings . . . Detective, pardon me for saying this, but I'm still puzzled as to why you left your former job in . . . Chicago, was it? Why take a position on this tiny little force in a town that is kindly called 'quaint,' instead of staying where career advancement would occur at a rate quicker than glacial?"

He smirked. "Trying to deflect my questions?" he asked, circling her. "Why would you do that?"

"When have I done that, not answered questions?" She turned away, trying to ignore his towering masculine presence in her old-fashioned kitchen. The man just plain made her nervous. "Do you want something?" she demanded, feeling a prickling at the back of her eyelids that foreshadowed tears. She plunked down in a chair at the table. "I'm a little down right now. I was just out at Kathy Cooper's mother's house, out in the country, and that poor woman . . . I don't know what she's going to do now that Kathy is dead. I'm just . . ." Her voice choked off. She swallowed hard, cleared her throat and twisted to look up at the detective. "I just can't understand why someone killed Kathy. I mean, I understand, I guess; she angered a lot of folks. But to kill her? That's extreme. And why there, at the Fourth picnic?"

"Don't you believe that Stanko did it?"

She hesitated, thinking about it seriously. "I don't know. It seems logical, you know? He's violent, I get that. He threatened Kathy. I get that, too. But the sheer number of people who benefited from her death . . . it's staggering."

"We know that; we've investigated all of them. But Stanko is the only one of them to have that bowl in his hands."

"I would bet that you're not so sure of that," she said, watching his eyes, fiddling with the runner in the middle of the trestle table. Hoppy settled at her feet and stared up at him, too. Even Denver prowled into the kitchen from one of his hidey-holes and sat by the stove, glaring at the detective. "I would bet," she said, slowly, "that there are a whole lot of fingerprints on that bowl, and maybe a lot of smudging, too. I don't know much about fingerprints, but I know it's not always easy to tell who had an item and when."

"We do know that *you* had the bowl in your hands. *And* you fought with Kathy Cooper. Freeing Stanko would put you back in the spotlight." He was watching her, his gray gaze flicking unsettlingly over her eyes, down to her mouth, back up to her eyes.

She gazed at him steadily, hoping her eye wasn't twitching. "We both know I didn't have a true motive, Detective. A high school feud? You couldn't arrest me for supposedly saying something nasty to someone seventeen years ago." She saw in his expression that it was true. Relaxing a bit, she said, "Stanko has a history of violent behavior from what I understand, but lately he's been trying to change his life. He certainly walked away from Kathy even when she was belligerent toward him. He said enough, though, that he sure looks like a good suspect."

It began to make sense. "In fact, maybe I've been looking at this all wrong," she said, as a light bulb began to dimly glimmer in her brain. "I thought the use of the bowl was to implicate *me*, but maybe they were really trying to implicate *Johnny*."

He nodded. "That's possible."

So, he was still investigating even after having arrested Stanko. Had he been pressured into making an arrest? Had he even been the arresting officer? She didn't remember seeing him there that day.

"Who else wanted Kathy dead?" he asked.

"Let's see . . . offhand? I can't say these folks wanted her *dead*, necessarily, but Kathy was a contentious sort; she seemed to thrive on conflict. Have you looked at her nephew's grandfather, Andy Walker? Kathy was trying to get custody of Connor, and I'm sure that didn't sit well with him. Kylie's motives are much the same, only stronger for a mother." She wasn't about to tell him about the insurance policy Kathy had taken out for Connor's benefit. She was pretty sure he'd already know anyway. "And the husband is always a possibility, isn't that true?"

She stopped. To tell, or not to tell, that Craig had a lover on the side? On the one hand, it was a contributing factor to thinking Craig might have done it, but on the other hand . . . what kind of a gossiping snitch was she? It didn't feel right, not when she didn't have any concrete reason to think Craig had killed Kathy.

"What are you thinking right now?" he asked.

"I'm just . . ." She shook her head. "Look, this isn't fun, informing on my friends and neighbors. Did you come here for anything specific?"

"I understand Dan Collins had to leave town, and your sister is away, too."

"Yes. And?"

He crouched down beside her and turned her face toward him, his fingers warm on her cheek. He gazed up into her eyes. "I'm being serious, Jaymie. Stop trying to do my job. It's dangerous. If you ask the wrong question of the wrong person, he—or she—could see you as a threat and come after you. I really don't want to see this pretty face in the morgue." He patted her cheek and stood.

"Who has been complaining about me asking questions?" She watched his face after she asked that question. "Let me guess . . . Could it be Craig Cooper?"

"Look, Jaymie, I believe Stanko did it despite what your friend Valetta thinks. It's the simplest answer, and simplest is usually right."

"Occam's razor," she murmured.

He stared at her, eyebrows raised. "Okay, yes. The theory that the simplest explanation is actually correct applies."

She shouldn't have been surprised that he understood her

allusion. "That's not really what Occam's razor means, and I'd bet you know that. So let me use it correctly: Yes, Stanko's fingerprints are on the bowl, and he was heard to threaten Kathy. She's dead. Simplicity suggests that there is a correlation." She thought for a moment. "However, I would say that his motive is weak: anger. But if we accept that he had a problem with impulse control, then surely he would have attacked her then and there, rather than waiting hours?"

Christian nodded and sat down opposite her, elbow on the table, chin in his hand. "Go on, Miss Leighton. I'm fascinated."

He was laughing at her, but she didn't mind. "Yes, Stanko's got a record," she continued, "and some of the charges are for violence. He threatened her. But he's never been a planner. I don't know for sure, but I would bet that all of his offenses in the past have been where he was insulted or criticized, and he struck out then and there. So other explanations may end up being less simple, but more correct."

The detective sat back in his chair and put his ankle on his other knee. "The DA is happy, and the judge agreed with us that he is a flight risk."

"Look, logically, if you're right, and Stanko is guilty, then I'm not getting into any trouble asking questions."

He shook his head. "You don't know that. There are secrets that people will kill to keep, and if you stir up the muck, you might inspire another killer to come out of the woodwork."

She couldn't disagree with anything he said, and she shrugged. "Valetta just doesn't think Stanko is guilty, and she's backing that up with her own money."

"Hey, I'm glad he's got friends, but the best lawyer in the world isn't going to help with his fingerprints on the murder weapon and his footpr—" He stopped and shook his head. "Never mind."

She watched his face, and the scene of the crime came back to her. "His footprints were in the mud near the ladies' washroom, weren't they?" she said. She could see the truth in his eyes and how the noose of justice was closing around Stanko's neck with each bit of circumstantial evidence gathered against him.

"I didn't say that," he said, his brows drawn down over his gray eyes. He bolted to his feet and headed to the back door. "And now I need to get out of here before you figure out our whole case!"

He left, and Hoppy gave a final bark at the back door, sending him on his way. Jaymie was on the phone to Valetta in seconds, updating her on what she had learned and what the detective had *not* said. Valetta was grateful. The lawyer would get all of that information, she said, from what was called "discovery," when the prosecution would have to reveal what evidence they had on Stanko, but it was good to have it earlier.

"I'm just guessing," Jaymie said. "He wouldn't confirm it, but ask Johnny why his footprints would be there, at the scene of the crime."

When she hung up, she felt an urge to call her mother, and Joy Leighton was home, for once. She told her mother all that had happened and about her day and, finally, about Mrs. Hofstadter's farm.

"Oh, honey, I'm so sorry! Look, Alan and I are coming up two weeks early to visit Mom Leighton and Becca in London. I think we'll come to Queensville and stay at the house for a week before the cottage is vacant. Maybe I can get some of the girls together and we can go help Martha out."

It was a stunning offer from her mom, who disliked housewifely chores. In Florida, she hired a local woman to do all the heavy cleaning, and Jaymie's dad did dishes and cooked, now that he was retired. "Would you, Mom? That would be awesome!"

"Honey, don't say *awesome*. You're not eighteen."

"I don't know if you realize how much work it will be, though."

"I think I do. Did I say we'd do it alone? You and Becca and Valetta and Dee will all be there, along with Mimi and me and the other older women. Trust me, I wouldn't tackle it by myself. But Martha won't know that until we all show up."

"Mom, she's going to resist. She's become a bit of a hoarder." She took a deep breath and decided to be completely honest. "Actually, she's a *terrible* hoarder. She didn't even want to give me my casserole dish back."

There was silence for a moment. "Jaymie, maybe you don't remember this, but I've been chair of more committees than you can shake a stick at, and I've wanted to shake a stick at many of them. If I can steamroller twenty fractious women into a smooth-running organization, I can handle Martha Hofstadter. You leave that up to me. We'll be up in two or three weeks. In the meantime, I will rally the girls and make sure Martha has someone dropping in on her every day. Now, how are you and that young man doing? Becca told me all about Daniel Collins, and my advice is, grab him before he marries someone else!"

Jaymie rolled her eyes and sat down, knowing she would not get off the phone until her mother had given her advice on "Husband Hunting: How to Catch and Tame the Bachelor Male." After a half hour, she finally managed to get her mother off the phone and made dinner, just a salad. Her shorts were far too tight, and she needed to fit back into her summer clothes instead of having to buy a whole new wardrobe. She sat in the garden to eat, reading a romance book to try to calm herself after Detective Christian's unsettling visit and her mother's lengthy monologue. The coming meeting between her mother and Daniel, and maybe even Daniel's parents, was going to be simply awful, no matter how much she tried to believe otherwise. Her mother wanted grandkids, and Jaymie was her only shot at it.

Instead, she would think about something less intimidating than her determined mother, like the murder investigation. After dinner she was going to tackle something she just wasn't sure about. She decided to go over and talk to Ella Douglas about Kathy Cooper's July Fourth visit.

But first, the phone messages.

She listened to them; Becca had called, asking how things were going. Dee Stubbs had called to ask about Kathy Cooper's memorial service. Heidi had called and simply asked her to call back, but when Jaymie did, there was no answer. And Daniel had called to say he missed her already. She hadn't really thought about him much, but that might be because of how busy she'd been. Shouldn't she think of him anyway, if he was her boyfriend, as people seemed to figure?

She'd definitely have to put some thought into that. How much should she miss Daniel when he wasn't around?

❧ Sixteen ❧

IT WAS A lovely evening, with a light breeze that tossed the tops of the poplars but was gentle as a caress down at street level. As she walked toward Ella and Bob Douglas's home, Jaymie pondered the day. The tangled threads of the mystery of Kathy Cooper's murder seemed knotted even tighter. Was she being a fool? Was Johnny Stanko the real villain after all?

What Detective Christian had said to her earlier remained in her mind. He warned her not to go asking the wrong questions of the wrong people. But how did one know what was safe and what wasn't with a murderer in their midst? Some innocent remark could be misconstrued, and *wham!*—she was the next victim. She pondered his contention that even if Stanko was guilty, it wasn't good to go asking awkward questions, because you never knew what trouble you were stirring up. But heck, if you went around with that thought in your mind, you'd never talk to anyone about anything!

She threaded her way through town, admiring gardens, enjoying the summer air. She had looked up where the Douglases lived, on a street in the older section of town. When she got to the house, she stopped and examined it. An old frame cottage-style home not far from Johnny Stanko's house, it was modified to take into account Ella's motorized wheelchair. A lift had been added to one end of the porch, which stretched the whole width of the house.

There was no vehicle in the drive, but that only meant that Bob was out, because Jaymie knew Ella didn't drive. It was Ella she wanted to talk to anyway, so she mounted the steps and knocked on the door. After a few minutes, she was about to turn and leave when she heard the deadbolt click, and the door creaked open.

"Yes?" Ella Douglas said, weakly, peering out at her.

"Hi, Ella. It's Jaymie Leighton. How are you this evening?"

"I'm all right."

"Can I come in? I'd like to talk to you."

There was silence for a long minute. "Okay. For a few minutes."

"I won't keep you long," Jaymie said, slipping through the open door. She heard a *beep beep* and saw Ella motoring down the hallway. She followed her to the living room, a cramped space with just enough room for the wheelchair to wend its way to a spot cleared for it. By her wheelchair there was a floor lamp, a low shelf filled with books pushed in haphazardly and a small table with a plate of uneaten toast and jam on it. A book was overturned in the jumbled mess.

"Bob's at a Rotary club meeting," she said. "He usually does the dishes after supper, but he was in a hurry tonight."

"Can I help? Would you like a cup of tea?"

Ella eyed her warily. "Tea would be okay, but please don't

disturb anything in the kitchen; Bob likes things just as they are."

"No problem." She made her way to the kitchen, past a multitude of bookcases stuffed with books on holistic medicine, herbal remedies and the philosophy of medicine.

The kitchen was a bit of a mess—toast crumbs, an open jar of homemade jam, a dirty plate in the sink—but Jaymie had said she wouldn't touch anything. She looked for the kettle, found some tea bags—there were dozens of boxes of different types of herbal teas as well as some orange pekoe—and a teapot. She dropped the teapot lid, but luckily it didn't break.

"What's going on in there?" Ella called. "Did you break something? What are you doing?"

Jaymie came to the living room door and said, keeping her tone cheerful, "Just being clumsy. I dropped the lid of the teapot, but it's fine. No damage."

"Try to be more careful," the woman said, flexing her fingers on the armrests of her wheelchair.

Jaymie didn't reply, opting to go back and finish making the tea, using the orange pekoe bags instead of the more risky herbal teas, because she didn't know how they tasted. She found a tray, and put the teapot, two mugs and the bowl of raw sugar and a pitcher of soy milk on it, and carried it into the living room.

"Where would you like me to put this?" Jaymie said.

Ella blinked and looked around. "I don't know. Wherever you can find room, I guess."

Setting the tray temporarily on the floor, Jaymie moved a stack of books that were on the coffee table to a spot on the floor, and put the tray up on the table.

"You'll put that back, won't you? The books? Before you leave?"

"Yes, of course. How do you like your tea?"

"I don't really like black tea. Wasn't there some chamomile, or mint?"

Jaymie stifled a sigh of exasperation. She reminded herself of how difficult it would be to be confined to a wheelchair. The Eleanor Grimshaw she remembered had been a strapping, energetic girl. She took one of the cups back to the kitchen, made a mug of chamomile and brought it back in, removing the uneaten toast and setting the tea in the pool of yellow light from the floor lamp. She made up her own mug and sat back in one of the overstuffed armchairs.

Eyeing her with suspicion, Ella said, "If you want to know if I know anything about poor Kathy's tragedy, then you've come to the wrong place."

Okay, so no subterfuge, no sneaky way of interrogating Ella. "I just wondered, I guess, if you've had any dealings with her other than that confrontation in the Emporium." Jaymie watched the woman's face, noting sallow cheeks, ashen skin and wary, sunken eyes. A nerve jumped in Ella's temple, but other than that, her expression didn't change. "Someone told me that she intended to drop in on you the morning of the Fourth," Jaymie pressed. "Did she?"

"Who told you that?" Ella said, sharply. Her gaze was dubious, her eyes narrowed.

"A friend," Jaymie said, slowly, wondering why Ella was so suspicious.

"Whose friend? Yours or Kathy's?"

"Kathy's. Why does it matter?"

"What were you doing talking to a friend of Kathy's about me?"

Jaymie sighed. She now remembered more about Eleanor Grimshaw's years at Wolverhampton High. Eleanor—now Ella—didn't have many friends. She seemed to exist on the fringes of school activities and rarely mixed with others. Maybe her current sparkling personality was just an extension of her teenage self and not the result of her illness at all.

"I wasn't specifically talking about you at all. It just came out. Did she drop in here on the morning of the Fourth?"

"Well, yes."

"What did she want?"

"Why are you asking?"

Jaymie let that question lie and just sipped her tea, watching Ella, trying to figure her out. Finally, she asked, "Why did you move to Queensville, Ella? Is your family still here?"

"I don't have a lot of family left. Bob and I just wanted a fresh start. I don't know how much of a fresh start you can have when you're as sick as I am, but . . ." She shrugged. "Queensville is the only place I was ever happy."

"It must be so tough. I'm sorry."

"Bob has been amazing. I don't know what I'd do without him. The sicker I get, the more he loves me!"

"What an odd thing to say!" Jaymie blurted, then reddened. "I'm sorry; I shouldn't have said that."

"No, you shouldn't." Ella shrugged and put her cup down. "Sometimes I think that Bob's too good for me, but he's a nurturer, you know? Someone desperate to help others."

"There are men like that," Jaymie said, reflecting on an acquaintance, a fellow who had married a party girl. They had three kids together, and he looked after every need of the babies they had while she went out barhopping most nights of the week. He seemed content with the arrangement, and the children adored him. Maybe Bob was that kind of guy. "It's good that you found one."

"No point in not telling you, I guess. Kathy did come here the morning of the Fourth," Ella said, picking at the fluffy gray afghan that covered her knees. "She said she was sorry about yelling at me in the Emporium. At least it gave me the chance to say I was sorry too, and make sure little Connor was okay. I told her that my eyesight isn't very good."

"I think she was distracted that morning, and maybe upset. Did you two talk about old times at Wolverhampton High?"

Ella's cheeks took on a faint pink tinge. "No, not really. What's to talk about? The fact that we were both outcasts?" she said, bitterly, then she looked ashamed. "I don't know if she remembered, but I was kind of hard on her in high school. I bullied her a bit. I keep trying to be a better person, but . . ." She shrugged. "We sat and talked, mostly about my health."

"She planned on being a nurse, back when we were kids," Jaymie murmured. This was proving to be a dead end.

"So she said. She wanted to make sure I was getting the right foods and taking the right supplements. I got the feeling she was interested in natural remedies." She chuckled, but it was a mirthless sound. "I told her I've tried everything known to man! And a few things that aren't."

"Was there anything odd about Kathy that morning? Did she mention that something was bothering her?"

Ella shrugged. "Not really. My eyesight is bad, though, so I don't notice a lot about expressions and such. Some days I just can't even stand light in my eyes, it's so bad."

"I'm so sorry," Jaymie murmured.

"Could you get me a glass of water? I'm so thirsty. It's dry in here."

Jaymie retrieved a glass of cold water for her, and the woman drank it down. Jaymie watched, then asked, "What did Kathy do while she was here? Did she stay long?"

"Not really. We talked for a while. Kathy made some tea,

got the mail for me, went to the washroom. Bob came home, and Kathy said she had to go, that she and some friends were getting together in the park. I said I wished I could go, and Bob said maybe we would. That's why we went for a walk there."

"And then you came home?"

"Why are you asking questions like that? Where else would I go?"

"I'm just trying to figure out what happened to Kathy, if anyone saw anything."

"Well, we sure wouldn't have!" Ella snapped. "We came home and stayed home for the rest of the day."

It seemed that there was nothing here. Ella certainly had no reason to wish Kathy harm, nor did her husband. "I'll leave you be, then," Jaymie said.

"Make sure you leave everything the way it should be," Ella fretted. "Except, can you take that toast and throw it out? I'm just not hungry tonight."

"I will." She took the plate and their mugs to the kitchen, tidied everything back to how it was and rinsed out the teapot, then took her leave, feeling deeply sorry for someone whose health was so compromised. Ella was peevish and demanding, but who wouldn't be in that situation?

As she left, Jaymie took a look at the wheelchair lift attached to the vine-covered porch. It was certainly likely, looking at the thing, that Ella could work it herself. It was intended for the wheelchair-bound person to use alone, in fact. It was barely possible, then, that Ella could have left the house without Bob knowing, and gone to the park to confront Kathy. But why? The theory didn't make much sense.

The phone was ringing as she got home, and it was Wendi, her university friend in Port Huron, the one she had called about Matt Laskan.

"Girl, you caught yourself a humdinger," she said.

"What do you mean?" Jaymie said, walking to the back door and sitting down on the step to watch Hoppy take his last piddle of the evening, then scratch grass over the spot.

"This Matt Laskan fellow? He was arrested on charges of assault and, get this, attempted kidnapping in January. Charges were dropped, but still! That is serious stuff."

"Assault? Attempted kidnapping? Matt Laskan?" Jaymie sat, mouth open, thinking of the buoyant yet calm fellow she had only met a few times. "Was he drunk?"

"No record of any blood alcohol level."

"Who was the victim?"

"I wondered if you'd ask that. Thirty-nine-year-old female by the name of Janet Broadhouse."

"I wonder why she dropped the charges."

"Maybe the girl's got more important things to worry about."

"Like what? What do you mean?"

"Oh, maybe like the drug and prostitution charges she's facing in court next month?"

JAYMIE HAD A difficult time getting to sleep and kept waking up. It was a restless night. She was trying to reconcile the calm accountant that Matt Laskan seemed to be, with someone who would get himself into such a spot that he would be arrested on assault and attempted kidnapping charges with a druggie prostitute.

The next morning, as she drank her first cup of coffee and got ready to go over to the bed-and-breakfast, she still pondered it all. He was *really* lucky the charges were dropped, because attempted kidnapping could be hard time. Was this what Kathy had over his head? And would he kill to keep secret that he associated with a prostitute? His girlfriend would surely not be too happy about that, Jaymie imagined, on *any* level. The possible health consequences and the damage to their relationship aside, if she was thinking of a senate run, Matt's legal problems could kill that for her. But how would Kathy have found out about the arrest?

Valetta called just as she was on her way out. "I'm off again today. Have you figured anything out, Jaymie?"

"We should talk. I'm trying to work things out, but I *have* found some interesting information, and I want to see what you think. I'm taking a run to the thrift store in Wolverhampton when I get done at the B&B. I desperately need more vintage melamine and wicker baskets for the rental business, if I can find any. Can we get together after that?"

"Why don't you pick me up and we'll go to town together, if you don't mind."

"Works for me." Jaymie got done quickly at Anna's and took Becca's car to pick up Valetta. It was going to be hot, and her van didn't have air-conditioning, unless you counted an open window. She didn't mind, but she didn't want to subject Valetta to the heat.

"So what's new?" her friend said, slamming the door shut. "Sounded on the phone like you found out something juicy."

Jaymie retraced her steps from the day before, ending with the shocking call she'd gotten from her friend in Port Huron.

"Kidnapping? Assault? How did Matt hide that?"

"The charges have been dropped," Jaymie said.

"Dropped. Hmm."

"Wendi speculated that the woman has so much on her plate—other legal problems of her own—that she doesn't want to go to court to follow up on the charges."

"Or the charges are baloney, and she doesn't want to get caught lying."

"Possible. Matt Laskan does not seem the type to get physical. But then he doesn't seem the type to use prostitutes, either."

"You can never tell," Valetta said, her mouth setting in a grim line.

They parked on the main street in Wolverhampton and went into Dollar Dan's Thrift Store and More. As usual, Valetta tried to get Jaymie to buy every kitchen utensil or bowl that looked to be more than ten years old, and Jaymie resisted. She did her best to keep her mind off the vintage bowl used to kill Kathy, but the murder was like a dark blotch in her brain, a spot that she couldn't ignore, one that filled her with horror.

Instead, she haunted the kitchenware aisle, gathering some vintage melamine, and even found a couple of nice willow baskets that she could transform into picnic baskets with vintage gingham linens and the right accompaniments. Acrylic wineglasses and a couple of straw wine-bottle holders attracted her attention, and she snatched them up to use in the Lover's Lane basket. In no time, her cart was full, and she took a deep breath. Retail therapy for her was a trip to a junk or antique store.

She moved on to the furniture, examining a nice wood bookcase. Jaymie's romance novel collection was almost as large as her cookbook collection and needed its own home. As Valetta approached with a full cart herself, she said to her friend, "I think I need this for my collection of Mary Baloghs and Jo Beverleys."

"Then you should get it."

Jaymie stole a look at Valetta, and said, "Not to beat a

dead horse, but you're really sure Johnny Stanko didn't kill Kathy, aren't you?"

"I believe him," she said promptly. "Whenever he's done stuff in the past, he's always admitted it. He's adamant he didn't do this."

"So where was he? What was he doing?"

"He says he was just sitting alone watching the fireworks."

Jaymie nodded. It wasn't an alibi, but it was an explanation. "I think I will take this bookcase. Can you help me haul it out to the car?"

"Becca's going to have your guts for garters when she finds out you've been carrying stuff home from the thrift store in her Lexus."

"What she doesn't know won't hurt her." She chuckled, shaking her head. "Where do you get those phrases, Valetta? Guts for garters?"

"I read," she replied, her tone dry. "Kinda like you, kiddo. Okay, let's get out of here. I've got so much stuff here, we'll be lucky if we fit it all in Becca's car."

"I should have brought the van. It doesn't have air-conditioning, though, and it's going to be blazing today. You want to get lunch?"

"I'll buy," Valetta said, and suggested a new tearoom she had been dying to go to. "Violet wants to go on her birthday, but I want to be sure she'll enjoy it. You know what *tearoom* means to most. Pathetic pallid tea and dry cake." Valetta's sister-in-law, wife to her and Brock's late brother, was English. She had stayed in North America even after her husband died, relocating across the river to Canada to be closer to some of her own family, who had moved to Sarnia, Ontario, in the eighties.

They made their purchases and exited to the car. By the time they managed to stuff everything into the car, including the bookcase into the trunk, they were dripping with sweat. They walked down the block to the tearoom, Wellington's Retreat. It was faux snug, with a fireplace that was thankfully not on, pretty shelves lined with teapots and teacups, and smallish tables. A chalkboard menu at the cashier's desk stated that the lunch special was cold cucumber soup and watercress sandwiches.

"I think I'll go with the special," Jaymie said doubtfully, as they approached the cash desk to order.

The cashier, a polite older woman, wrote that down, then looked to Valetta.

"Me, too," she said. "The special. And one of the coconut jam tarts for dessert."

"And tea," Jaymie added. "Black, nothing fancy."

"Tea?" Valetta said, raising her eyebrows and mopping at the perspiration on her brow with a tissue.

"Tea!" Jaymie said firmly. "Even on a hot day I like tea. You can't bring Violet here if you haven't tried the tea."

"I'll take your word for it and have an iced tea, instead."

They took a seat at a table near the window, and the air-conditioning gradually cooled them down. Talking desultorily about the murder, trying to come to some conclusions, they took each person in turn and laid out the case against them. Jaymie took a notebook out of her handbag and began to jot down what they were saying. "You know," she said, glancing up at her friend, "it is entirely possible that it was a complete stranger who killed her."

"How would a stranger get your bowl, though?"

Jaymie pondered that. "I don't know. Chance? Was it just sitting somewhere? I'll have to think about it. Let's stick with who we've got, so far. Kylie Hofstadter. Motive: to stop the custody suit her sister was bringing against her, and maybe to get the insurance payout."

"Insurance payout?"

"Oh right! I haven't told you." She related to Valetta what she had learned from Mrs. Hofstadter about the large insurance policy Kathy had purchased to benefit her nephew. "I'm not sure, but it is probably in Kylie's name. Anyway, means: Kylie was close enough to pick up the bowl at some point. Opportunity: her alibi is Andy Walker, I guess, and she is his, but I've never yet established where they were at the time of the murder. And how did they lose sight of Connor?" She jotted that down. "That seems odd to me."

"Now, Johnny Stanko," Valetta said.

"But you don't think he did it."

"That doesn't matter. Write it down."

Jaymie obeyed, and unfortunately he had no alibi and all the motive, means and opportunity in the world. "Now, Craig. I have no clue where he was; he said he was working, but he wasn't at the office. Matt Laskan looked at him oddly when he flubbed about that. He doesn't appear to have means or opportunity, if he's telling the truth about where he was, but he could be lying and I wouldn't know." She thought about it. "I really do think he was lying, but why? I have to establish his alibi. I'm sure the police know where he was—or at least where he says he was—but Detective Christian is not going to tell me." She filled Valetta in on his visit to her and his warning to her to stop asking questions.

"It's just like a romance mystery novel," Valetta said, her eyes wide behind her thick lenses. "You know, the kind where the plucky girl detective keeps getting into trouble and the handsome cop warns her to stay out of it."

"Except I'm not getting into trouble. Now, Matt Laskan.

Given what I found out about his run-in with the cops, he's looking better as a suspect. No alibi that we know of, so his means and opportunity are the same as Craig. But motive? Well, pretty good, actually, now. If anyone finds out about him being arrested on kidnapping charges, who is going to go to him to do their books? And his girlfriend . . . if she wants to run for senate, Matt's problems would not look good at all, so if Kathy threatened to talk . . ." Jaymie thought about it. It was sounding better and better all the time.

"But you're assuming that the charges in Port Huron, and him being involved with a prostitute, is what Kathy was holding over him," Valetta said.

"You're right. I guess it could be something completely different."

Just then the tearoom door opened, and a pretty blonde dressed in a skirt suit walked in. The waitress, who was bringing Jaymie and Valetta's order, greeted her. "Hey, Lily. The usual?"

"Sure. I'll take a booth."

Jaymie sat, stunned. Lily? Could this be Matt Laskan's girlfriend? It sure looked like the person in the photo on his desk. While Jaymie accepted her lunch plate, she watched the young woman, and then, when the waitress had gone over to her, she whispered her thoughts to Valetta. Between them they decided it must be her.

A car pulled up to one of the metered parking spaces just outside of the tea shop, and a man got out and fed the meter. When he turned, Jaymie smiled. "Hey, there's Craig," she said. She waved out the window, but when he saw her, he stood stock-still for a moment, then whirled on his heel and headed across the street. "I wonder why he did that?" she said.

They ate lunch and puzzled it out. Jaymie decided that after her run-in with Craig the day before, he didn't want to see her. Lily kept looking toward the door, expecting a lunch date, perhaps. It appeared she was being stood up, Jaymie thought, as she finished her tea and last bite of sandwich. Was she waiting for Matt to come in?

The young woman's phone rang, and she looked at it, clicked the button and picked it up. She spoke for a moment, then whipped her head around, meeting Jaymie's gaze head-on. For a moment, Jaymie was embarrassed to be caught examining her, but then she realized that the other woman was even more mortified than she was. Lily whispered something into the phone, closed it and stuck it in her handbag. She threw a five on the table, got up and hustled out of the tea shop without another word, not meeting Jaymie's gaze again.

It came together in that moment who her lunch date was to have been. Lily, Matt Laskan's girlfriend, had been about to meet Craig Cooper for lunch. Lily was beautiful, tall, willowy and blonde. Lily, Matt's lovely girlfriend, was Craig Cooper's mystery mistress.

❧ Seventeen ❧

SHE SHARED HER theory with Valetta, then Jaymie hustled up to the cash desk to pay, even though Valetta had told her lunch was on her. "I thought I recognized that woman who just left," she said to the cashier/waitress, as she handed her a twenty. "Was that Lily . . . oh, what is her last name? Lily something or other."

"Lily Fogarty? Yes!" the woman said, making change.

"Town councilwoman, right? Isn't she usually here with a fellow? Kind of medium height, medium hair, gray eyes, wears glasses. A button-down kind of guy?"

The middle-aged woman cooled perceptibly. "I've never seen you here before. What's your interest in Lily and her boyfriend?"

It was an acknowledgment of sorts. So Craig *was* sneaking around with Councilwoman Lily, his partner's girlfriend! "I . . . uh, I just know him, that's all."

"Then you don't need *me* to tell you if she's been here with him or not."

"My friend didn't mean any harm," Valetta said, sticking a generous tip in the tip jar. "She's just naturally inquisitive. Craig's a neighbor of ours in Queensville."

The woman relaxed. "Craig . . . yeah, that's her new guy. I'm hoping it turns out well for her. She's such a great gal; she could go all the way to becoming president if she put her mind to it!"

On the sidewalk outside, Jaymie said to Valetta, "Thanks for bailing me out in there; I got a little overexuberant. And nice move, getting her to acknowledge Craig's name! So now we know for sure. But really . . . President Fogarty? Not if folks find out about her rotten taste in men. First someone who almost went to jail for assault and kidnapping, and then a married man!"

"Do you think one has to do with the other?"

"What do you mean?"

"Do you think Lily found out about Matt's trouble in Port Huron and turned to Craig?"

Jaymie thought for a moment. "Interesting theory, but it still doesn't seem to have anything to do with Kathy's death, unless . . . unless Craig's relationship with Lily was his motive for killing his wife. He wouldn't be the first guy to think of murder as a way to avoid splitting up the marital assets." She shivered. "I can't believe we're talking about neighbors, fellow Queensvillians, as potential murder suspects."

"We're trying to do them a favor, trying to eliminate them!" Valetta looked up and down the street. "I'll bet those two arranged to meet somewhere else."

"Maybe, but it's a big town. They could be anywhere." Jaymie thought about it for a long minute. "I wonder if their relationship explains why Craig is being so shady about where he was at the time of the murder, and why Matt's girlfriend canceled on him when she was supposed to have a picnic dinner with him?"

"You think Craig and Lily were together on the Fourth?"

"It's possible."

"Well, let's find out," Valetta said. She whipped out her cell phone and did a search, found Laskan Cooper's website and Craig's cell number. "What should we say to him? Should we ask him about Lily?"

"No, not by text. I want to see his face. Ask him to meet us at . . ." Jaymie looked around. "At the donut shop," she said, pointing down the street at the Tastee D's coffee and donut shop.

"Craig, we know you're in W; meet us @ Tastee D's," Valetta typed, then hit send. "Let's go to the donut shop and see if he shows up."

They waited and waited, and finally Craig, a sullen expression on his face, walked in, saw them and slowly walked over to their table.

"Pull up a chair, Craig," Jaymie said.

"Why are you following me?" he said, towering over them, glaring down at Jaymie. "I told the cops to make you leave me alone."

So that explained Detective Christian's visit the day before. Jaymie picked her words carefully. "Craig, I am not following you. Valetta and I came to Wolverhampton to shop. We have a carload of bags and a four-foot bookcase, if you want to see it all."

Valetta added, "You don't have a *reason* to be paranoid, do you?"

Jaymie watched his face as his gaze flicked from one of them to the other and back. He was trying to figure out how much they knew. "Why'd you walk away when I waved to you from the tea shop?" she asked.

"I . . . I didn't see you there. I just thought of something I'd forgotten to do."

"I'm not buying it, Craig. What were you really doing July Fourth when you told Kathy you were going to work?"

He leaned toward her, his breath sour, his pupils pinpoints in the cold gray irises. He poked a finger in Jaymie's face and said, "You stop trying to pin Kathy's murder on me, or I'll . . ." He stopped and shook his head.

"Or you'll what?" Jaymie asked, her heart pounding, curious about what he'd come up with as a threat.

But he said nothing, and whirled, stomping out of the donut shop as everyone in there watched.

"I've never seen him that angry," Valetta said, her eyes wide behind her glasses. "Why? All you did was ask why he walked away from the tea shop." She paused and thought, then said, "And what he was *really* doing on July Fourth. Guilty conscience, maybe?"

"I never even got to ask him about his relationship with Lily Fogarty."

"I think we know enough about that, don't you?" Valetta said.

"Not really. We don't *know* anything, we've only guessed."

"What do you mean? It was so clear he was in Wolverhampton to meet her."

"But *why* was he meeting her?" Jaymie asked, tightening her ponytail with a yank. This was irritating, having just to guess about things. "For all we know he's . . . I don't know, blackmailing her, or giving her a message from Matt, or saying good-bye forever, or that he never really cared for her anyway. We don't *know* anything."

"True. Darn you! Why do you have to ruin a perfectly good theory with common sense?"

"I guess we may as well go home."

Jaymie dropped Valetta and her bags from the thrift store off at her cottage, then trundled home, got her own bags inside and wrestled her bookcase upstairs to her bedroom with encouragement from Hoppy, who yapped at her the whole way. It was such a girly room, she thought, looking around as she huffed and puffed, catching her breath. It had been her room since she was little, and she loved it, from the butter yellow walls to the iron bed with the handmade quilt.

But she didn't know another woman her age who was still living in her childhood home. Becca had once said in exasperation that Jaymie was living in a bubble, protected from real life by the safety of their childhood home. She didn't agree, but in fairness, Becca did have a point. Could she picture marrying and living with her husband, leaving this house? Or was she like Jane Austen's Emma, only with an old house in place of an old father? Would her husband have to agree to put aside his own preferences to live with her in her geriatric home?

She'd never find a Knightley, she feared.

The thought of books spurred her on to find a home for the new bookcase. She first needed to thoroughly clean it, though. The rest of her afternoon was spent in that soothing occupation, and by the time she went to bed that night, her collection of Mary Balogh, Mary Jo Putney and Jo Beverley historical romance novels snuggled alongside her Brontë and Austen collections.

THE NEXT MORNING was Shady Rest time, of course. She cooked eggs, sausage and bacon to order for Anna's guests, then sat down for a coffee and muffin with her friend, a ritual that had become their version of "girl time," while Tabitha had her own "tea time" at her little table in the corner of the kitchen. This morning she had noticed that Anna's eyes gleamed with excitement at something, and she whispered once that she had news for Jaymie that she couldn't wait to tell her. As Jaymie made them both coffee, Anna finally closed the door on her guests, allowing them to eat in peace.

"So what's got you all worked up?" Jaymie asked. It must be something about the baby-to-be, or something about Clive's job, Jaymie thought. Maybe he was up for a promotion that would help with their two-home lifestyle.

Anna grabbed a newspaper that was folded off to the side of the round kitchen table. "This is the woman, the one I told you about, who I saw kissing Craig Cooper in his office," she said, tapping the front-page photo of the *Wolverhampton Howler.*

Jaymie grabbed the paper and stared down at a photo of Lily Fogarty at a public event. The caption explained that she was shaking hands with a well-wisher at the Fourth of July evening parade in Wolverhampton. But it was a face in the crowd near her, watching her with burning intensity, that caught Jaymie's attention: Craig Cooper. If this was an evening parade and went on to an event in the town square, as it stated, and if Craig Cooper was with Lily there, as it seemed, then he could not have been in Queensville in time to kill Kathy behind the washroom.

"Well, this confirms it!"

"So at least I did you some good?"

"You sure did." She told Anna about her trip into Wolverhampton the day before and her sighting of Lily Fogarty and Craig Cooper. She also explained how the photo cleared

Kathy's husband, pointing to him in the crowd, all the while wondering why Craig hadn't just told her and Valetta that he had been with Lily that evening. Of course, why should he? He had probably told the police, and that's all he needed to do.

"So he was—*is*, I guess—serious about Lily Fogarty," Jaymie mused. "Wonder how that's going to affect his and Matt's partnership? What a mess. I suppose that's one reason why Craig called off the hunt for commercial property in Toledo. He knew he was going to leave his wife." It made her sad to think of it. Kathy would have had a lot to go through if she had lived, but she would have made it, because she was stronger than she seemed. "Poor Kathy."

When Jaymie got home, she checked her e-mail. There was a message from Heidi to call her, but just as she was reaching for the phone, it rang.

"Jaymie?" Valetta said. "I found something out, but I don't know what it means. Johnny told his lawyer he gave the bowl to Uncle Sam."

"What? Why would he say that?"

"I don't know!"

"But he originally said that he brought the bowl back to our table." To Jaymie it sounded an awful lot like scrambling to try to disassociate himself with the bowl. There were probably ten men—and a couple of women and a dog or two—in the park dressed up like Uncle Sam. It was a clever excuse, or it could be the truth, she supposed. Was he smart enough to make that up?

"I just don't know what he means. I told the lawyer about all the people dressed up as Uncle Sam in the park that day. I wanted to ask specific questions, get a better description, but the lawyer doesn't want me talking to Johnny. Says it will taint his recollection if I ask him questions. He told me he'll tell the cops, and they can ask Johnny about it, with him there, of course."

"I guess he knows what's best." Jaymie thought there was probably another very good reason his lawyer didn't want Johnny talking to Valetta. He was likely afraid his client was guilty and didn't want him confessing to the one woman in the world who would still, despite her friendship with the guy, feel compelled to tell the truth to the police, for better or worse. If Johnny was guilty, Valetta would not try to keep him out of jail. "One thing we can try to do is find out who all was dressed up as Uncle Sam."

"I know a few right away, but there were bound to be some I didn't know about."

"Maybe you can find out more. I'll try, too."

"Oh, and another thing," Valetta said. "That other insurance policy that Kathy had? The money goes directly to Kylie for her to use. It's not in trust for Connor. She gets the full million."

"Wow. Really?" Jaymie needed to see Kylie again. She was so confused.

She told Valetta what she had found out about Craig's Fourth of July photo in the paper and what it implied, and Valetta seemed relieved.

"I'm glad. I didn't want to think Craig had killed Kathy, but with him being so evasive . . . you never know with couples, especially when there's cheating involved."

"I know you don't want to think it's Johnny Stanko, but I don't think we're any closer to knowing who else it could be, do you?"

"Let me sniff around."

"I really would like to talk to Kylie again. Where does she live?"

"She moved into Andy Walker's house last year. Kathy

threatened to call child protective services, I heard, if Connor and she kept living in the farmhouse. She told Kylie it wasn't a fit situation for a child. I don't think she foresaw Kylie and Andy Walker becoming friends, though, because they'd had such a falling-out after Drew's death. Kylie moved in to room at Andy's house and, as far as I know, she's still there."

"As sad as it sounds, I have to go with Kathy on this; you haven't seen it, but that farmhouse was not a healthy or safe environment for Connor. As a matter of fact, it's not healthy for Mrs. H., either. My mom is going to get together with some ladies—and us younger women too—to help the poor woman clean her place up."

"You can count on me, but it may be a bit of a struggle. If Mrs. H. is a hoarder, like you say, she won't give up her junk without a fight." Valetta watched a lot of reality shows, among them *The Hoarder Chronicles*, kind of a cross between the shows about antique hunters and troubled hoarders. "Mrs. H. is a senior citizen. Let me see if there are any agencies that could help her with emotional support."

"Thanks so much, Valetta," Jaymie said. "Mom said that she'd get some of the ladies she knows to check in on Mrs. H., too. I feel so bad for the woman, knowing that Kathy was really her only connection to the world most of the time. Kylie can't possibly fill in."

"Then it's up to the rest of us," Valetta said. "Kylie's got work and Connor, so her time is taken up, for sure."

"Where does she work?"

"She works evenings at the Wolf Whistle restaurant. That's why living with Andy works so well, I guess. He's a mechanic at the marina down by the docks, strictly a day job, so he can babysit Connor at night while Kylie waitresses."

"The Wolf Whistle? Kind of like Hooters without the class, isn't it?"

"I know, I know," Valetta said. "Gross to work someplace where your main attribute is a good-size bra, but Kylie needs the tips to survive. Brock says she does a good job."

"Brock?"

"He goes there for the spicy chicken wings, he *says*."

"Sounds like you don't believe him," Jaymie said with a chuckle.

"I don't, but he's my brother. I don't think I *want* to know any more. Anyway, he says Kylie is a good waitress, and not as flirtatious as some of the others. Maybe because of having a kid, or maybe she's just not that flirtatious by nature. It was so hard on her when Drew died; she really loved that guy."

From there they went on to talk about Jaymie's bookcase, and finally signed off, as Valetta had a customer walk in. Jaymie immediately called Heidi and caught her at home, for once.

"I'm so glad you called!" Heidi said.

"What's up?"

"Can I come over?"

"Sure. Is Joel home?"

"He was, but he's off again," Heidi said. "Some kind of sales conference at headquarters in Atlanta. He actually wanted to know if I wanted to go. To Atlanta? In the *summer*? No way! I'm getting heatstroke just thinking about it."

Jaymie laughed. "Come here for dinner, then," she said. "Give me a couple of hours, then come on over."

Heidi walked over, arriving at about six, and Jaymie already had dinner made. It was informal, just salads and hot dogs, so they ate out in the garden, sitting in the vintage Adirondack chairs Jaymie kept carefully repaired. Heidi seemed to have something to say, but she waited until after dinner, when she'd opened the bottle of wine she had brought and popped in the fridge. "How are you and Daniel getting along?" she asked, pouring a couple of glasses.

"All right. He had to go to put out some fire at headquarters in Phoenix. He's called a couple of times, and we've talked, but it sounds like he hasn't figured it all out yet."

"What about that sexy detective fellow?" Heidi asked, waggling her eyebrows.

"What about him?"

"Have you thought any more about what Bernie said? That he likes you?"

"I think she was mistaken, or it's just a stupid rumor," Jaymie replied. "He's not interested in me. In my limited experience, if a guy likes you, he'll make sure you know it." She did briefly think about him, his palm gentle against her cheek, concern warming his gray eyes. Then she shook her head.

"Unless the guy is gun-shy," Heidi said. "Bernie said that the rumor is, the detective got fired from his last job for getting involved with a witness, and now he's super wary. She says that he's trying to get back onto a big-city police force, and until then, he isn't putting down any roots."

"All the more reason not to get too excited about some vague rumor that he likes me." Heidi opened her mouth, but Jaymie put up one hand. "No, Heidi, that's enough. I've got my hands full with Daniel, and I don't even know how serious I want to get with him."

"Because of Joel?" she asked, her voice soft and her blue eyes wide.

Jaymie thought about it for a moment. "I guess at first that was true, but now . . . I'm just beginning to figure myself out. I don't think I've ever stopped to do that before. I coasted. But now I'm getting to a point where I know that I want something out of life, something more than a boyfriend or even a husband. But I'm still not completely sure what." She shrugged irritably. "I just don't know. Can we change the subject?"

"Sure. I've got another one lined up," Heidi said with a chuckle. She took a long drink of her wine and set it down. "I talked to Joel while he was home. I wondered why he was so evasive about Craig and Kathy and Matt and Lily. I mean, we all did have dinner together. We hung out a little. Why didn't he say that to you when you asked?"

"And . . . ?"

"He says he knows too much, but he doesn't feel comfortable spilling the beans."

"What does he know?"

"He knows what Matt Laskan's big secret is."

❧ Eighteen ❧

"WHAT IS IT?" Jaymie asked. She knew already, but she wondered what Joel knew and how.

"That's just it, he won't tell me. He says it has nothing to do with anything."

Darn. No new info, then, unless . . . "Heidi, do you call or text Joel while he's away?"

"Sure, all the time."

"Can you text him now?"

Heidi whipped out her cell phone and was ready, the dipping sun glinting off the screen. "What shall I say?"

Jaymie thought about it for a moment. "Ask him if he knows about ML's legal trouble in PH."

Heidi tapped away and hit send. "What does that mean? I get that ML is Matt Laskan, but what is PH?"

"Tell you in a minute." They talked for a while longer with a few pleasant silences as the air cooled to comfortable and the animals came out of the shade to roll around at their feet. Heidi's phone rang, a funky little popular tune. She picked it up, looked at the display and answered.

"Hey, baby, what's up? What do you mean, how did I find out about Matt? That was a message from Jaymie. How does *she* know? I don't have a single clue. Do you want to talk to her? Sure, she's right here. *Why* is she right here? I'm at her place; she invited me over for dinner. Okay, wait a minute." Heidi covered the phone with one hand and made a face. "Joel's kind of angry. He wants to talk to you."

She took the phone. "Hi, Joel."

"How'd you find out about Matt's trouble in Port Huron?" he said.

"Nice to talk to you, too! We're just sitting here outside with some wine. How's it going in Hotlanta?"

"Very funny. I'm serious, Jaymie. Leave the poor guy alone!"

Jaymie sighed. "I'm kind of tired of being warned to leave things alone. First Craig and now you, on Matt's behalf."

"What do you mean, 'first Craig'?" he said.

"Nothing." She was not about to blow Craig and Lily's little secret; that was up to them. "Look, I just found out that Matt had some legal trouble in Port Huron. I know what the charges were going to be. Until they were dropped."

"I mean it, Jaymie; you should really keep your nose out of other people's business. It's not what it sounds like."

She thought about it for a moment. "If it's not what it sounds like, why don't you tell me what it *is*, then?"

There was silence on the other end. "Let me think about it," he said. "I'll be home tomorrow or the day after tomorrow, and I'll decide before then what I should tell you."

"Fine," she said tightly. "You decide. I'm handing you back to Heidi." She thrust the phone back to Heidi and took their wineglasses back to the kitchen to refill. It wasn't fair, she supposed, to be angry, because Joel was clearly torn between telling her and keeping a secret for a friend. But it was frustrating to be so close to an answer and yet not to get it. He said it wasn't what it sounded like. What else could attempted kidnapping be but what it sounded like?

When she came back out, Heidi was staring down at the phone in her hand with a perplexed frown. "You really got him mad!" she said. "Joel told me to get away from you, that you're a bad influence."

"Really? Me, a bad influence?"

"Yeah."

"Cool. Are you going?"

"No way!" Heidi said, accepting the refilled wineglass from Jaymie. She grinned, her eyes glittering. "This is too much fun, getting him riled."

"Good for you!" So there was some spirit in pretty little Heidi after all. "Okay, now about Lily Fogarty . . . What do you know about her? Do you like her?"

"Not really. She's too . . . oh, she's too darn smart!"

"And that's a bad thing?"

"It is when she makes me feel like a dumb bunny."

Jaymie watched her expression, halfway between a pout and a grimace. Denver hopped up onto her lap and settled. "I can't imagine you feeling threatened," Jaymie said, petting her cat and watching Heidi's face. "But are you?"

She shrugged. "Joel really admires her. They sit and talk about politics, and I don't know anything about politics."

"Neither does Joel," Jaymie said, sitting back, the magic of a purring cat on her lap calming her down. "He just talks a good line. Half of what he says is crap."

"Really?"

"Sure, and I'll bet Lily knows it. Joel doesn't care about

any of it; he just pretends if it's something he thinks he *should* care about. In reality, he's as shallow as any of us."

"But you're not shallow, Jaymie," Heidi said, reaching across and putting her hand on Jaymie's wrist. "You're smart. Maybe that's why Joel left you for me. You don't think Joel likes Lily in that way?"

Jaymie needed to pick her words carefully so she didn't hurt Heidi's feelings. In truth, Joel always wanted to feel intellectually superior to his girlfriend. Heidi was right; Jaymie's intelligence and willingness to challenge him were why Joel had left her, at least in part. She had begun to catch on to the fact that he pretended to know a lot more than he really did. Heidi hadn't—so far anyway—caught on to that. Of course, now that Jaymie had outed him as a fraud, it might only be a matter of time. Heidi was smarter than she realized. "You suit him. Lily doesn't."

Heidi seemed content with that. Their conversation wandered off to other topics. The Heritage Society had been given an extremely valuable item, a genuine letter belonging to Button Gwinnett (he was a "first signer," one of those founding fathers who'd signed the Declaration of Independence), and it was due to be auctioned off at Christie's in New York in September. Talk had moved to what could be done with the possible one million dollars it would bring. "Mrs. Bellwood thinks the Heritage Society should buy Dumpe Manor," Jaymie said about a Queen Anne manor house on the edge of town.

"Dumpe Manor?" Heidi chirped. "You're kidding me, right? Dump, as in, 'take a'?"

Jaymie giggled and wondered if the wine was getting to her. "Dumpe with an *e* on the end. Can you imagine? We get a million dollars and buy the Dumpe?"

"But then you could open up the Dumpe to the public," Heidi said, choking on laughter.

"How do you furnish a Dumpe?" Jaymie laughed so hard that Denver jumped off her lap and glared up at her. "Would you come to the grand opening of a Dumpe?"

Heidi was laughing so hard, she spilled her wine down her chambray blouse. "The slogan . . . it could be, Come to the Dumpe and Find History!"

"Genius! We could have a world-famous Dumpe!" Jaymie exclaimed. "And Tea with the Queen could be moved to the Dumpe!"

Heidi held her stomach and roared, her hysterical laughter echoing in the growing darkness. "All dressed up to go to the Dumpe!"

"Hey, rumor has it there's a ghost of the last family member to own it!" Jaymie said. "We'd have the world's first haunted Dumpe!"

That was it for them; both laughed until tears streamed down their faces. When they parted a half hour later, Heidi was still giggling. She phoned to tell Jaymie she'd gotten home all right, and Jaymie changed into a nightgown and headed to bed a while later to relax with a book and try to keep the good feeling she had going.

She woke up the next morning with a headache; not exactly a hangover, but close. A mild feeling of depression settled over her as she wondered if they would ever know for sure who killed Kathy Cooper. She did her job at Anna's, then learned she wouldn't need to come over for a while because Clive was taking a few vacation days and coming to Queensville to give his wife a hand in the breakfast department. It would be good to have a break from that responsibility. Her pseudo-investigation into Kathy's murder was weighing her down. Kathy's memorial service was going to take place Friday afternoon, she'd learned, and it was one more hurdle to get past, one emotional trial she was not looking forward to. How would she manage, after harassing Craig and suspecting Matt? She called Becca and left her the message that the memorial service was set to be held at the Methodist church. She, Becca, Valetta and Dee would go together.

Her mind teemed with questions, most of them with no easy answers. They ranged from the unanswerable—Why had she put off making it up with Kathy?—to the impossible— Why did such rotten things happen in life?

She had to concentrate on questions to which there may be answers. She sat in her office, trying to work on her recipes, but that seemed as confusing as anything at the moment. Did she have a clear grasp on what she was doing? Was she rewriting vintage recipes or merely decoding them for the modern cook? It was a fine line she was walking. And what if no one wanted yet another cookbook? She shut down her computer, grabbed a notebook and went outside to sit in the shade of the backyard to try to clear her mind of the turmoil that was troubling her.

She wrote down a series of questions having to do with her suspects and others with whom Kathy had contact.

One: Why had Matt Laskan not been formally charged on the serious counts of attempted kidnapping and assault? If Kathy threatened him with revealing all about the charges, would Matt have snapped? Did anyone have evidence of where Matt actually was during the evening fireworks in Boardwalk Park?

Two: Why did Kathy go to Ella and Bob's the morning of July Fourth? Did she really apologize to Ella? Was that the only reason she went?

Three: Why did Andy and Kylie lose track of where Connor was during the fireworks? Were they together during that time, or was one of them busy elsewhere?

Four: Did anyone see Stanko give the bowl to an Uncle Sam impersonator? What did the Uncle Sam do with the bowl if that was the case? Could the impersonator have been one of the other suspects in Kathy's death?

Craig seemed to be off the hook as far as Kathy's murder was concerned, as were other peripheral folks Jaymie had never really suspected anyway: Lily Fogarty and Chloe Cooper, who both had unshakable alibis. But she would take the other questions one by one and try to figure them out.

She looked up Matt Laskan's number in the phone book, but when she called, the receptionist at Laskan Cooper said he was out. The girl mumbled something about him being over at Heartbreak Island seeing a client, and when Jaymie asked when he'd be back, she said about noon. That meant he must be coming back on one of the half-hour ferry jaunts before lunchtime.

"Come on, Hoppy. We're going for a walk," she said. It was early yet. The day was sparkling with sunshine and there was no sign of the humidity that would build by afternoon. Hoppy greeted the opportunity to check his pee-mail with boundless enthusiasm, but his social networking made the walk a longer one than strictly necessary. Jaymie hoped she hadn't missed Matt's ferry return to Queensville.

She descended the long, sloping pathway to the marina north of the ferry dock and sat down on one of the benches, lifting Hoppy up to sit by her. A sturdy man in dirty jeans and a torn, grease-smeared T-shirt was working on one of the boats. It was Andy Walker! Well, she had a few questions for him, so maybe she would take the time to somehow befriend him. But just as she was about to get up and saunter over, she saw Kylie and Connor walking from the other direction, hand in hand, down the path to Andy.

He was happy to be interrupted, it was clear, and he swung Connor up on his shoulder and pretended to lose hold of him once, which sent the little boy into shrieks of laughter. The two adults moved to a shady spot by a marina shed, and Kylie handed over a paper bag and a take-out cup. He looked in the bag and seemed pleased, because he leaned over and kissed Kylie Hofstadter . . . full on the mouth. Even from a distance it was clear that it was not the kiss of a father-in-law to a woman he thought of as a daughter; it was the kiss of a man in love.

❧ Nineteen ❧

JAYMIE WAS ROCKED back on her bench, the breath gone from her as if she had suffered a blow to the stomach. She must have made some noise, because Kylie looked over and saw her. Even from a distance, it was clear the young mother's face was red. She said something to Andy, and he looked sharply over at Jaymie and said something back to Kylie.

She got up and approached Jaymie, holding her gaze over the hundred feet or so she had to walk. "Hey, didn't see you there. You look, uh . . . shocked," Kylie said.

"I guess I am," Jaymie replied, as Hoppy jumped off the bench and danced around Kylie's feet, begging for attention. "I didn't know you two were involved in that way."

"We weren't until . . . well, until real recently." She was uneasy, shifting from one foot to the other, looking back at the two fellows in her life.

"Recently? When?"

Hoppy gave up on getting attention from Kylie and drifted to the end of his leash, sniffing the railing at the boardwalk that overlooked the dock.

"It just . . . happened," Kylie said softly, shrugging. She waved at Connor, who didn't seem to notice.

"*When* did it happen?"

Kylie turned back and stared at her. "Why do you want to know?"

Jaymie couldn't think of a single reason to insist, and maybe it wasn't important. "Kylie, why don't you sit for a minute?" she said, patting the seat of the bench. "I didn't get a chance last time I saw you to really say how much I regretted missing so many years in Kathy's life. You two had your problems, but were you close growing up?"

Her chin had firmed at Jaymie's mention of her and her sister's troubles. She didn't sit. She glared down at Jaymie, her intensity unsettling. "Haven't you disagreed with your sister over the years? If one of you had a kid, you'd know that just makes the disagreements more . . . I don't know, more involved. Kathy thought I should be raising Connor one way, and I have my own opinions."

"But she didn't want you raising him at all, did she?"

"Look, as hard as it was that she was trying to take Connor away from me, I understood where she was coming from. In a way she did me a favor. It was a wake-up call, big-time. Her custody suit shocked me out of that awful blackness I was living in after Drew died. And then she forced me to take a good, hard look at how Connor and I were living, in that dirty, disgusting old farmhouse." She looked off down the river, and a deep sigh escaped her.

"Kathy tried everything first," she continued. "She tried to get Mama to let her put the farm up for sale and have someone come in and clean it, but Mama said no. She can't help it, I guess, but that farm is a big old millstone around all of our necks. She just won't let go of it." She shook her head, sadness in her eyes. "We can't look after it, or at least I know *I* can't. I tried to get Mama to sell it so we could all move into town and she could be more comfortable, but she wouldn't budge. Anyway, because of Kathy and her custody suit, I ended up moving in with Andy, to give Connor a better environment. We started raising Connor together." Again she looked back at the two of them, sitting together, Connor copying Andy's sitting position and mannerisms, and her mouth softened into a smile. "Andy's great; Connor may be his grandson, but he loves my boy as if he's his own son."

Jaymie pressed her advantage, now that she had Kylie talking. "But did you think Kathy would ultimately manage to take Connor away from you?"

"My lawyer didn't think so," Kylie said, her gaze settling back on Jaymie, her expression sober. "A year ago, maybe, but not now that I'm getting things straightened out."

Jaymie watched her face. "Do you think Kathy would have been okay with you and Andy becoming a couple?"

Two red spots flared on Kylie's cheeks, and she sucked in her breath. She stuck her hands in the pockets of her shorts and rocked back on her heels. "It wouldn't have been any of her business."

Jaymie was silent. She had hit a sore spot, talking about Kylie and Andy's relationship. Maybe Kylie had worried about how Kathy would take it. On an impulse, Jaymie said, "Well, at least you won't have to work as hard now, with the insurance Kathy left you."

Kylie gasped. "How do you know about that?"

"Uh, I just . . . your mother said something about it when I went out to get the casserole dish."

"I don't know what you're saying, but that money is for Connor, and it'll all be there when he's old enough to use it."

"I wasn't saying . . . Kylie, I'm sorry! I didn't mean—"

"Just leave us alone," the young mother said, whirling and stomping away.

Unfortunately, Jaymie hadn't had a chance to ask where Kylie and Andy were the night of the murder. How did Connor get away from them?

The ferry came and went once, but Matt wasn't on it. Jaymie watched Kylie, Connor and Andy for a while as they ate their early lunch together; Andy and Kylie eyed her on occasion. Finally he was done, and Kylie and her son departed. She was silent as the little boy stopped to play with Hoppy, who yapped and dashed about, making him laugh. As Jaymie tried to think of some way to ask how Connor got away from Kylie and Andy that fateful evening, the young woman pulled Connor away, saying she had to get some things at the Emporium for supper.

This time, when the ferry pulled up to dock, Matt Laskan was aboard. He was dressed in suit pants and a short-sleeve shirt, open at the throat, and he carried a briefcase. He waved to the ferry captain and began up the pathway to the boardwalk.

Jaymie rose, stretched and began to walk, slowly enough that he overtook her. She looked over at him as he passed, and said, "Oh, hi, Matt. How are you today?"

He looked up, a worried frown on his drawn face. "Oh. Hi, uh, Jaymie."

She matched her footsteps to his and made small talk until they were away from the dock and could not be overheard. "You know, Matt," she said. "I was surprised to learn about the real reason Kathy threatened you on the Fourth of July. I would never have pictured you as the kind of guy

who would end up in jail on assault and kidnapping charges."
It was a calculated risk, and his reaction was all she could
have hoped for.

"How did you know about that?" he said, stopping dead
in his tracks. "Who told you?"

She watched his face. "I didn't know it was a *real* secret!
Those things are a matter of public record. Though I suppose
since it happened in Port Huron, nobody here would have a
reason to know about it. Craig did, though, right? And he
told Kathy? Is that how she found out?"

"No," he muttered, looking around with a guilty frown.
"Craig didn't tell her anything. Kathy was digging around
for dirt. She was an awful woman!"

"I'm so sorry," Jaymie said, infusing sympathy into her
tone. "It must have been infuriating, her holding it over you
like that! To think she threatened to reveal it to your
girlfriend!"

He stared at her, his eyes narrowed and his brows pinched
together. There was silence for a long moment, and Hoppy
whined, then tugged to the end of his leash and yapped at
some gulls that were wheeling around above them,
screeching.

"Why would Lily be concerned?" he finally said, blink-
ing rapidly.

She watched him, trying to figure him out. Was he saying
she wouldn't have cared because their relationship was
already over? Because she had moved on to Craig? What?
"You don't think she'd be concerned? Are you sure of that?"
Hoppy got bored with barking at gulls and sniffed around
Matt's feet.

"Why are you talking to me about this?" He squared his
shoulders and stared down at her, pushing Hoppy away gently with one foot. "What's going on?"

"How did Kathy find out, if Craig didn't tell her?"

He looked down at the dirt and scuffed his wingtip in the dust. "Kathy figured out somehow about my trips to Port Huron, and she followed me, the witch. I don't know why she cared, but she did."

"And she was using it against you? Using it as leverage in her campaign to move to Toledo and open a branch office?"

"Can you believe it? In this economy, she still thought *that* was a good idea!"

"I think she just wanted to move away from Queensville to get a fresh start. She intended to get custody of Connor. I suppose she needed you to go along with her plan, right, if she was going to convince Craig?"

"I just don't know why she thought her feeble attempt at blackmail would work. Kathy was some kind of weird woman."

"But Craig had other reasons for *not* wanting to move, right?" She watched him. Did he know about Craig and Lily?

But no hint of anger twisted his handsome face. "What do you mean?"

Okay, so he didn't know about Lily cheating on him, but that only made it more likely that he would have killed Kathy, not less. If he had known, he surely would not have wanted to kill Kathy and leave the way open for Craig and Lily to be together. But she was wandering off the path. "Never mind. You really didn't care if Lily found out about what happened in Port Huron?"

"Why would *she* care about it?"

Jaymie watched him, puzzled. His girlfriend wouldn't care that he'd been accused of assaulting and trying to kidnap a prostitute? She was flustered and puzzled.

Matt shifted his briefcase to his other hand. "That was all just a misunderstanding. It's in the past now."

"Really? Are you still making trips into Port Huron?"

"That is none of your business!" he said. "Look, I gotta go. Lily said she's washed those dishes and she'll bring the picnic basket in to the store today or tomorrow. We're having lunch at Ambrosio," he said, naming a little bistro that had recently opened along the river just outside of Queensville.

"Oh. That's nice."

"I don't know. She sounded down, and said she had something to tell me." He looked into her eyes. "Do women *ever* mean anything good when they say they have something to tell you?"

She saw pain in his eyes, and fear. Gently, she answered, "Sometimes. Maybe she just needs to . . . I don't know, go out of town or something."

He shook his head. "It sounded serious. I gotta go, if I'm going to meet her." He trotted off, briefcase swinging as he jogged.

It sounded like Lily was going to drop a bomb on him, either telling him about her and Craig or just breaking up with him. Jaymie walked to the Emporium, hoping to catch Valetta on her lunch break. She was in luck, and she sat on the front step as Valetta brought out a cup of tea.

"So, did you make any headway in finding out who was dressed up like Uncle Sam at the picnic?" she asked her inquisitive friend.

Valetta sighed and said, "Well, yes and no. I have seven names, but everyone agrees there were more like a dozen Uncle Sams and four or five Betsy Rosses." She named everyone she had so far found out about, but not one of them was on the list of suspects. "The trouble is, we'll never know if we got them all. One of our suspects could have been dressed up at some point, and we'd never know."

"Hmm. There's got to be a way to figure this out! Did Johnny notice anything in particular about the Uncle Sam? Was the person short or tall, man or woman, pale complected, anything at *all*?"

Valetta shook her head in regret. "He said the person was a man, for sure, but he couldn't say anything else."

"That leaves us pretty much where we started, with Johnny's uncorroborated story of handing the bowl to Uncle Sam. It would have been better if he hadn't lied first and told us he'd put the bowl back on our table."

"I know, but Johnny lies by instinct."

That didn't bode well for his court case, Jaymie thought, even if he was innocent. Lots of people lied, even when they didn't do anything wrong, she guessed, but mature people didn't. In the next moment she realized that, in all fairness, wasn't true at all. *Everybody* lied, and one only had to look at the mess among Craig, Kathy, Lily and Matt to see dishonesty in action.

"I feel like I'm wandering around in circles," Jaymie said. She told Valetta what she had written down and what she had seen that morning and what Kylie had said about her and Andy falling in love and just realizing it. "My problem is, I have no official reason to ask people these questions, and so I have to try to talk around it, and I never get the information I need. How did Andy and Kylie lose track of Connor during the fireworks? How does a three-year-old boy wander off in the dark and you don't notice? That's a sticking point for me, especially now that I know that Kylie is getting that huge insurance payout."

"Can you see Kylie killing Kathy, though?"

Jaymie thought about it for a minute. "I just don't know.

I keep wondering if Connor followed his mom, Kylie, when she went to meet Kathy. It's one of the few explanations that makes sense."

"But how would Kylie have gotten the bowl?"

"I don't know. Could Andy Walker have been one of those dressed up as Uncle Sam later? You know, it would be pretty easy to go somewhere, slip on a tailcoat, wig, beard, hat and gloves, and wander around. What do you know about him?"

"Andy Walker? Let's see . . . single dad, wife passed away about twenty years ago, when Drew was just seven or eight. He lived on a farm, then, but sold it and moved into town. I can't say that I know a whole lot more about him, other than that he's worked as a mechanic at the marina for years. Our paths haven't crossed much."

"Can you see him killing Kathy?"

"I wouldn't have thought so," Valetta said. "But I can't see anyone killing *anyone*!"

"I know what you mean. It seems so barbaric." She pondered the problem. "But there is one person we know who has been involved in a violent confrontation recently. I'm still puzzled as to why Matt Laskan wasn't charged with the assault and attempted kidnapping he was arrested for. And why does he seem so relaxed about it? Do you know anyone who can find out anything about the charges and why they were dropped?"

Valetta thought about it. "Maybe. I'll have to call in a favor."

Jaymie stood and dusted off her butt as Hoppy pranced around in circles, waiting to continue their walk. "Okay. Are there any new picnic basket rentals today?"

"Not yet."

"I'll call you later and see if you found anything out."

She headed home and did some cleaning and some

garden upkeep and then mowed the lawn. She confirmed
the next reservation for Rose Tree Cottage—the last one
before her parents' two-week stay—and arranged for a
plumber to check out the cottage drainage while the Leightons
were there to oversee the work, then called Dee to confirm
that she was going with them to the memorial service for
Kathy Cooper. She spent an hour cleaning and organizing all
the items she'd just bought at the thrift store in Wolverhampton. Valetta didn't have any new information, Jaymie discovered, when she called her friend to check in.

And then another early, solitary dinner. She made herself
some of her grandmother's mac and cheese, sharing it with
Hoppy. She kept thinking about Kathy, how she had so many
loose ends in her life. Would she ever have become the nurse
she wanted to be? And why had nursing appealed to her so
much? Would she have finally made it all up with her sister,
as it seemed she might have been on her way to doing? How
would it have gone down between her and Craig?

Something was sticking in Jaymie's mind, something she
had overlooked. Or something she had taken for granted.
Was it something about Kathy? Or . . . wait. It was something about the murder scene. Something not quite right.
But what?

Restless, not ready for bed but with no desire to do anything else, she slipped her flip-flops on and went for a walk.
She threaded her way through the village and up to the boardwalk, then stood for a while, watching the lights on Heartbreak Island. The occasional sounds of folks having a drink
on the decks of their boats in the marina, laughter and even
the occasional splash, drifted to her on the light breeze.

A splash. As she had approached the figure she thought
was Kylie behind the ladies' washroom, she had heard a
faint splash. The river was about ten feet below the railing.

What could it have been? A fish? Fish didn't generally jump at night. Could have been a duck, she supposed. The fireworks upset the ducks and sent them scurrying. But this was several minutes after the fireworks had ended.

Had someone jumped in? Not a big enough splash for that. Someone could have thrown something in, but from where? She might never know, and it more than likely had nothing to do with the murder.

SHE WORKED AT the Emporium again the next day and made up the rental baskets for the next few days. The winery idea had taken off, and after an ad on an online classifieds website, she had three Lover's Lane rentals booked, so she called the Queensville Inn to order the food hampers.

During their tea break, Valetta told her that she still hadn't found anything out about Matt Laskan's trouble in Port Huron. After lunch with Valetta at the front counter, Jaymie was perched on a high stool by the cash register doing a crossword puzzle. A long-legged blonde walked in the front door, her handbag under one arm and a rattan basket swinging from the other. "I'm returning this rental basket," she said, her voice clear and melodious. She plunked the basket on the counter and turned to walk away.

Jaymie recognized the woman right away from the tea shop in Wolverhampton, but she grabbed the book from the display, and said, "Please wait a moment while I find the entry. Now, what was your name?"

She turned back toward Jaymie. "Lily Fogarty," she said, toying nervously with her gold necklace. "But the basket is probably checked out under a different name."

"And that would be?" Jaymie said, looking up into her smooth face.

She sighed. "Craig Cooper."

Was there any point in delaying Lily, or in trying to find out about her and Craig? She already knew that neither Lily nor Craig was guilty of killing Kathy, but it occurred to her for the first time that though they hadn't done it themselves, they could have had someone else kill Kathy. In fact, wasn't it mighty suspicious that they had photo proof of the fact that both of them had an alibi? "Oh, so this is Craig's basket. I was at the picnic here in Queensville, and he didn't stay." She examined the other woman's face. "I wonder why?"

"I don't know," Lily said, impatiently. "He was busy, I suppose."

"Busy in Wolverhampton at your local evening parade, I understand," Jaymie said, calmly watching the woman's eyes.

"How do you know that?"

"His photo was in the paper, and he was in the crowd looking up at *you*."

"I don't have to stand for this. At least all you snoopy Queensvillians know Craig didn't do it, right?" she retorted crisply, and picked her purse up off the counter.

"Didn't kill his wife? Well, not directly. But there *are* other ways. You know, the husband is always the first suspect, especially if he had motive."

"This is not a topic I know anything about, so you'll excuse me if I don't get involved in local crime stories." She started toward the door.

Jaymie took a deep breath, and said, "But you're already involved, Ms. Fogarty, since you and Craig have been seen spending a lot of time together."

Lily whirled, her face red, and pointed at Jaymie with her handbag. "You're the one who was lurking at the tea shop, you and your snoopy old-maid friend," she snarled. "If you so much as breathe a word of this, I'll . . . I'll sue you for defamation of character!" She spun and headed out the door, the bells overhead jingling at her frantic departure.

"I guess I'm your snoopy old-maid friend," Valetta said, joining Jaymie at the cash desk and watching through the big front window as Lily got into a sedan and skidded out of the gravel parking space. "She was really mad."

"I know. I got to thinking, isn't it a real coincidence that the photo with both of them in it happened to make the front page? Did they know they'd both need an alibi? Did they *know* Kathy would be dead?"

"Oooh, I never thought of that," Valetta said, her eyes big and round behind her thick glasses.

"Neither did I, until now." Jaymie didn't add that it was still possible that Johnny Stanko was guilty, and that he'd been hired by Craig Cooper.

❋ Twenty ❋

THE REST OF the day trickled by minute by minute, with a flurry of customers at the last moment buying things for their dinners. There was only one minor addition to Jaymie's collection of information. Valetta made a call to an editor at the *Wolverhampton Howler*, and found out, to both Jaymie's and her interest, that Lily Fogarty had been proactive in making sure there was a photo of her in the paper, specifically the one from the Fourth of July events in Wolverhampton. It begged the question: Had she wanted to make sure both she and Craig had a good and verifiable alibi for the time of Kathy's murder? There were still too many unanswered questions to know for sure.

Jaymie walked home alone and let Hoppy out. She sat on the back step and watched as Hoppy snooped and sniffed. She and Valetta had talked it over, thoroughly exhausting the topic of the possibility of Lily and Craig hiring someone to kill Kathy. Jaymie had even brought up Johnny's name, and Valetta honestly examined the possibility. Nothing indicated it, they decided. Craig and Johnny's past relationship as bullied and bullier probably precluded Craig going to him for such a big job.

But it was still something Jaymie couldn't just dismiss.

The village was abuzz with the gossip about the police questioning. Spending the day at the Emporium, she had heard the tale a dozen times from different folks, how one police officer or another had asked them questions about the picnic in Boardwalk Park: if they had noticed anything, who was sitting near Kathy Cooper, et cetera. Trouble was, from what Jaymie could tell, no one had seen anything of importance, except for her and Kathy's argument.

She sat on the back step, enjoying the moment as a gentle evening breeze wafted over her. She too often took such a simple pleasure for granted, she thought, looking down at her strong legs, sticking out from her denim cutoffs. She was so lucky, especially compared to Ella Douglas; it was terribly sad how sickly Ella had become. It was as if she were fading away, the mystery illness attacking her from every angle and leaving her weak. Jaymie had speculated that Ella might be faking her illness and could be stronger than she looked, but visiting her had dispelled that notion.

It was just too bad that Kathy hadn't lived. Jaymie clung to the belief that she could have resolved things with her former friend, because Kathy sure seemed willing to forgive and forget, as far as Ella was concerned anyway. Maybe it was sympathy for Ella's illness that made it possible for Kathy to apologize for the incident in the Emporium and also forgive the bullying Ella had inflicted on her back in high school, when she had never been able to forgive one rumored nasty comment, something that Jaymie had never even said. No one wants to be mean to someone so desperately ill, Jaymie supposed, not even Kathy Cooper, the queen of holding grudges. It occurred to Jaymie then that Ella was one person who might know who had spread the nasty rumor.

Jaymie called her house, but there was no answer. She made a sandwich for dinner and went up to her office for a while. The "office" was really the spare bedroom, a tiny little closet of space about eight by ten, with her desk, computer and bookshelves. All through the long Michigan winter she had kept herself sane—and from fixating too much on Joel and Heidi—by going through her grandmother's old cookbooks from the second World War and beyond. She was now trying to organize the recipes into categories and collections. There were stacks of loose pages, many of them in her grandmother's spidery, elegant handwriting, the India ink fading but still legible on the sixty-year-old paper.

Among the papers was a list of herbal remedies for everything from premenstrual cramps to headaches. Another sheet listed a lot of poisonous plants in the garden to stay away from. Who knew that rhubarb leaves were so deadly? She'd have to remember that. Her grandmother had written that one of her friends from childhood had a relative in England who died from eating the rhubarb leaves they were turning to as a source of nutrition during the Great War, a time of deprivation. She read the long list of other poisonous plants and the horrible symptoms they brought on. One in particular stopped her dead. It was awful to think that a plant that was so hardy and prevalent—and so common locally—could be *so* dangerous.

She tried Ella's number again, anxious now to talk to her, but there was still no answer. She remembered suddenly what she had heard at the Emporium earlier: there was another Rotary club meeting that evening, an emergency one called to deal with the fallout from a recent fund-raising effort that had gone terribly wrong and had actually lost money. Bob, who was the secretary-treasurer for the local chapter, would be at that meeting, and it would go on for hours. So why was Ella not answering?

Jaymie remembered the last time she'd seen Ella, the pallid skin, the sunken eyes, the aura of desperate illness that clung to Ella. Uneasy, she tried calling again. There could be a thousand reasons why someone wouldn't answer the phone. She could be sleeping. She could be watching TV. She could have the ringer turned off. It was stupid to feel so worried.

But it wouldn't hurt to walk over there. If she saw Ella inside, or if she tapped on the door and Ella came to answer it, she would make some excuse, or say she was just passing by. All the way over she tried to allay her fears; it was silly to get so worked up over nothing. Becca had done that before when their grandma had not answered the phone, only to find that the woman was over at a friend's apartment watching an old movie or in bed sleeping soundly. Maybe Ella was over at someone else's house or . . . there were a million other possibilities.

She walked through the rapidly darkening streets, her palms sweating, the darkness increased by gathering clouds. A low rumble of thunder rolled across the heavens. It was going to rain, and she hadn't brought an umbrella. If she found out Ella was fine, it would be worth a soaking.

As she walked she thought back: Was Kathy's apology to Ella for overreacting to the incident at the Emporium just an excuse to check in on her? Kathy had always wanted to be a nurse, her lifelong passion. Jaymie remembered Kathy's request for an herbal products catalog at the Emporium. She was interested in natural remedies. She probably knew all the information Jaymie had just discovered among her grandmother's papers.

Her thoughts began tumbling over one another like com-
petitors at a gymnastics meet: natural remedies, symptoms
of poisoning, Mrs. Bellwood saying that nightshade was terribly dangerous. And from her own reading: symptoms of
nightshade poisoning included vision problems, rapid pulse
and lots more. Ella, her vision affected to the point that she'd
run over little Connor's foot . . .

"I don't eat potatoes or tomatoes," Ella had said at the
Fourth of July picnic. Why not tomatoes or potatoes?
Grandma had said never to eat green potatoes, because they're
poisonous. Solanine poisoning. A phrase from her earlier
reading, about tomatoes and potatoes belonging to the nightshade family, leaped out.

Her thoughts teemed. Nightshade; where all had she seen
it recently? At Mrs. Bellwood's. In her own backyard. At
Johnny Stanko's and . . . winding up the porch near the lift
at Ella and Bob's home!

She increased her pace, her heart pounding. This was
ridiculous; she was getting worked up over nothing. But still,
she couldn't stop worrying. She saw Bob and Ella's home
and broke into a sprint. A dog nearby barked. She trotted
up to the porch and knocked. And knocked. No answer, no
car in the drive. Bob wasn't home. If Ella was in trouble,
there was no one to help her, because Bob was at the Rotary
club meeting!

She pounded on the door, then went to the window and
cupped her hands around her eyes, looking through the
glass. It was hard to see; a curtain was in the way, almost
closed, but through a sliver Jaymie could see Ella, slumped
sideways in her wheelchair in her favorite spot, a book on
the floor near her. Crap! She didn't look well.

Jaymie tried the door, but it was locked securely. She
raced up the laneway toward the garage, let herself through

a gate and climbed the stoop to the back door. She rattled the knob, but it too was locked. But there was an open window with a screen. If she was wrong—please God let her be—then she would pay to have it repaired, but she took her keys and slit the screen, reaching in and around to the door and finding the lock on the knob engaged. She twisted it and tried the door. It was still locked. She twisted it again and rattled the knob, and the door finally swung open and banged against the wall.

Jaymie darted through the shadowy house, stubbing her toe along the way and yelping with pain. When she got to the living room, Ella was still slumped over. But she was alive, her breathing rapid but shallow, her skin hot and dry to the touch! A plate with a crust of toast on it smeared with bright red jam was on the table beside her.

Homemade jam. Bob was experimenting with homemade jam! Could it be . . . no, *no one* could do this by accident. She pictured Bob slyly gathering nightshade berries and cooking them. Did cooking kill the poison? But even if it did, that didn't matter; he could mash up uncooked berries to add to the cooked jam.

"Ella! Ella, wake up," she said, gently pulling the woman upright. She had to call 911. She snatched up the phone, but when she hit the button to call, there was nothing, no sound at all. No dial tone. But it had rung, earlier, when she called from her place. Was it dead?

A sound behind her alerted her, and she whirled, ducking just in time to avoid Bob's walking stick. It whistled past her head. She screamed, horrified by the sight of Bob's pale, sweaty face and bulging eyes. She raced past him toward the front door, shrieking, "Help! Help, someone!"

"Shut up! You're not getting away with this," he yelled, lunging after her.

"Bob, I didn't do anything," she screamed, confused. Did he think she was hurting Ella? Or . . . no! She was right in her supposition; Bob was trying to poison his wife! She ducked as he lashed out at her with the stick again. He was blocking her route to the back door, and the front door was securely locked; it would take time to undo the deadbolt. She made a split-second decision and sprinted up the stairs into the darkness above.

"Damn you!" he shouted, and began up the stairs after her, but more slowly.

She felt her way along the hallway and came to a door; she opened it, and crept inside what seemed to be a linen closet from the feel of piled towels and the smell of fabric softener.

"Jaymie, come out *now*!" he shouted. A hall light went on, a sliver of light under the doorway. "There aren't too many places you can be, so save us both time and come out so we can talk about this."

Talk about how he had poisoned his wife systematically with deadly nightshade–laced jam? Her glands ran water, and her stomach revolted. Kathy had suspected or even figured out what he was doing; that had to be the solution! Bob had killed her because she had figured out that he was poisoning his wife! But why hadn't she turned him in to the cops if she knew?

"Jaymie?" he called, his tone softer. The floor in the hallway creaked as he crept around, trying to figure out where she was. "Come on, I won't hurt you," he coaxed. "Let's talk about this." The sound of his voice changed, becoming distant and muffled; he must be in another room.

She slipped out of the linen closet and down the hall, but she heard him moving around, opening a door. She dashed into the closest room and softly closed the door, locking it with the knob lock. Luckily it was an old house like hers, and had the same kind of doorknobs. As far as she knew, all he had was the walking stick as a weapon, and how was he going to explain to the cops bashing her over the head upstairs while his wife lay dying in the living room?

He was in the hall again; he tried the knob of the door of the room she was in. "Aha, that's where you are!" he said. "Come on out, Jaymie. Let's talk!"

"Kathy figured it out, didn't she?" she said, raising her voice. "She figured out that you were poisoning Ella!"

He tried the knob again, rattling it. "She wasn't sure. She thought Ella may have been ingesting the berries accidentally. I placated her, told her I had just learned that the berries I had used in some homemade jam were harmful."

"So why did she meet you behind the washroom in the park?"

There was silence for a long minute. It sounded like he was leaning against the door. "Oh dear. You've figured that out, huh?"

"You were dressed up as Uncle Sam, weren't you? You came back to the park—after taking Ella home—dressed up as Uncle Sam! Poor Johnny handed you the bowl when you asked for it . . . or . . . or told him you'd take it back to our table for him. You knew that bowl was mine, and you knew Kathy and I were enemies!"

In a thoughtful tone, he said, "Too clever by half, that's what my mom always said when I caught on to something I wasn't supposed to know. Come on out, Jaymie. Let's talk. We need to discuss this face-to-face."

Right. As if. "And you had gloves on, didn't you?" Some Uncle Sam costumes included white gloves. "Come on, Bob; why did Kathy meet you behind the washroom?"

"I told her I had some legal contacts, someone who could

help her get custody of Connor. I knew what she wanted. She almost didn't agree, though; said she was going to give up on the custody suit. "Don't give up yet," I said to her. "Think it over and meet me there," I said, "just to tell me what you've decided."

"Just let me go, Bob," Jaymie said, a sob welling up in her throat. She leaned against the door, palm against the wood. What could she say to get out of this mess? "Ella will be all right if she gets some help. You don't need to do this."

He rattled the doorknob again. "I'm afraid it's too late for that. You've figured out too much. Just like Kathy . . . you're too clever! She was like a darned terrier, tenacious, once she had a bit of information."

"Bob, I don't have proof. Really!" Oh crap. Probably not a good thing to say, because if he was planning to kill her, he now knew he didn't need to worry about her leaving behind any brilliant musings about his role in the killing.

"But you're a lifelong citizen of good character in this boring little burg, aren't you? One word from you . . . I've been through the ringer with my first wife and the insurance company. How would it look if I was suspected in another murder?"

Another . . . ? "You *killed* your first wife?" Oh God, what was she going to do? If she kept running into murderers, she was really going to have to start carrying a cell phone.

"Bitch figured out I had embezzled some money from the charity we ran on her dime, and she was going to turn me in! I couldn't let her do that. We had a little 'accident,' and she died. Insurance and my inheritance was enough to pay off our debts *and* take care of me for a while," he mused. "But not long enough. Ella and her nice, fat insurance settlement came around just in time!"

"Insurance settlement?"

"Of course! She was in a car accident, a bad one; that's why she's in a wheelchair!"

"I thought she was sick with some endocrine disease!"

"Glad you bought that crap," he grunted, trying the door. "Ella sure did. She was finally convinced she was really sick, not just injured. I hope everyone else buys it, including that snoop, Valetta Nibley. It'll make it easier for the coroner to pronounce natural causes."

"Why are you doing this?"

"Oh, come on! Surely you can figure this out. She has a million-dollar annuity. When she's gone, I'll get insurance money again—like any loving couple, we bought policies to benefit each other, you know, even though her premiums were through the roof—*and* I'll inherit the entire annuity as a lump-sum settlement." He paused, then said, his tone sly, "Just come on out, Jaymie, and we'll talk! Maybe we can make a deal."

There was a pounding at the door downstairs.

"Damn it!" Bob growled, striking at the door with his walking stick. More pounding from downstairs echoed through the house. "I've got to go and send whoever that is away."

Jaymie heard a loud screeching, like furniture on a wood floor. Darn! She unlocked the door and pulled it open, but he had shoved some extremely large piece of furniture against it, a wardrobe or armoire! She flicked the light on to find that she was in some kind of spare bedroom, which was stuffy from disuse. And hanging on a coat rack? An Uncle Sam costume, minus the wig, beard and top hat!

A splash; something tossed into the river; and gray hairs clasped in Kathy's dead hand. That's what it must have been.

He couldn't risk the beard being found at his place, because the police would be able to match the fibers in her hand to his Uncle Sam costume.

But she couldn't just stand there gaping. She had to get out. There was a window! She dashed across the room and tried to open it, but the old sash was either warped with time or painted or nailed shut. Should she break a pane? That wouldn't do a bit of good, since it was an old six-over-six type, and one pane was barely big enough to get her arm through.

She dashed back across the room to the door and flung it open, shouting past the huge wooden wardrobe, "Help, help!" and hoping whoever was at the door could hear her. It wasn't enough. She put her shoulder to the wardrobe and pushed, and it budged. If *he* could move it, so could she. She did it again, throwing herself against it hard enough that her shoulder felt bruised already. She shoved again, harder, and it screeched, catching on a floorboard and tipping, crashing over against a wall.

She climbed over it and dashed down the stairs to the landing. The front door was open slightly, and she could see Bob's figure silhouetted by the faint porch light. Was he with someone? It didn't matter. The door was open, and she was going to have to take her chances. She bolted down the last flight of stairs and flung herself through the door, sending Bob flying down on the porch just as a fire truck and a cop car, sirens blazing, screeched to a stop. A man in boxer shorts and a sleeveless T-shirt stood near the steps, phone in hand, eyes wide with shock.

"He tried to kill me," Jaymie shouted, panting and pointing toward Bob as the cops came out, guns drawn. "His wife is inside, and she's very ill, and he was trying to kill her," she gasped. "He killed Kathy Cooper and tried to kill me!"

And then everything went black.

SHE WOKE UP as the paramedics were loading Ella into the back of the ambulance. One paramedic was by her side, and she looked up and smiled. "I'm okay," she said, trying to sit up.

The woman pushed her back down. "Just be calm, miss, and we'll—"

"I'm okay, really!" Jaymie insisted, shrugging away from the paramedic's insistent, gloved hands and sitting up. "I just hyperventilated. My shoulder is bruised, and I have a few scratches, but I'm fine."

Bob Douglas was sitting in the back of the cruiser, and when Bernice Jenkins, the officer standing by the cruiser, saw her, she bustled over. "Can you tell me what the hell is going on?" she asked.

"Bernie! Thank God you're here. Bob Douglas murdered Kathy Cooper."

"Well, that's funny, because that's what he's saying about you!" she said, hands on hips. "He said he caught you in his house trying to kill his wife—he says you fed her some poisoned jam or something—and when he tried to ward you off, you went berserk."

"Right. *Not* funny."

The neighbor came over, and hovered, saying, his tone querulous, "I never did trust that Bob Douglas. He kept trying to get rid of me tonight, when I came to the door about his house alarm and the alarm company. If this girl"—he pointed at Jaymie—was trying to kill his wife, would Bob be trying to get rid of me and keep me from calling the cops?"

He stepped closer to Bernice. "Well, would he? I don't *think* so! The Douglas's alarm company called me—I was their contact, you know, because they didn't know anyone else—and they said that there was some kind of malfunction with the alarms in the Douglas home, so I came over and banged on the door. No one answered at first, so I called 911, and then Bob comes to the door and gets mad! And then I heard someone screaming upstairs, and he's trying to get rid of me, saying it's all a mistake. But I said, what kind of mistake has a woman screaming inside your house?"

He said it all in one long stream, and Bernice nodded, listening intently, and finally said, "Okay, sir, let me get your name. We'll need to talk to you down at the station."

"I'll go right now. This minute, if you want. I have important information, and I know my duty as a citizen."

Another car pulled up, and Detective Christian jumped out of it, dashing over to Jaymie. "Are you okay? What the hell is going on here?"

She put up one hand, and said, "Help me get up, Detective. I think I bruised my butt falling down."

"I think you ought to stay right there for a minute, until we know you're okay," he said.

Bernice eyed the detective and Jaymie. She swiftly hid a smile, but not before Jaymie caught that look. Christian knelt beside her, his arm around her, and she looked up into his gray eyes. This was not going to quell the rumors that he liked her, she supposed. But did she care? "I'm okay, really," she said, her heart pounding again. She pulled away.

The detective's concerned expression was soon shielded by a mask of professionalism. As the ambulance carrying poor Ella Douglas roared away, Christian took Bernice aside. The officer talked to him nonstop, pointing out the neighbor, who now sat on the front step of the Douglases' home, and Jaymie, who hugged herself, feeling chilled and damp from the night air.

At that moment, Valetta, her face slathered in white cream and her glasses askew, came running down the street, shrieking when she saw Jaymie sitting on the ground. "Jaymie, Jaymie, are you okay?"

"I'm fine, Valetta, relax!" She explained what had happened, beginning to shiver halfway through. "Why am I so cold all of a sudden?"

"Shock," Valetta said. "You just had an awful scare." She whipped off her housecoat to reveal a shorty set underneath, pink with gray Parisian poodles and Eiffel Towers all over the top and shorts. "Put this on," she said, wrapping it around Jaymie.

It was warm from her friend's body and smelled of Jergens and Noxzema. The shivering settled. Valetta marched over to the detective, and said, "Jaymie needs to get someplace and have a cup of tea or something. I'll take her home, then meet you over the police station, okay?" She didn't wait for the detective's answer, she just grabbed Jaymie's arm, hauled her to her feet and marched off with as much dignity as a woman in shorty pajamas and her face slathered in cream could muster.

❋ Twenty-one ❋

SUGARY TEA AND a sweater from Valetta's closet made Jaymie feel better, and after that, Valetta insisted on driving her to the police station. Jaymie had made one call, though, before they'd left Valetta's cottage. She just wasn't sure that she had gotten through to the paramedics, so she called Wolverhampton General Hospital, insisted on talking to the nurse in charge of Ella Douglas and told her that Ella might be suffering from solanine poisoning. If they pumped her stomach, they'd probably find the residue of red berries, deadly nightshade.

At the police station she was faced with a weary-looking Detective Christian, who eyed her cherry red sweater adorned with fluffy kittens gamboling with balls of yarn. She didn't feel like explaining that it was Valetta's. The almost-fifty-year-old woman had some peculiar fashion tastes, as evidenced by the Parisian-puppies nightwear. "I know you've probably got a million questions," she said to the detective, "but I have to be sure I was clear. Solanine poisoning . . . look at the crust of toast with red berry jam that's on the little table in the living room by Ella Douglas's motorized wheelchair."

"Solanine. What is that?"

"Atropine. Belladonna. Deadly nightshade," Jaymie said tersely, scrubbing her gritty-feeling eyes. "I've done a lot of research lately, and I believe Kathy Cooper had gone down the same research paths, given her interest in herbal medicine. Maybe check her computer?" She paused, as a bit of information came back to her. "You know, she may even have been talking to someone at the Payne Institute. I was at her house a couple of days ago when they left a message for her to contact them, so maybe she was asking around. I remember seeing advertised in the *Howler* that they have a course on the poisonous plants of Michigan.

"Bob Douglas was poisoning his wife with deadly nightshade. I think Ella was sensitive to it anyway, which sped up the process." Jaymie stopped and thought back. "I went to visit her a few evenings ago, and there was some uneaten toast on her side table, and Bob was out *that* evening at a Rotary club meeting, too. Oh my gosh! I think he tried to kill her then, but she didn't eat it!"

Jaymie, with the detective's thorough questioning, took him and Bernice Jenkins, who sat in taking notes, through her last few hours, how it all had come together, from Kathy Cooper's naturopathy catalog through her interest in nursing. She told them about her worries for Ella, when she hadn't gotten an answer on the phone, and about finding the Uncle Sam costume in the spare room. She went through how she'd figured out about the splash she'd heard that night, and got a surprising admission from Detective Christian that they had found an Uncle Sam beard and wig in the river near the crime, and it matched the fibers found in Kathy's hand. They had been trying to trace it to someone ever since.

"We're going to have to put you on a retainer if you keep solving crimes," he said, finally, with a rueful smile.

"I've got another one for you," Jaymie said. She told him what Bob Douglas had said concerning the death of his first wife.

The detective and Bernie left the room. Jaymie got up to look in the big mirror that lined one wall. Good heavens! She looked a fright: smears of dirt on her cheek, her hair like a rat's nest. She jammed her fingers through it, trying to comb it out. Why didn't Valetta tell her she looked like crap? Detective Christian came back in, quickly hiding a smirk. Was that a two-way glass, she wondered? Had he seen her primping? Red flooded her cheeks.

Sobering, he said, "You'll be happy to know that Miss Nibley called Mr. Stanko's lawyer, who is, at this very minute, at the jail. His client will be released as soon as the paperwork is done."

"Johnny sure didn't help himself, did he?" Jaymie said. "I thought he was probably guilty, you know. But Valetta was *so* sure he wasn't, and I thought I'd sniff around. He's really lucky to have a friend like her."

"She's the kind of friend you'd want on your side."

"One question I had was, how did Johnny Stanko know about my bowl being the murder weapon?"

"Ah yes, you found out about that—him knowing the bowl was the murder weapon—on your visit to him, which you never told me about."

She flushed and wisely remained silent.

"He apparently got an anonymous call about it—we think that was from Bob Douglas, but we're not sure—its purpose to incriminate Stanko by making him too knowledgeable or making him run. We think Bob is the one too who called us and told us about Stanko being in his house, resulting in the arrest. He was seen skulking around the neighborhood." He gazed at her steadily, his gray eyes warm. "Jaymie, you need to keep your nose out of investigations, though, and I'm serious. It could be really dangerous. It *was* really dangerous. Bob Douglas intended to kill you."

"I know. But I was just poking around," she said. "There were things I wanted to know, but most of them had *nothing* to do with Kathy's murder."

"You didn't know that at the time," he pointed out. "That turned out not to be the case!"

"But I didn't go to Ella's because I was investigating. She hasn't been well, and I was worried about her when she didn't answer the phone. I didn't figure out about Bob until I found her half-dead and saw that berry jam smeared on the toast. That's when it all came together."

He finally let her go. Valetta took her home, made sure she was all right and left her with Hoppy and Denver guarding her well-being.

The next couple of days were busy, and the town was buzzing with the news. The memorial service for Kathy was postponed, and a funeral was planned for Monday, after the arrest of Bob Douglas, first on charges of attempted murder of his wife, then finally—as the news came to Jaymie through the Queensville telegraph, i.e., Valetta—with Kathy Cooper's murder.

Jaymie attended Kathy's funeral with Becca—she had returned without Kevin—and Dee and Valetta. Dani Brougham and Emma Spangler were there, Dani weeping softly, leaning on Emma's shoulder. Craig Cooper sat with his sister and Lily Fogarty. Matt Laskan sat alone, eyeing Lily with a heartbroken expression. Kylie, Connor and Andy

Walker were there, as was Mrs. Hofstadter, also weeping inconsolably. Kylie, Jaymie heard, had prevailed upon her mother to stay at the Walker home for a few days. She would try to talk to Kylie and tell her that her mother wanted to help Mrs. Hofstadter, but she wasn't sure how Kylie would receive what could possibly be viewed as interference.

The Methodist church was crowded, and the hymns chosen appropriate. Matt Laskan glowered over at Craig and Lily as the choir sang, from "Depth of Mercy": "Now incline me to repent, / Let me now my sins lament, / Now my foul revolt deplore, / Weep, believe, and sin no more."

"I found something out," Valetta murmured to Jaymie after a prayer. "About Matt Laskan and his arrest. Remember I told you I might have a contact? I know a girl who does booking and admin at the jail. We can't say a word about this to anyone, but the kerfuffle with Matt Laskan? It was a big mistake. Word is, he goes to Port Huron once a week to visit his sister!"

"His *sister*? Okay . . . but—"

"Shush. Just listen. She's on the street," Valetta said, casting the fellow a glance. Matt was still focused on Lily, but with a softened look and a trembling lip. "She's an addict, and she hooks to support her habit. He goes to the city once a week to make sure she has been eating, and to try to talk her into going into rehab. Her pimp interrupted them, and Matt took a swing at him, then tried to take off with his sister in the car. The cops were called, and in front of her pimp she had to say Matt tried to kidnap her. But the charges were dropped when it was all sorted out."

"Wow. In a million years I would never have guessed that explanation. So that's why he was so puzzled, and asked why Lily would care? It's no one's business, really; he's just a nice guy trying to save his sister from herself." She felt awful for him. His sister was an addict, and his fiancée had dumped him for his business partner; all in all, not a great week for Matt Laskan.

The service was finally over, and everyone adjourned for coffee and cake in the rectory hall. Matt Laskan disappeared, though Craig and Lily were conspicuous by their solidarity in the face of disapproval. One generally did not attend one's wife's funeral with one's girlfriend, but if they had a future together, maybe it was the best strategy to move forward.

The next afternoon, Jaymie picked some roses from her garden and took them to Wolverhampton General Hospital. Becca offered to go with her, but Jaymie really wanted to talk to Ella alone. When she entered the invalid's room, Jaymie paused a moment, watching her. She was lying in bed staring out the window to the blue sky, streaks of sunshine blazing through the horizontal blinds, laying bars of shadow across her blankets. Her color was so much better than it had been that it was startling. She was hooked up to an IV, probably fluids, since the solanine poisoning had taken so much out of her.

"Hi," Jaymie said, coming in, flowers thrust forward.

"Hi! My savior. I'm so glad to see you!" Tears gathered in her pale eyes and trickled down her cheeks, soaking into the neck of her blue-patterned hospital gown. She took the roses and buried her nose in the bouquet.

Jaymie pulled a chair up to the bed. "How are you feeling?"

"Better than I was. I'm back to being just a cripple!"

Not knowing how to answer, Jaymie was silent.

"So . . . I understand Kathy has been buried," Ella said, a catch in her voice.

"Yes, just yesterday. It was a lovely service. Everyone talked about how much she'll be missed."

There was silence between them for a while. Then Ella said, her tone pensive, "You know, I'm the one who told the guy that Kathy liked, back in high school, that you said she and her whole family stank."

Jaymie felt the gut punch, but in the last few days she had begun to wonder. "Why did you do that, Ella?" She searched the other woman's face.

"I'll tell you. I'll tell you the whole stupid, sad story." Eleanor Grimshaw was new in school that year, and she wasn't cool, the way some kids were, nor pretty, nor popular, nor smart or athletic. She was just "the new kid." Her family's farm was down the road from the Hofstadter farm, and Eleanor began to fantasize how nice it would be to have Kathy as a friend, to be able to hang out at each other's places and ride the school bus together, to go to school dances as buddies. "But she had you. The last thing she wanted was another farm girl as a friend, because Kathy never wanted to be a farm girl, she wanted to be a townie." Her voice faltered; Ella was clearly weary.

"You don't have to do this right now, you know," Jaymie said. "You can tell me this another day."

"No, I need to do this today. I almost died, Jaymie. I was almost murdered! I married a murderer. I'm never *not* saying anything again. I'm never leaving anything to tomorrow." She stopped and caught her breath, the roses lying on her legs, the buds starting to droop. "Anyway, I figured if I broke up your friendship with Kathy, then she'd want to be *my* friend. So I started the rumor that you said she and her family and her home stank like pigs. I knew telling that guy was the way to go, because he'd spread it to all his buddies. It worked! It got back to her that you had said it, just like I planned. I was there to console her when she needed a friend."

"So you did become real friends?"

"For a while. But Kathy was obsessed. All she talked about was you, and your friends, and your family. She was so intense! And she wanted to get back at you. It's all she talked about! I got sick of it. Sometimes when you get what you want, it turns out to be not what you want at all."

Ella must have been really lonely to have played such a mean trick.

"I wish I'd known," Jaymie said. "I wish I'd known how lonely you were and had reached out. But I was in my own little bubble back then."

"Don't be sorry for me. I was not a healthy kid, not in any way. There was a lot going on at home, and I couldn't know then that I was just . . ." She sighed, her eyelids drooping. "I was *so* unhappy. Anyway, when I couldn't get her to lay off talking about you, I just turned around and became the meanest bully! I was so angry and miserable, and saying nasty things was all I could do. It felt better while I was doing it, but afterward it was awful."

"I wish my mom had let Mrs. Hofstadter say something, like she wanted to," Jaymie said. "Some adult intervention might have helped us all. Please don't feel bad. You were a kid too, just like Kathy and me, and it sounds like you had enough going on in your life that we weren't aware of. I wish we'd *all* been friends."

"I came back to Queensville hoping that it was all over, that I hadn't done irreparable damage, but there you were, years later, you and Kathy, still enemies. When I found out it wasn't over, I didn't know how to fix it. I was trying to summon up the courage to tell Kathy the truth, hoping that would fix things. I was going to that morning when she came over, but I was getting so sick. And then she apologized for being mean in the Emporium. I thought, if she can apologize to me, maybe she would to you, too."

"But that wasn't all she talked to you about, that morning, was it?"

"No. She went into the kitchen and was gone for a few minutes." Ella closed her eyes, and sighed. When she opened them again, there was a profound sadness in the depths. "Kathy came back to the living room and asked me about the homemade jam in the fridge. I was surprised that she was in my fridge. In fact, I was a little put off—I don't like people rummaging through my things—and maybe I snapped at her. I told her Bob made it, and that he was experimenting with local berries. *Now* I know what that was about. If she'd just told me . . . but I guess she only had suspicions at that point."

Jaymie remembered how Ella acted about her belongings, her insistence that things be put back exactly as they were. Maybe that prickliness had made Kathy hesitant to confide her worries or suspicions to her old nemesis, which perhaps went back to overhearing Ella's complaints in the Emporium about her vision problems, dry mouth, et cetera. Kathy, interested in all things medical, probably did some research on those symptoms, and discovered the correlation with atropine poisoning, Her hypothesis would have been confirmed by finding the deadly nightshade–laden jam. Kathy had had lots of time between the visit to Ella and the afternoon's events in the park to do more research, and even to phone the Payne Institute.

But still . . . "You'd think she would have said something, like, *don't eat the jam!*"

"Maybe she didn't want to alarm me. I told her flat out I wasn't planning on eating any more of it because I didn't like the taste. She asked if Bob was due home, said she wanted to talk to him, that maybe she'd catch him that day, if we were going to be at the park."

"Perhaps she wasn't sure until she saw how he reacted

to her questions about the jam." Jaymie didn't elaborate on that, though she knew from Bob what went down that evening when Kathy confronted him. "Why did you eat more of it, if you didn't like the taste?"

"Bob begged me . . . said he'd made it better. I ate it to please him. He'd been so helpful. I wish Kathy had just said something. Now she's gone forever." Ella lay back, weakened by talking so long. Tears trickled from her closed eyes. "I wish I'd told her the truth, apologized for the past. I'm such a coward."

"Ella, we're adults now. If Kathy had just told me what was said about me back in high school, I could have told her that I'd never said it. We could have solved it. Once we grew up, it was *our* responsibility, not yours." Jaymie thought back through the years. While they were friends, Kathy had rarely invited her to come out to the farm; she always wanted to spend time at Jaymie's house or the cottage. "You know, I think she was hanging out with me, trying to become the 'townie' she wanted to be. And so her pride was hurt when she thought I dissed her. Injured feelings can be mended, but pride . . ."

Pride. When Joel left her, Jaymie's pride had taken a big hit. She had figured out a lot since he'd left, though, and she was better now. It was *his* weakness—his inability to deal with a smart, independent woman—not hers, that had led him to leave her. She turned the conversation to other things, Ella's plans now that Bob was incarcerated with no bail set.

"Glynnis, a cousin of mine, is coming to stay here for a while," Ella said. Her cousin was a few years her senior and had just lost her job as a loans manager at a savings and loan. She needed someplace to live for a while. "She can help me, at least until she gets back on her feet."

"I'm happy you won't be alone," Jaymie said. Ella was

still heartbroken over Bob's awful betrayal, but she almost seemed stronger without him, more decisive and with a better outlook on life. "I hope you feel better soon."

"I hope so, too. They're still doing tests to see if there has been any permanent organ damage."

"Good luck. I'll see you soon." Ella's eyes were drooping, and they closed as Jaymie left the room. She returned home, had lunch with Becca, then walked over to Stowe House. Daniel had just gotten in late the night before, and she wanted to talk to him. He greeted her at the door with a big hug and a kiss.

"I missed you!" he said, holding her close. "I can't believe what happened while I was away."

"Let's go for a walk."

It was a beautiful summer day, and they walked hand in hand toward the river, as if by common consent, not talking much. She told him her side of what had happened. It was only a few days ago, but it felt like quite a while.

"Daniel, I don't think I've been very fair to you," she said, stopping and indicating a shaded bench along the boardwalk path.

They sat. "What do you mean?"

She thought about what she wanted to say. "First, I want to tell you about my feelings for Joel."

He tensed.

She glanced at him, saying, "I loved him; I really did. But that's over."

He relaxed.

"He was the wrong guy for me. He tried to make me feel inferior. He interrupted me all the time, corrected whatever I said."

"He's a jerk," Daniel said sharply.

"You're right; he's a bit of a jerk, and I'm *so* over it. But, that said, I'm just not ready to get serious again. I don't get there easily, Daniel. Joel and I dated for almost a year before . . . before anything happened. And he was only my second real boyfriend. I'm kind of a stick-in-the-mud."

He was pensive and stared out over the river.

"Really, Daniel, it's not y—"

"Please don't say, it's not you, it's me," he said tightly.

"Okay." She paused. He was still tense, like he was waiting for the other shoe to fall. "I'm not saying I don't want to go out with you, I'm just . . ." She shrugged, unable to form the thought into words. She watched his face. "Why did you move to Queensville, Daniel? You've never really told me."

"Why does that matter?"

She watched him for a long moment and cocked her head to one side. "When was the last real relationship you had?"

He shrugged and was silent, staring still toward the river. She turned toward him, putting her knee up on the bench and her arm along the back. "Tell me," she said, gently, squeezing his shoulder. "Did someone hurt you?"

"Has anyone gotten away unscathed?" he asked. "We've all been brokenhearted at some point."

"Then tell me about *your* broken heart."

He glanced over at her, and something he saw in her expression seemed to relax him. He talked. It was a long conversation, one that delved back five years before to a woman who'd worked with him and in whom he had placed a lot of trust. But she'd left him, breaking their engagement, telling him she didn't want what he wanted: a home, a family . . . kids. "You want children, don't you, Jaymie?" He turned toward her, and the longing on his face, the absolute yearning, was heartbreaking.

Her heart sank. "You came to Queensville looking for something, didn't you?"

He nodded. "Yeah, I was just . . . driving. And when I came through Queensville, it was the weekend of the Queen's Tea three years ago. Stowe House was up for sale, but the Realtor had allowed the event to go on. I stopped and had tea. You served me; do you remember?"

She shook her head.

"I asked you about the house, and even though you were busy, you talked to me. I called the Realtor that day and bought Stowe House."

Oh crap. Jaymie felt her heart drop. He bought Stowe House because of her? How had she never known this? Was that creepy or sweet? She considered the implications. "You thought because I was a small-town girl with no career that I was just waiting for Mr. Right to marry me and give me children, didn't you?"

"Is there anything wrong with getting married and having kids?" he asked, his tone exasperated.

"Of course not. But if that's what I am to you, then I'm not the right girl." She searched his eyes. "I might want kids, but not yet. I can't even promise in the next five years."

He held her gaze. "I get it," he said, taking her hand. "I do. But since then, since I fell in love with Stowe House and bought it, it's been three years. I found out you were going out with Joel, and I just got on with my life. Stowe House has become a project of sorts, I guess. I like Queensville, and I'm good, now. I've gotten to know you, Jaymie. I really like you. Honestly. Down to my heart."

"And I like you, too."

"So can we still go out?"

"No expectations, at least not for . . . oh, six months?"

He smiled. "Six months; let's see, that takes us up to Joel and Heidi's wedding, doesn't it?"

She laughed out loud. "It does! I had completely forgotten about it."

"Good. Okay, six months. We'll go out when I'm in town, and see where it takes us."

"That's totally reasonable."

They walked back to Jaymie's house in amicable silence.

❧ Twenty-two ❧

"**S**O YOU'RE NOT engaged?" Becca asked the next morning, turning the Lexus onto the highway out of Queensville.

"I am *not* engaged," Jaymie replied. Again.

"I thought for sure when you and Daniel came walking into the house hand in hand yesterday that you were engaged."

"Becca, we've only really known each other a few months!"

"You've known each other for three years!" Becca retorted.

"I've known him as an acquaintance for three years, but as a friend for a couple of months."

They were on their way into Wolverhampton for shopping and lunch, at Becca's request. Jaymie explained what Daniel and she had talked about and the decision they had come to.

"You can't keep him hanging on forever," Becca said.

"I'm *not* going to keep him hanging on forever. We're giving it six months before we make any decisions." She hadn't said anything about him buying Stowe House after talking to her at the tea. She didn't need any additional pressure, and Becca would think that was just *too* romantic, Jaymie feared. Sometimes she wondered why, when she was the one who read romance novels, Becca was the one who did the most romance-novel-heroine-like things. Like getting married on a whim.

Becca grumbled some more about Jaymie being a commitment-phobe, then was silent for the rest of the drive. Jaymie watched the summer landscape slip by outside the car window. *If only* haunted her, like a bad dream, and it was getting worse. *If only* she had made a more concerted effort to mend her fences with Kathy, maybe all of this wouldn't have happened. Maybe Kathy wouldn't have been so alone in her last days, when her world was crumbling around her. Heidi had learned from Joel, who was walking the tightrope, now, of being friends with both Matt and Craig, that Kathy had indeed found intimate text messages on Craig's phone from Lily, and a photo of them kissing. Kathy and Craig had it out on July Fourth, finally, and were going to break up.

Even as that happened, even as she learned about her husband's betrayal, Kathy still reached out to try to help Ella. Jaymie sighed. She shouldn't have had to do it alone.

Becca reached over and squeezed her arm. "It's over, Jaymie. I know you wish you could have helped, but it wasn't meant to be, and Kathy is gone. I feel bad too, but in a lot of ways, she made her own bed, alienated people, you know?"

Jaymie didn't reply. The pain she felt in her heart was not going to go away quickly, she feared. And maybe it shouldn't.

It would always be a reminder to not let a day pass with misunderstandings between her and others.

They pulled into town and swung onto a back street in Wolverhampton, pulling up to the back of a row of shops. Becca grabbed her purse and said, "Come on. Let's shop!"

"Okay. What are you looking for?"

"A dress."

"Okay." She followed Becca through a back door of a shop called Her Special Day. As the back hall opened out to the shop floor, Jaymie glanced around and got a sinking feeling.

Becca surged forward and snagged a saleslady. It was a wedding-gown shop.

"Becca. *Becca*!" She raced after her sister and grabbed her sleeve, tugging it. "I told you, Daniel and I aren't serious. We're just going to see where dating goes!"

Becca, diving into a line of pretty white dresses, fingered a lace sleeve and looked over at her sister. "Who said this is for *you*?"

"What?"

"Kevin asked me to marry him." She blushed bright pink and studied the row of dresses, clanking the hangers along the rod.

"But . . ." Jaymie grabbed her arm. "Becca, please tell me you haven't said yes! You haven't known him that long."

A saleslady hovered, listening in.

"I haven't said yes," Becca admitted, shooting the woman a glance. "But I haven't said no, either. How much is this one?" She held up an ivory skirt suit with pearl detailing.

"Isn't it just lovely? Perfect for the older bride. That is twelve hundred dollars," the woman said, and went into a long sales spiel.

Jaymie was in enough shock that she was pretty much

speechless for the rest of the shopping trip. Becca did not buy a wedding outfit, which Jaymie took as a hopeful sign. She had nothing against Kevin, but it had only been a couple of months!

Later that afternoon, Jaymie sat at the trestle table in the kitchen with a mound of cookbooks. The last couple of weeks had been so unhappy and off track that she needed to reconnect with part two of her project, *More Recipes from the Vintage Kitchen*.

Becca was doing laundry and texting back and forth with Kevin. When their phone rang, she grabbed it. "Hello?" After a moment she handed it to Jaymie. "It's for you. An Alexander Engle?"

The name vaguely rang a bell. Jaymie took the phone. "Hello?"

"Ms. Jaymie Leighton?"

"Yes."

"This is Alexander Engle, cookbook editor at Adelaide Publishing."

Her heart thudded. "Mr. Engle!" He was an editor at the publisher to whom she had sent *Recipes from the Vintage Kitchen*.

"Jaymie? What's wrong? You look sick," Becca said.

She waved her sister away. "So nice to hear from you, Mr. Engle!" Heart thumping, she got up and paced the length of the kitchen. An editor didn't just phone to say he didn't want to publish you, did he?

"I received your proposal for *Recipes from the Vintage Kitchen*. It's very interesting."

"You find my cookbook interesting? Thank you so much." She repeated his words so Becca would stop looking at her with concern. Her older sister's expression changed to one of shock and hope.

"Unfortunately, though it's very interesting and, may I say, entertaining, it is nowhere *near* what it needs to be, for it to be publishable."

Her heart sank and she sat down. "Oh."

"But I am still *tentatively* interested. I have some questions for you, if you have a moment?"

"I have all the time in the world," she said.

"Good. We get a lot of cookbook proposals. Right now on my desk I have a few dozen. I'm accepting two for publication."

She sighed, trying to quell the disappointment that welled up within her. "I understand. It's a very competitive business."

"But very popular. I do like your concept, but there just isn't enough here right now to carry a book."

"What does it need?"

"A lot, to be frank. It needs more of everything: more recipes, more tips, more anecdotes, more history. I'd like some personal narrative from you about your vintage kitchen, and how the tools and kitchenware you collect influence the cooking. I'm assuming you collect?"

"I do."

"And do you write?"

"Write? Uh, what do you mean?"

"Do you write a cooking column for anyone?"

"No."

"You should. You need more seasoning, Ms. Leighton, to use a pun."

"What do you look for in a cookbook writer?"

"Very good, right to the point. Well, a proposal should include information on how you plan to promote your cookbook. Do you have any TV experience? A cooking show? Even just guest spots? What connections do you have in the industry? Have you even *considered* doing a cooking column? In other words, what are your plans, and what is your background? How does it make you a salable cookbook author?"

"Oh," she said, her voice small.

"I know, it sounds like hard work, and it is. Are you willing to work hard?"

"Yes, yes I am."

"I think you could do it, if you're as passionate about it as you seem in your cover letter."

"I am! I love everything about vintage kitchenware and recipes. That's what I'm doing this moment, looking at my grandmother's old handwritten recipes."

"You need more than passion, though, and more than just mulling through old recipes. You need to prove yourself, and you need an agent, one who knows the cookbook genre. Not a romance agent, or a science fiction agent—a *cookbook* agent. And you need to sharpen your focus. I couldn't really tell from your proposal whether your book would just be recipes that are clarified for the modern cook or if they will be reinvented."

There was a difference? She'd have to think about that. "Which do you think is best?"

"Oh no, that's not up to me," he chastised. "You need to be able to give me a precise answer to that question. I have to go. I have a conference call in two minutes. Good luck, Ms. Leighton, and I hope I hear from you again with a new and improved proposal."

"Mr. Engle, may I e-mail you with a question from time to time?" she asked, speaking rapidly. "I promise I won't take up too much of your time."

"Certainly. I'll do my best to get back to you. Alexander Engle at AdelaidePub dot com." He hung up.

Her head was reeling as she laid the phone down. It had all happened so fast!

"Well? Well?" Becca said, grabbing her wrist. "Talk to me! What did he say?"

She told Becca everything. Her sister was disappointed, and went back to her laundry and texting, but the more Jaymie thought about it, the more hopeful she became. An actual editor took the time to call her from New York City to say he liked her idea and to give her advice and encouragement. That surely didn't happen to everyone!

She had hope, and a lot of work to do, if she was going to build a career as a cookbook author. Sighing happily, she glanced around her cluttered kitchen. "Six months," she muttered. "If I can figure out in that time whether I'm interested in Daniel long-term, then I can certainly get further on in the cookbook publishing game. Starting now."

Jaymie's Fourth of July Potato Salad

8 medium potatoes, cooked until just tender and diced
   (leave the peel on for best nutrition)
1 ½ cups mayonnaise
2 tablespoons cider vinegar OR substitute dill pickle juice,
   as you like
1 tablespoon yellow mustard
1 teaspoon garlic powder
1 teaspoon celery salt
½ teaspoon pepper
1 or 2 celery ribs, diced
1 carrot, grated coarsely
2 green onions, chopped
5 hard-boiled eggs, coarsely chopped
paprika and chives

1—Boil potatoes in salted water until just tender. Cool to room temperature. Dice, however small you want the chunks, and place in a large bowl.

2—Mix mayonnaise, cider vinegar (or pickle juice), mustard, garlic powder, celery salt and pepper in another bowl.

3—Pour mixture over potatoes. Add celery, grated carrot and onions, and mix well. Stir in chopped eggs.

4—Turn into a pretty bowl, and sprinkle a little paprika and chopped chives on top.

Best done the night before for the flavors to meld and develop. Do not let this potato salad stay at room temperature for long! Mayonnaise spoils quickly in the heat.

Jaymie's Notes

Everyone likes potato salad! But as with most recipes, you can make it your own by using whatever ingredients you like best. This one is based on my grandma Leighton's old recipe, but I changed it up just a bit. Next time, I think I'll use new potatoes halved for this recipe, and add some diced seedless cucumber and chopped red pepper.

Remember, presentation is everything! The beauty of vintage is, you can find the most amazing serving pieces for next to nothing in thrift shops and secondhand stores. Go with an open mind and open eyes, and don't confine yourself to the kitchen department. Check out the tablecloths; vintage linens really do finish the look of your retro picnic!

Victoria Hamilton is a pseudonym for national bestselling author Donna Lea Simpson, who is also a collector of vintage cookware and recipes.

The first slice is magic . . .
The second slice is murder . . .

FROM
Ellery Adams

Pies and Prejudice
A Charmed Pie Shoppe Mystery

When the going gets tough, Ella Mae LeFaye bakes pie. So when she catches her husband cheating in New York, she heads back home to Havenwood, Georgia, where she can drown her sorrows in fresh fruit filling and flaky crust. But her pies aren't just delicious. They're having magical effects on the people who eat them—and the public is hungry for more.

Ella Mae decides to grant her own wish by opening The Charmed Pie Shoppe. But with her old nemesis Loralyn Gaynor making trouble, and her old crush Hugh Dylan making nice, she has more than pie on her plate. And when Loralyn's fiancé is found dead—killed with Ella Mae's rolling pin—it'll take all her sweet magic to clear her name.

Includes pie recipes!

facebook.com/ellery.adams
facebook.com/TheCrimeSceneBooks
penguin.com